To Winnie
Hope you like this
E. Comp

The Heartbreak of Josie Whitt

by

E. COMPTON LEE

Lavender Press
an imprint of Blue Fortune Enterprises, LLC

THE HEARTBREAK OF JOSIE WHITT

This book is a work of fiction. Names, characters, businesses, organizations, places, events and incidents either are the product of the author's imagination or are used fictitiously. Any resemblance to actual persons, living or dead, events, or locales is entirely coincidental.

For information contact :
Blue Fortune Enterprises, LLC
Lavender Press
P.O. Box 554
Yorktown, VA 23690
http://blue-fortune.com

Cover design by WAMCreate

ISBN: 978-1-948979-81-8
First Edition: September 2022

This book is dedicated to my grandson,

Gus Lee

www.thegusleefund.org

CHAPTER ONE

Josie Whitt sat in her car, studying the cottage. The grayish-green clapboard exterior was plain, but the proportions were pleasing. Josie knew, though, from her visits here with the realtor Steve Getz, that the paint around the windows was peeling and the wooden sills were cracked by weather. She would have preferred a trailer with aluminum siding and rusted metal windows, some of them loose or falling out, but the roof on this cottage showed signs of leaking and one corner of the house appeared lower than the others. Three tall oak trees hung their branches dangerously close to the roof.

It would do.

Eventually, Rambles poked her in the back of the head with her nose. "Okay, okay." Josie roused herself and stepped from the SUV followed by her Husky. The dog trotted off into the tall grass, which closed around her.

Getz, after looking into the rear-view mirror of his sedan and smoothing his hair, left his car and stood beside Josie. "I'm not sure why we're here again, Josie. I'm really not."

"We're here because I asked you to bring me back. By the way, what's that building we passed down close to the road? We didn't look at it the last time."

"A shed of some sort, I would assume."

"Let's go look." Josie walked around Getz and started down the dirt path that served as a driveway.

The wooden shed clearly leaned to the left. Inside were a few broken garden tools covered with rust and dirt and around twenty bales of moldy hay. Josie ducked through the low door and called half-heartedly to the dog, who was nowhere in sight. Sitting on a bale, she put a stalk of dried grass in her mouth. Getz had tried to discourage her from even looking at this place. In the kindest manner, he patiently pointed out that the plumbing was ancient and not even close to code, the roof iffy, the foundation iffier, and the location far too isolated for a woman alone. Three hundred and sixty degrees and not a sign of humanity. The cottage and its thirty wild acres were located one hundred miles northwest of New York City, fifteen miles from Hudson, New York, and two miles from the village of Hollandtown. The roads leading here were so uncared for and rough most of the villagers never used them.

Getz looked around the inside of the shed, brushed at the top of the hay bale, and sat gingerly next to Josie. "With your budget, you could find something closer to town. Something nice. Comfortable, with all the amenities and little to no upkeep."

"I like this one."

"Who's going to clear the property? Thirty acres of weeds and saplings. The house is a money pit. You'll never get a loan."

Josie sat, kicking the hay bale with the heel of her sneaker.

"You shouldn't be isolated like this. What if something happened? A woman alone needs neighbors. You're still young. What—twenty-seven, twenty-eight? You should meet new people, make a new life for yourself."

"I don't want neighbors. And I'm paying cash. And I'm twenty-six."

Getz was considered one of the best realtors in the area. Cheerful, diligent, prompt in returning phone calls, he took on the most difficult properties in the county and somehow managed to turn them over, often at a profit. Even so, today, he said, "Let me take you to three other listings

I have. I promise you'll like them."

"That's not necessary. I like it here."

"Even $65,000 is too much for this place."

"Offer fifty."

Reluctantly, Getz followed Josie's instructions and the owners accepted. They didn't even bother with a counteroffer.

Two weeks later, Josie moved to Willow Bark.

Her first evening there, she went poking around in the shed looking for gardening tools. Not finding anything useful, she meandered back to the cottage, picking the tops of wild daisies as she made her way along the driveway to her new home. When she noticed what she was doing, she threw the flowers down. It was a perfect evening, not too warm and not too cool, the air clean and dry. At around seven it was still light but heading toward dusk. Someone had planted ivy and climbing bush roses around the house, but now they were taken over by brambles and opportunistic, highly allergenic weeds. An occasional rose poked through the overgrowth. About three yards from the kitchen stood a claw foot tub. Next to it, a willow tree draped its lacy branches over the rim and onto the enamel bottom. Nailed above the cottage door a simple, faded wooden sign in black letters read "Willow Bark." Getz couldn't tell her from whom or why the name had come. Perhaps, whoever they were, they had found healing here. Josie was touched by the whimsy of the idea that the humble aspirin, made from the bark of a tree, could possibly heal what ailed her or anyone else whose guilt was a wound that would never close. Still, she found the name sadly comforting. The back door stuck, and she kicked it open into a square room that served as a kitchen. It was as bare bones as any kitchen she had seen. White shiplap walls, a stained old enamel sink and drain board, two wooden cabinets and a three-by-three Formica counter. The white gas stove and oven hadn't been touched by the digital age, equipped with a dial to adjust the temperature. A little refrigerator, no more than five feet, with a tiny top freezer stood next to the stove and featured an elaborate rust stain on the entire front door. Josie stared at it for a moment, but no painting formed in her mind as it once would have. The linoleum floor, worn through in places, torn in others, also sported stains: brown, orange, and strangely, a bright green. Her grandmother's tavern table and a straight-backed chair took up the middle of the room.

She poured herself a vodka and orange juice, went through the living room into the bedroom across the hall, and laid on the bed, pulling a light blanket over her. She'd find the sheets tomorrow. Her brother, grumbling about how he should be getting ready for his next show, had helped move her furniture into the house: an iron bed, a couch, one very old oriental rug so worn that the nap was completely gone in places, leaving only the colored threads to hold it together, one over-stuffed chair, the tavern table, a few wooden chairs, and a chest of drawers. Her clothes, along with her books, were in boxes scattered around the room, the hall, and on into the second bedroom. She had stuffed her painting supplies under the bed.

A straight-back chair with several books piled on the seat served as a bedside table. Josie stretched her legs and looked out the large window. The light coming through the dusty panes lit the scarred pine floor, making it glow with golden warmth. She raised her eyes to the ceiling where a water stain spread in the corner next to the window, almost but not quite, making up for the lovely floor. She sighed. She didn't deserve anything remotely picturesque.

The vodka and orange juice tasted sweet and spicy. Josie picked up a book from the stash on the chair. The words formed in her head but made no sense. Even so, she kept at it, sipping vodka and turning pages until it became too dark. She leaned over the bed and turned on a tarnished brass lamp with a one-hundred-watt bulb and no shade. Enough to read by. But this movement, simple and brief as it was, broke her concentration and there it came. The image that followed Josie everywhere. The one she battled against by using all her energy to focus on whatever was in front of her: the sight of the blueberry pie her twin sister was carrying flying into the air, the sound of crunching bones and the painful electrical surge of neurons firing along Josie's skin.

Tossing the book down, Josie leaped out of bed and kicked the boxes around the floor, looking for her overnight bag. Finding it, she retrieved a blue and white make-up bag which held toothbrush, toothpaste, deodorant, shampoo, and a prescription bottle of sleeping pills. Josie had never taken this kind of medicine. In fact, except for the penicillin she took for childhood strep throats, she had never taken any medicine at all. She was healthy as a horse. With that thought, she felt herself reel and nearly lost her balance. Spreading her feet for stability, she opened the bottle and looked at the pills inside. It would be so easy. But then she thought of Sylvia Plath, stuffed into a cranny in the cellar and still found by those determined to keep her alive. There was no guarantee of success this way. Besides, she didn't deserve easy.

Putting her index finger inside the bottle, she retrieved one pill and bit it in half. Back in bed, she turned off the light, punched her pillow, curled into a ball, and waited. It didn't take the medicine long to overcome her gaunt body, and soon Josie Whitt slipped into a drugged slumber.

Sometime in the night, Rambles pushed open the kitchen door, walked silently through the house into the bedroom and sprang up next to her owner, something she had never done before. The Husky tucked her tail around herself, sighed, settled into the mattress, and she too fell asleep.

CHAPTER TWO

Tristan peeked around the bedroom door. "Have you found it yet?"

"Dude. We just got here for Christ's sake," Shadaisy said from inside the closet. She batted clothes around, rattling hangers and in Tristan's mind making too much noise. "Maybe you should quiet down a little."

"Well, I can't hurry up and quiet down at the same time, now can I?"

The boy left to go to the front room and look out the window at the Giovanni's driveway. Shadaisy had lived with them during one of her thirteen foster home placements.

The boy trotted back to the bedroom, calling out, "All clear still."

"Push that chair over here."

Tristan shoved a pink, badly stained upholstered chair over to the closet door. The girl put her hand on his shoulder, stood on the lumpy seat and began shoving cardboard boxes, heaps of winter hats and scarves, piles of clothes and a few unknown objects around on the shelf. "Okay, it's not here. I'm going to have to stand on your shoulders. To reach the higher shelf."

"I can't do that."

"Hell, I only weigh a hundred pounds." Putting a hand on each side of the door frame for balance, Shadaisy placed a sneakered foot on the boy's far shoulder and with a little grunt placed the other foot on the near one and straightened upright, grabbing hold of the upper shelf.

"Oh God," said Tristan.

There was more rummaging. A box fell on the floor.

"You're going to have to pick that up."

"I know that. Hold on to my legs, will you, so I don't fall. Jesus! Got it!" Shadaisy jumped off Tristan's shoulders to the floor, turned to face him with a wide grin, deep dimples in each cheek, her blond cherubic curls making her look as innocent as the day she was born. She held a double-barrel shotgun over her head. "Bingo. I knew it was here. Now look through the dresser. I'll put everything here back, so they'll never know."

Tristan knelt on the floor in front of the dresser and pulled out the bottom drawer, patted around the clothes, retrieved a box of shells, held them out so Shadaisy could see them. "Done," he said, grinning from ear to ear.

"That was quick. Not bad, Mouse, not bad at all."

Shadaisy had brought supplies: two blankets from her bed and some duct tape. Tristan wrapped the blankets around the gun and secured them with the tape while his friend tried to put everything back where it had been. She stepped away and held out her arms. "How does it look?"

"Fine. How does this look?"

"Like a shotgun wrapped in blankets."

"Well, I don't know what else to do."

"If you see any cops, just act nonchalant."

"Oh, sure. That'll work."

"You got any better ideas?"

Tristan rested the gun on his shoulder. "Forward march, Captain," he said with no enthusiasm at all. He picked up his backpack, slung it over his shoulder, and saluted.

Tristan and Shadaisy had met four years ago when they were eleven and thirteen and living with the same foster family. She'd been living in this particular house for a month when she saw a new boy sitting on the front porch steps. She sat next to him. "Hey," she said. "What's your name? Mine's Shadaisy."

Shadaisy? What kind of ghetto name is that?"

"A ghetto one, asshole. What's yours?"

"Tristan."

"Tristan? What kind of faggoty name is that?"

"My mother loved opera. Especially Tristan and Isolde."

Shadaisy was about to make a comment implying that no way would a boy whose mother loved opera end up in foster care when she noticed the look on his face. It was one of such love and longing that she knew then and there he would be her best friend for as long as she could manage it. "How old are you?"

"Eleven."

"Really? You look more like eight. Anyway, I'm thirteen and I think you're cute. A little small, but cute. You look like a mouse."

"I do not."

"Yes, you do. You're small and have big ears and a pointed nose and dark, round eyes." Shadaisy put out her hand. "Let's be friends."

The boy stared at her in disbelief. Never had someone offered him their friendship. He shook her hand.

They'd been living in that house for six months when Shadaisy was returned to her mother. Tristan stayed for the next four years. They kept in touch via prepaid cell phones, letters, meetings, and emails, even though Shadaisy was placed in five other homes during that time. It was at the Giovanni's, the fifth of these placements, she learned there was a shotgun in the house. A damned shotgun. What fool kept a shotgun in the city? What happened to a good old Glock? Still, it was better than nothing. Before she could use it, however, she was sent home again. A week later, she and Tristan made their way to the Giovanni's to "liberate" the gun.

Once they had successfully exited the Giovanni's with everything hopefully back in place, they took alleys and back streets to the house where Shadaisy's mother lived. No one seemed to notice the strange package the boy carried. They came across no police. When they arrived at what was considered Shadaisy's official home, a run-down, rent controlled house on a shabby street in the Bronx, Tristan went around to the back with the shotgun and hunkered under Shadaisy's bedroom window while she went in the front door. The boards on the porch were so rotten and ragged, Shadaisy always wondered if she would make it inside. It was a shotgun house. The door opened into the living room, followed by the same sized kitchen and behind that a bedroom. Shadaisy had separated the bedroom in two with a sheet nailed to the ceiling. The furniture was utilitarian, old, and spiky. Linoleum covered the floor throughout, some of it two layers thick and in different patterns where someone had covered over the holes. Mrs. O'Brian, the girl's mother, sat at the kitchen table, smoking. Her hands shook. Shadaisy realized she was tweaking and tweaking hard. She'd been a meth addict for fifteen years. Mr. Lederer supplied the drugs. He was Mrs. O'Brian's social worker and traded drugs for sex.

Shadaisy had never gone farther down that road than pot. Choosing to chill out and puff languidly on a toke was one thing. The stinking business of mixing and cooking shit was another. The dirty spoons, needles and syringes were disgusting enough. But the rotten teeth, the oozing facial sores, and skanky, dirty hair were so revolting, Shadaisy could barely look at her mother. She knew it was vanity that saved her, vanity about her looks but also vanity about not needing anyone or anything. Nothing would get the hold on her that meth had on her mother.

Mrs. O'Brian lit another cigarette. Her hands shook badly. "He's coming today. He'll be here soon. Anytime." She inhaled deeply. Smoke puffed out of her mouth as she said, "You better be going. He'll be here any minute."

"I'm going, I'm going." Shadaisy put her hand on her mother's shoulder, but the woman jerked away. "Don't wait up for me, Mom. Okay? I won't be in till very late." She headed to the bedroom then turned back. "Mom, I love you."

"Yes, yes, I know. You better go, okay."

Her mother had been a beauty once. Now Shadaisy couldn't imagine what Mr. Lederer saw in her, but he was at the house every other week, like clockwork.

Two years ago, during one of those visits, Shadaisy had burst from behind the sheet separating her bed from her mother's and stood, hands on hips, watching the horrified look flow across Lederer's face as he tried to stop his climax. While he pulled on his socks and shoes and hopped awkwardly out of the room, Shadaisy formulated a plan.

"I'll make you a deal," she said.

After that, the good social worker always left an envelope hidden under the sink where Mrs. O'Brian never looked. Inside was a fifty-dollar bill. Today, with her mother in the kitchen, Shadaisy would not be retrieving those fifty dollars. Having said goodbye to her mother, she grabbed her backpack, climbed out the bedroom window, crept with Tristan to the side of the house, and settled beside him amongst the garbage bags and plastic cans in the alley. Shadaisy unwrapped the shotgun and, worried about fingerprints, balled up the duct tape and stuffed it in her backpack. Reasoning that the blankets were too rough to lift prints from, she threw one into a garbage can and used the other to cover the gun while she waited for Mr. Lederer.

Each youngster had brought underwear, a pair of jeans, a long-sleeved t-shirt, and extra socks. Shadaisy had included toothpaste, toothbrush, and some aspirin. They leaned against the house shoulder to shoulder, their knees up. Shadaisy held the shotgun across her lap. The sun was setting, lighting the New York city skyline and turning the first several feet of the alley into bright relief. The youngsters sat just beyond this illumination in the dusk. Shadaisy wondered how much she was going to miss this city with its filth and crime and energy and excitement.

She'd never been anywhere else. She nudged Tristan with her shoulder. "You nervous?"

The boy shrugged. "Not yet."

Mr. Lederer generally stayed less than an hour. The plan was, once he was disposed of, she and Mouse would take the train out of town and hide in the wilds of upstate New York. The thought of being in the empty country was unsettling but seemed the safest way to be on the lam. They would stay away for the rest of the spring and through the summer and fall, then return before it turned freezing cold to fetch her mother. Shadaisy had been gone longer than this at times when she was in foster care. She figured her mother would barely notice her absence. Once they returned, she would gage the atmosphere and decide if it were possible to stay in the city. She doubted it would be, certainly not in the same neighborhood, and finding a new one would leave a paper trail any dope could follow. Undoubtedly, they would have to take her mother back out into the country. They would probably be out of money by then, but Shadaisy couldn't worry about that now. She also couldn't worry about how she was going to get and keep her mother clean.

"You okay?" she asked.

"Dude. Stop asking me that or I won't be."

They talked desultorily about nothing much for a while then fell silent. The stretch of sunlight in the alley lengthened, and the two moved back farther into the dark. Eventually, Shadaisy said, "It should be about ten more minutes." Her mouth was dry, but she relaxed into thinking she still had time when she heard familiar footsteps going down the porch steps. "Oh, shit." Her first impulse was to jump to her feet, but Tristan put a hand on her shoulder. Moving very carefully, the girl slid her back up the wall of her house and slowly moved her feet underneath her. Tristan did the same, the side of his body from his shoulder to his sneakers touching the girl's until she stepped into the last of the evening light. At the unmistakable click of handle and gun barrels coming together, Mr. Lederer turned. Shadaisy stood with a shotgun pointed at his face.

Blinded by the final rays of the setting sun, she shot wild. The kick from the gun knocked her backward into Tristan, who grabbed the back of her arms and stood her upright while Lederer screamed and screamed.

The youngsters didn't wait to see the result of the shot and scrambled to get away from the ear-shattering screams, which turned Shadaisy's stomach. Fortunately, in this neighborhood, no one was likely to look out the window much less come outside. The teenagers ran as fast as their legs would carry them, their sneakers slapping the pavement. They had planned their route again and again and walked it until they could do it in their sleep or at least in the dark without the need for a flashlight or any other kind of light. Just as they turned left into another alley, the sun settled behind the horizon, leaving them and everything else in the dark. They made their way, alley by alley, to the Hudson River, where they tossed the gun. After several subway rides circling back and forth, they reached Penn Station and boarded the train to Rhinecliff.

CHAPTER THREE

Josie Whitt woke early her first morning at Willow Bark. She put on her shoes and socks and made her way, stepping over boxes, into the kitchen. Now, where was the tea? Oh right. Knowing the chaos the house would be in, she'd put a few tea bags and her special cup in her purse. Porcelain with a large bowl and graceful lip, the teacup appealed to Josie so much she had painted pink roses on it. She drank her tea from it every morning. Good, she thought, taking it unbroken from her bag. Searching through boxes would be torture today. She could do that later when the errands didn't loom.

She turned on a burner on the old stove, smelled gas, and was about to turn it off when a flame whooshed around the burner. The box where she had tossed her pots and pans was overfull and open. It was easy to find the right size. She filled it with water and placed it on the burner. When the water boiled, she dunked a tea bag into it, until it was the right color. She filled the cup and put it on the tavern table. She would make a list while the tea cooled. Lists were good. They gave her a sense of accomplishment without actually doing anything. They required concentration and very little movement. Let's see: a rototiller, a shovel, garden rake, a small spade, and clippers with long blades, a weed wacker, the stronger the better, tomato and zucchini plants. And a garden tractor.

She would also need some groceries. Butter, milk, Italian sausage, bread, pasta, marinara sauce, and cereal. Somewhere in these boxes were spices and canned goods she could supplement her purchases with for several weeks.

She felt sick to her stomach, and underneath her skin, the muscles shivered. She'd end up back in bed, unable to move. The trick was to keep the number of items she needed to buy small. This list was already too long, but she wanted to get them now so she wouldn't have to think about it later. Steam rose out of the cup. Josie sipped at it. Still too hot. Well, it would be there when she returned. Grabbing her purse along with the list, she left the kitchen and opened her car door, slid in, and turned on the engine. Rambles appeared out of nowhere. Josie got out of the car and let the dog in the back seat, slamming it shut harder than she meant to. She drove out of the driveway and turned onto the road heading toward Hudson. She still wore the clothes she'd slept in.

The weather was glorious, a perfect day in May, with only traces of winter left in the air, the sun dazzling, high white cumulus clouds in a pristine blue sky. At first, there were miles of fields gone wild with tall brown weeds then a few untidy farms looking as though the people who lived there existed below the poverty level. Closer to Hudson, Josie noticed ranch houses, mostly brick, set back on large lawns. Along the road were daffodils, their blooms faded to limp translucence or gone, picked by a conscientious homeowner. The lawns hadn't yet achieved emerald green, but bright patches were here and there. The gardens around the houses still looked raw and uncertain. She and Jaylene had collaborated on their own gardens, giving advice and sharing plants. Josie felt a sharp squeeze in her chest and snapped her thoughts away from this subject, returned her attention fiercely onto the road, not letting her eyes drift from side to side. She couldn't seem to remember where the grocery and hardware stores were. Leaving in such haste, Josie hadn't thought to Google directions. In fact, she hadn't even remembered to bring her phone. She hated the thought of having to stop her forward momentum and get out of the car, approach someone, possibly even having to wait in line, and then trying to decipher the directions, something she was hopeless at. The idea was to keep moving forward, no hesitating, and return home as fast as possible. Odd. She'd only spent one night at Willow Bark and already thought of it as home. She began steeling herself to stop at a gas station when she drove around a bend and suddenly on her left was a new shopping mall with a ShopRite, Lowes, and Walmart anchoring a bleak and vast parking lot. Thank God. She hadn't heard about this new development, but then she wouldn't have been likely to. Not this year. She would go to Lowes first, then to ShopRite for food supplies.

A man in an orange vest appeared at her side as soon as she entered the building. That's because it's brand new, she thought. Give it a few years and it will be hard to locate anyone for help finding things. "I need a rototiller, a shovel, shears, a rake, spade, a weed wacker, some vegetable plants, and a garden tractor." The man, whose nametag said Vince, looked startled for a moment, then recovered himself and grinned as though this was the best news he'd heard in a long time. "Come right this way," he said.

There were three different rototillers. Josie chose the mid-sized one. She didn't know the first thing about these machines except that they broke up the ground to prepare it for planting. She didn't even know how to turn it on or if it was run by electricity or gas or what. This one apparently used regular gas.

Vince went over the instructions carefully, glancing at Josie to make sure she understood. She tried her best to follow what he was saying, nodding and smiling, but most of the time she was lost in a haze of anxiety. Finally, he straightened and looked at her closely. "Do you have any questions?"

She had no questions because she hadn't really been able to listen to what he was saying. Also, she knew that her concentration was so shaky it would do no good to repeat the tutorial, so she shook her head. Maybe her brother, if she bribed him with food, could be persuaded to help her get it started. She said, "Should we leave it here while we look at shovels?"

"This is just a display. I'll have someone bring one in a box from the back."

Next, they looked at weed wackers. Josie had weed wacked. Once. After that, Will had done all the weed wacking and Josie rode the garden tractor around their large lawn. She had loved driving it, glancing over her shoulder to see the progress behind her. They had bought the tractor from Sears and Will kept it fueled and did the minor repairs.

Vince told her John Deeres were the best.

"Okay, I'll take one of those."

He looked at her cautiously. "They're also the most expensive."

"That's okay. I'll take the middle size."

"Excuse me, but what are you buying this equipment for? If I can ask?"

Josie was nearly weeping at this point. "I need to clear some land. That's all." Though normally she would have taken offense, she didn't care about the change in Vince's demeanor.

"Do you have anyone to help you with this?"

"Oh, yes. Of course."

Vince consulted his phone. "It can't be delivered until next week."

"That's fine." Josie hadn't even thought about how she would get all this stuff back to Willow Bark.

They went to the tools section next. Josie chose the medium range shovel, rake, and spade. She picked out the biggest pair of clippers available, then grabbed fifteen Big Boy tomato plants and three unknown varieties of zucchinis. Vince had fetched a low, rectangular cart with a long handle to pull it. "Getting a jump start on your garden, I imagine."

"Yes."

Vince followed her, pulling the cart to the check out. He watched as she put the credit card into its slot and waited until the machine said, "Transaction complete."

"All right, then," he said, rubbing his hands together. "I'll get the rototiller."

There was a moment of panic when Josie drove the Jeep to the pickup-point. It had never occurred to her that all these items might not fit. At her signal, Rambles hopped into the passenger seat looking annoyed and refused to sit down, turning instead in tight circles, her feet making a tidy dance on the cushioned leather. Finally, Josie shoved the dog's hips down and said, "Sit." The dog lowered her haunches until they almost touched the seat but not quite, and there she hovered.

It took Vince some considerable juggling. He loaded the rototiller first, putting the back seats down. Then he arranged and rearranged the plants in empty spaces around the hardware. Finally, everything was inside and looking stable. Vince pushed here and there to make sure nothing would move in transit until Josie, thinking she might scream, tapped him on the shoulder. "It's fine. You've been great. Thank you."

"You sure you have someone at home to help with this stuff?"

"Of course."

"Well, you'll be fine. It's good equipment. And there is the year warranty on the tiller and the tractor, if you have any trouble."

Josie wondered miserably if she should tip him but no, certainly not, certainly it was against store policy. All the clerks would spend their time loading cars if they were allowed to take tips.

ShopRite loomed in front of her. A new store to get used to. A warehouse of a store. *I can't do this*, she thought then told herself, yes, you can, just go along the perimeter where the basics are then look for the bread. In and out. The thought of having to come back in a day or two if she didn't do this now pushed her out of the car and through the enormous automatic doors.

Butter, milk, Italian sausage, where the hell was the bread, oh, here it was. Josie nearly ran along the aisles, which were wide enough to steer around anyone in front of her. She found the cereal easily enough, but the Frosted Mini-Wheats remained elusive, so she grabbed Cheerios instead. Then on to the pasta, which was right where the sign said it would be, and the marinara sauce next to it. Encouraged, she sped on to the produce section for onions, garlic, and mushrooms. There. That should do it. Please, don't let there be a line.

There wasn't, and she was back in the car in less than twenty minutes. Josie placed the plastic bags on the floor in front of Rambles, knowing they would be fine there. She could leave a T-bone steak on the table and the dog wouldn't touch it, stealing food being beneath her. Josie said, "Really, you are a remarkably good dog, you know. I don't tell you often enough. I apologize." The dog flicked an ear at her and settled herself firmly on the seat.

CHAPTER FOUR

Shadaisy and Tristan had their pick of seats in the nearly empty train. They settled into the middle of the car, stowing their backpacks overhead and, happy to be alone, looked at each other and smiled. The doors to the train swished open and a man of average build, dressed in jeans and a black hoodie, walked down the aisle and sat in the seat in front of them. He looked to be in his late twenties, early thirties. Shadaisy and Tristan signaled to each other with their hands, wondering if they should move but, in the end, were too tired and soon forgot about him. They leaned into each other. "You're shaking," Shadaisy said.

"I'm cold."

"We should have brought those blankets."

"How would we have done that? No room in the packs." Then after a thoughtful pause, "Hard to run wrapped in a blanket."

"Very funny. Do you think this train carries any?"

"I never been on a train like this before." Tristan waited for Shadaisy to get up and look around, but she didn't.

Eventually, she sighed. "Me neither, and I don't want to do anything that would draw attention to us."

"Right. You scared?"

Shadaisy put her finger to her lips and pointed to the man in front of them. She turned in her seat, so her mouth was next to Tristan's ear. "No, not yet. It doesn't seem real… I wonder if he's dead. I couldn't see a thing."

"You got him. That's for sure. Never heard screams like that before."

"He might not be dead. I hope to God he is. I'm sure he knew who I was."

Tristan turned so he could look her in the face. "He's dead, Shadrack."

"That makes me a murderer. Or would it be a murderette?"

"Murderess. And I would be a murderesses' accomplice."

"I don't know."

"What?"

Shadaisy put her head against the back of her seat and sighed. "I'm not sure I want to be a murderer."

Tristan looked away from her. "It's a little late for that now."

"Tell me he deserved to die."

"Okay. He deserved to die."

"Yeah, I guess," the girl said bleakly.

The boy faced her again, his voice falsely chipper. "How much money you got?"

"Four hundred. You? You spend any of yours?"

"Dude. I got seven, like I told you."

When he was twelve, the children at Tristan's foster home were sent after school and weekends to a rooftop garden over a warehouse where at-risk-youth worked tending plants. The idea behind this government-funded program was that they would learn a trade and, more importantly, a solid work ethic and self-respect. In addition to this opportunity, they were paid a pittance, which Tristan's foster parents forced him to turn over.

Soon after he began, the boy found he liked the work and took to staying after the other children left for the day. Sometimes it was well after dark by the time he grabbed a bus for home. Tristan and the manager worked quietly together for nearly a week before Mr. Hartnett asked him if everything was all right at home. Tristan said, yes, it was fine, and, in truth, he didn't go hungry or at least not too hungry, wasn't beaten or raped, just ignored as much as possible. The work, outdoors and physical, gave him a sense of health and well-being and the plants responded to his care in a way that made him feel he existed, maybe even mattered a little. Mr. Hartnett shared his thermos of coffee with him and eventually, as the days lengthened, he brought extra sandwiches to share with the boy. Tristan and Hartnett talked about the plants, the boy a sponge for the information his manager gave him. They didn't stray from this topic much, for which Tristan was grateful, until one evening Hartnett said, "You're a good worker, you know. You have a feel for this. You must like it."

"I do."

"Do you plan to get into the business some day?"

Tristan, who had never thought much beyond the next time he would see Shadaisy (or Shadrack, as he called her) wasn't sure how to answer. He liked Mr. Hartnett and assumed the right thing to do was tell him, yes, he definitely wanted to work with plants in some way, but this wasn't true. Or maybe it was. Who knew? He certainly didn't, so he said nothing.

Hartnett sat up straighter and crumpled his sandwich paper. "I'm going to pay you for the extra time you put in here, ten dollars an hour, if that's okay. Cash. No one need know anything about it, if you don't mind."

Tristan went over and over this conversation on the bus ride home, finally convincing himself Hartnett would never come through with his promise. However, the man was more than good for his word, throwing in extra money on days when the work was especially strenuous and on holidays. That was four years ago.

Now, Shadaisy said, "Eleven hundred should take us a good distance if we're careful. We got to buy bikes, but we can get them cheap at

Walmart. We can eat peanut butter and canned peas. I heard somewhere peanut butter and peas have all the nutrition you need."

"Yuck," Tristan said.

"You're still shivery. You scared or cold?"

"I told you, I'm cold. I feel sick."

"You can't be sick. Not now. Not here." Shadaisy turned to the boy and laid her arm across his chest and drew him to her side, placing his head on her shoulder with the palm of her hand. He snuggled against her, and she rested her cheek on the top of his head. Suddenly exhausted, the two melted into each other and fell into a deep sleep, soothed by the train's gentle sway. The train stopped a few times to let off the other passengers, but the teenagers slept through it until the backward push of the brakes finally woke Shadaisy. Tristan moaned, then cuddled closer to her and dropped back into unconsciousness.

The girl, on the other hand, popped wide awake. Outside the window was total darkness. The door swished open and two men in suits entered and without hesitation walked down the aisle toward her and Mouse. Shadaisy rolled her head just enough to see them more clearly. They were moving shadows in the dark. Even so, by their suits, their posture, the way they held their shoulders, Shadaisy knew for certain they were detectives. How in the name of hell had they found them so quickly? She had seen enough *Law & Order* to know it shouldn't have been this easy. Now she was going to prison. At seventeen, it wouldn't be juvey, either. Probably Sing Sing. Did Sing Sing have a woman's unit? She didn't know, but anywhere they sent her would be hard core. Her babyish looks wouldn't help her there. Worse than no help. She would undoubtedly be raped, though how a woman raped another woman she hadn't figured out. But she was tough, tougher physically than most of the other women inmates, she bet, because she'd never done crack or meth and was healthier and therefore stronger. The men made their silent way toward the young criminals. She was going to prison for the rest of her life, for sure. Mouse might go to juvey, being only fifteen. Plus, he hadn't actually shot anyone. The men stopped just short of her seat. One was pointing a gun. "Let's make this easy. Just get up and come quietly." The man sitting in front of the youngsters rose to his feet and edged his way into the aisle in front of the two suits. One pulled his wrists behind his torso and put them in handcuffs. Then the three made their silent way to the train door, down the stairs and into the dark.

"What the hell?" said Tristan, who had jerked awake as the men were leaving. Shadaisy allowed herself to straighten her shoulders and sit up. She opened her mouth to tell Mouse what had just happened but only sobs came out. Her shoulders trembled, and she hiccupped while Tristan silently stroked her arm. The train shook itself into movement and on they went while the girl slowly regained control and told her friend, between hiccups, what had happened. There was no hope of going back to sleep and the two leaned against each other whispering, though there was no one to hear them. Tristan wondered where the police had come from, how did they know where to stop, how did the conductor know where to stop, why didn't they pick the dude up at the next station, who was that man anyway and what had he done? It must have been real bad to stop the train. "I mean, they stopped the train in the middle of nowhere."

Shadaisy shrugged. "It was so dark I couldn't see a thing. The train stopped and these dudes just got on and walked down the aisle like they did it every day."

"Why did he sit in front of us?"

"How should I know? Maybe he was lonely."

"Or thought they wouldn't nab him in front of two kids."

"They don't care about that." Shadaisy leaned her head against the back of her seat. "How long do you think we'll have to be on the lam?" She used to love this phrase, "on the lam" and said it often, with attitude.

Now Tristan thought she sounded sad. "I don't know," he said. "How long does it take for a case to grow cold? Three, six months?"

"I think we can go back around Thanksgiving. Maybe during the parade. When everyone is into doing the holiday shit."

"I wonder where we'll be in November. What we'll be doing. Like, will we have jobs? A place to live. Are you in shock?"

"What? No, I'm not in shock."

"I was just thinking you might be because… you know. It would be totally normal if you were."

"I don't want to talk about it. Let's just get off this train and get something to eat. I'm starving. Now, go to sleep."

Tristan didn't go to sleep and neither did Shadaisy. They sat in silence as the train swayed toward its destination.

Eventually, the brakes pushed them backwards as the train stopped in front of a dimly lit platform made of wood that looked black in the near dark. The conductor called out, "Rhinecliff, last stop."

Holding onto the edges of the seats, the youngsters made their way to the door and gingerly stepped off the train onto the empty platform. Shadaisy looked left then right. She turned around and took in the wooden stairs leading up the hill to the building at the top. The sides of this hill were covered in rocks and wild grasses, unkempt and uncared for.

"What is that?" she said. "Do you think it's a barn?"

"I think it's the station."

"Can't be." Shadaisy knew Penn Station, large and industrial, and Grand Central, a palace with statues and restaurants and oyster bars and shops and hallways to run along after you had stolen something. And there were people everywhere. Train stations didn't sit abandoned on top of a scruffy mountain. If this was Rhinecliff, they were lost. The whole plan worthless. They should never have left the city. Mouse said, "Look at this, Shadrack. This is great. We're actually in the Wild West. The Wild West! We're free. No one knows we're here. Come on, let's get something to eat."

The girl didn't answer but followed him up the long wooden steps and through some doors into a room with benches, a booth where you could buy tickets and very little else except a man walking slowly around turning off lights. "We close in five minutes," he said.

"Do you have anything to eat here?" asked Shadaisy.

"There are some vending machines over there, but you have to be out in five minutes."

The young criminals scrambled among the machines, selecting peanut butter crackers, Hershey bars and cans of Coke before they were hustled out into the night.

CHAPTER FIVE

Josie pitched herself out of bed, went straight through the kitchen without preparing tea, and started by taking the plants out of the SUV before they dried out and died. She put them under the oak trees. It took several trips. What had she been thinking? What could she possibly do with all those tomatoes? And zucchinis. Around here, one plant would produce more fruit than any family could consume. And she had six zucchinis and about twenty tomato plants. She'd had the notion that digging and working with mother earth would be healing. Now she couldn't think of gardening without Jaylene hovering in her mind, sometimes no more than a feeling, sometimes an image clear as day.

She should take everything back. But the thought of Vince, of driving to Hudson and finding someone to help her unload the plants, the tools, the rototiller was unbearable. The John Deere was already scheduled for delivery. She'd have to call and cancel, enduring one recorded message after another until finally some crab answered the phone and then put her on hold forever.

She used the hose to dribble water over the plants, turned off the water and surveyed the front of the cottage. The climbing bush roses and weeds had made their way about two feet up the clapboards. Josie began pulling them off. The roses came away easily, but the weeds were tenacious. She took a closer look. Three shiny leaves on each stem. Josie made an involuntary step backwards and looked at her hands. Poison Ivy. Some people were so allergic to it they would already face being covered with blisters all over their body. She, on the other hand, had only one or two small patches a summer even though she walked through it on the way to the swimming hole nearly every day. Still, Erik was coming tomorrow and though she didn't remember him ever having poison ivy, she felt she couldn't expect him to wade through the stuff while he rototilled the garden. Her gardening gloves were lost somewhere in the boxes that filled the cottage. She'd risk going bare handed. Fortunately, the cottage was small, and by pulling and using the clippers, it didn't take long to clear the vines off the building.

The weed wacking was another story. Josie had bought the kind that ran off a battery, making it heavy, but she didn't want to have a cord to tangle and trip over or prove to be too short. One fueled by gas meant trips to the gas station. Josie had plugged hers into an outlet in the kitchen to charge overnight. It took her a few moments to figure out how to turn it on, but once it roared to life, she began on the land in front of the kitchen. Holding the wand in front of her, the swirling plastic took down the tall grass easily, but then the poison ivy vines took hold, wrapping around the plastic strings and stalling out the motor. Josie tore them loose and started again. Within five minutes, the same thing happened, this time breaking off a long piece of plastic twine. She kept at it, stopping at least every five minutes to free the machine. It was slow progress, and after an hour she'd cleared only a six-by-six patch. The juice from the vines was all over her hands and she imagined invisible droplets filling the air.

She went inside to call Erik. The phone rang nine times before he answered.

"What?"

Josie had trouble slowing her breath. "I've made a terrible mistake. There's poison ivy everywhere, and it keeps clogging the weed wacker.

I've only gotten a small patch cleared, and it's taken me an hour. I don't even want to garden. I've got hundreds of tomato and zucchini plants, and I don't want any of them. I could give everyone in Hollandtown and half of Hudson tomatoes and zucchini and still have some for myself."

"That's not a bad idea." Erik was five years older than his twin sisters. Josie felt she hardly knew him. She and Jaylene had always been so bound together an older brother only existed on the periphery. She knew he was an artist, successful enough to have two or three one-man shows a year in the city, and that he was good looking with his dark blond, curly hair, sleepy blue eyes, and neatly carved mouth. Women found him attractive unless he was getting ready for a show and then his tension and anxiety showed in his face and tended to put people off. In general, he was distant and often irritable and cared more about his work than anything else.

"Or," Erik continued, "you could get pigs to feed them to."

When Josie didn't respond, he said, "That was a joke. Look, do what you can. I'll be over tomorrow, and we'll see what we can do."

Surprised by his helpfulness, Josie meekly said, "Okay" and hung up. Pushed forward by her brother's generosity, she went outside and started again.

The weed wacker felt heavier than it had before, and infinitesimal bits of flora somehow made their way underneath her nightgown, around her neck and down her back. Within five minutes, sweat broke out from her head to her feet. Droplets slid into her eyes, stinging them and making it difficult to see. It was terrible work, far more terrible than Josie had imagined. She paused, assessing the size she had designated for her garden and deemed it impossible to complete. That was when the tears started. They came without warning, flowing in a steady stream. She had never experienced tears like this before, not even after the accident or at the funeral. The tiny rivulets rolled down her cheeks, taking the bend of her jaw in their course before dropping onto her neck. Wiping them away had little effect, the supply was endless. From a distant and objective point, Josie noted the tears were not accompanied by sobs, which was a good thing as sobs would have made it impossible to continue with the weed wacker. Years ago, she'd read that crying burned more calories than any other activity. Josie envisioned the fluids flowing from her body, releasing the toxins she carried. By wiping her nose with the sleeve of her nightgown and her tears with the back of her hand, Josie was able to see where she was going. Her arms and shoulders stung, her back burned and her legs cramped. She focused on the birds singing, closing out of her mind everything but their lovely, passionate call for a mate. Refusing to pause, she entered into a trance consisting of birdsong, the wet working of her body, the pain, the tears, and a wavy, fluid view of the world. By the time the grass and weeds were more or less two inches high throughout the garden area, her limbs shook, and she had a splitting headache. She hadn't eaten all day. Ever since the accident, she'd been plagued with a persistent nausea, making food a challenge.

Once the willow branches were clipped and out of the clawfoot tub, she filled it by using a hose attached to the faucet in the kitchen sink. She stepped in and leaned back against the curved porcelain, slid down, completely submerged her head, then surfaced and scrubbed herself from head to toe with a bar of soap and wash cloth. She'd heard that not washing for an indeterminate amount of time was a cure for exposure to poison ivy because it reduced spreading the poison oil all over, but she stepped out of the tub, turned the nozzle on the hose, and sprayed herself for at least five minutes. She lifted the nightgown out of the willow tree where she had flung it, walked into the kitchen, turned off the water, dropped the nightgown on the bathroom floor, and grabbed a towel. Rambles jumped off the couch and followed her into the bedroom. When Josie dropped the towel on the floor and flopped on the bed, the dog jumped up next to her. Josie rolled on her side to look at her. "It's not like you to stay inside all day. Guess you didn't like the sound of the weed wacker, did you?" She rolled onto her back. "Neither did I."

CHAPTER SIX

The train station had overhead night lights and just out of their range, Shadaisy and Tristan saw the dark outline of an enormous oak tree. Its branches were so wide and thick the ground underneath stayed in perpetual shade. Nothing but moss grew there. Tristan dropped his pack on a mossy patch, leaned against the huge trunk, and slid to the ground. "No one will see us here," he said. "And the ground's pretty soft." He patted the moss. "Sit."

Shadaisy sat. "I don't want to walk another inch."

They ate their crackers and candy and drank their Coke in silence before curling up and falling into a twilight sleep. They tossed and moaned and dozed. They spooned in a futile effort to keep warm until shortly before daybreak, when they finally fell into a real sleep only to jolt awake when the sun came up. Shadaisy reached into her pack and retrieved the tube of toothpaste, squeezed some into her mouth then passed it to Tristan. He made a face. "You just sucked on that."

"You'd better suck on it, too. Or I won't let you get near me. Oh God, I hurt all over." She rummaged around in her pack until she found the map. She spread it out on her lap. "Here's the station. Not too far away is this place called Rhinebeck. We can walk it. We can buy bikes there."

"And sleeping bags. I can't do another night like this."

Shadaisy glanced over at Tristan slumped miserably against the oak. "I feel sick," he said.

"You're such a baby. You're not sick. Just overwhelmed." The girl surveyed the area. There was the station, the empty parking lot, and trees, trees, trees. Nothing else. This is the wild west all right, she thought. She stood. "Come on, we might as well get going. We'll get a hot breakfast in Rhinebeck. And bikes."

"And sleeping bags."

"Okay. And sleeping bags." She reached out and yanked the boy to his feet.

It was nearly noon by the time the youngsters arrived at the village of Rhinebeck. It looked like a movie set depicting what Shadaisy thought of as a quaint English town. Beautiful old buildings of brick or stone, some with awnings, many with picturesque colored shutters. The place was bustling, but it didn't take a genius to figure out that there was a main street with a few side streets, well-kept back alleys, and that was pretty much it. They went into the first café they saw, called simply, The Corner Café. A black sign with white letters inside the door said, "Please Wait to be Seated." Round tables, chairs with curved backs. Soft lighting. No fluorescent overheads here. People glanced up at them, standing next to the door, then kept staring. Even the waitress stared as she approached. Her badge, black with white letters, said Sherrie. She put them in a corner nearest the kitchen. Tristan ordered three eggs, sausage, bacon, pancakes, hash browns, and a glass of milk. Sherrie eyed him over her pad. When the food arrived, he leaned over the plate, barely swallowing his food before taking another bite.

"Will you slow down. People are staring."

Tristan appeared confused for a moment, then continued eating with the same enthusiasm. "This place is crawling with New Yorkers," he whispered around a large bite of sausage. "And '*ladies*' from New Jersey." He wrinkled his nose. "What are they doing here?"

"Being posh. Apparently, this is a 'place in the country'. Don't stare.

We stick out like sore thumbs as it is." Shadaisy ate her cheese omelet and drank her orange juice with studied care then put a biscuit in her backpack. The two of them sighed, leaned back against their chairs, and smiled at each other. "A full belly—who knows when we'll have another meal like this?" Tristan said.

"Let's go find some bikes." Shadaisy signaled to the waitress. Sherrie went into the kitchen. Time passed. Then more time. Tristan stretched and glanced over his shoulder. "What's she doing in there? Can't take that long to get the bill." Finally, the waitress reappeared and dropped a piece of paper covered in handwritten words and numbers on the table.

Shadaisy smiled at her. "Can you tell us how to get to the nearest Walmart?"

"We don't have a Walmart in Rhinebeck."

"Seriously?" Tristan said.

"There might be one across the river."

Shadaisy looked Sherrie squarely in the eyes and said sweetly, "Where could we find some bicycles? We're biking cross country. Cycling Magazine is following us. It's going to be a huge story. Maybe even on TV."

Sherrie gaped at her for a minute. "There's a bicycle shop on Washington Street a block over. They sell mostly foreign bikes, but you might find a few American-mades… or secondhand."

Shadaisy picked up the bill, then stared at the waitress until she eventually turned to go back in the kitchen. Shadaisy counted out the exact amount of money, leaving a nickel tip.

Outside, Tristan said, "So much for keeping a low profile. That stupid story will be all over town in five minutes. And the nickel tip."

"I couldn't stop myself. There's nothing wrong with being a waitress, but being a stuck-up waitress is a sin. And you didn't help by inhaling enough food for a Russian army."

They found the bicycle shop easily. A flag with a World War 1 vintage bike on it flapped prettily above the door. A tall, blond, slimly built young man greeted them as they walked inside. "Hi there. What can I do for you?" He held out his hand. "My name is Rob."

Shadaisy took his hand, which was warm and dry and comfortable. "I'm Julie and this is Joe. We're new in town." She held it a beat longer than Americans usually do. "We want some bicycles so we can go exploring. Nothing fancy... we're, um, still growing. No point in investing a fortune." She produced her deepest dimples.

"Julie, Joe," Rob said, nodding to each in turn. "Do you plan to do anything other than explore? Any racing? Tours? Cross country?" He kept his eyes on Shadaisy as he spoke. He too smiled.

"No, no, not yet... maybe later. For now, we just want to ride around. See the country."

Rob lifted a beautifully proportioned, sleek bike off its rack. "This one is a beauty. It's French." He pushed it over to her. "Feel how light it is."

She angled it so that she could read the price tag. Forty-five hundred dollars.

"It's a great bike for that price. I think it would fit you perfectly. Do you want to sit on it?"

"It's a little too delicate for my taste. Do you have something a little... you know... more down to earth?"

Rob produced a BMX.

"No, that's a little too down to earth. I was thinking of something, oh I don't know. Unique. Maybe even secondhand. With an interesting history." Shadaisy did a little bounce up onto her toes and down again, smiling at Rob as though they shared a secret. He smiled back. "I do have something. A Dutch couple traded their bikes in yesterday. They might be too big for you." He glanced at Tristan. "We could put pedal enhancers on them. The Dutch, you know. Tallest people in the world. The men, at least." He walked them into a room at the back of the store where he propped up bikes that obviously had seen better days. "Haven't had a chance to clean them up. But they're quality bikes. The Dutch couple were serious bikers. Rode all over Europe."

"You can tell. How much?" said Tristan.

Shadaisy shot him a glare. To Rob she said, "You must be Dutch."

"Well, I am, actually." He beamed. "On both my mother and my father's side."

"I can see that. I don't see a price tag, though. How much for both? We can pay in cash."

"These are really good bikes. Let's say $800 for the two."

"These bikes look like they might break down at any time. We need something dependable. Any other used you can show us?" Shadaisy eyed the cluttered room.

"Tell you what, I'll fix anything you need for the next three months. All these others need repairs before I can let them leave the store. Trust me, they're sound."

"They look like they've been run over by a bus," Tristan mumbled.

Shadaisy ran her hand along the frame of the bike nearest her, positioning herself closer to Rob.

He leaned closer to her, bent over as though he might be going to tell her a secret. "If you take them as-is without my having to clean them up, I could work with you on the price."

Before either of them could say anything, Rob leaned the smaller bike against Tristan. "Here, see if you fit this one."

Tristan hesitated then stood on tiptoe and swung a leg over the frame. His feet barely touched the pedals.

"Pedal enhancers will fix that," Rob said. "Julie, try this." He held the underside of her arm as she swung her leg over the seat. "You fit yours a little better, but you still could use some help. Sit tight. I'll be right back." Rob hustled out of the room to the front of the store and returned with what appeared to be blocks connected to a complicated set of clamps. He unwrapped the plastic. "So, how long have you been in town?"

"Not long." Shadaisy grasped his shoulder to balance herself. Rob put his hand on the small of her back for support as she dismounted. Tristan remained straddling his bike. There then took place a series of negotiations, with much touching and smiling between Rob and Shadaisy, until it was agreed that $600 would cover the two bikes, two sets of enhancers (installed), two baskets (installed) and one extra cushioned seat for Tristan.

"Well, you've robbed me," said Rob, looking delighted. "It's been a long time since anyone has cut that good a deal with me. I'll even clean them up for you and deliver them this evening. If you don't live too far, that is." He raised his eyebrows into a question.

"Oh thanks, but we're going on a little excursion the minute we're out the door. Aren't we, Joe?"

Tristan nodded, wondering if Shadaisy's face ached from all that smiling.

"Do you live in town?" Rob asked innocently.

"Not quite." Shadaisy extended her hand for a shake, lowering her eyes as she did so. Rob took it, raised his other hand to cover hers, but before he could, she pulled away, shot a glance at Tristan, and they wheeled the bikes out the front door.

"You're shameless," the boy said once they were safely on the street. "I thought you were going to get married right there on the spot." Even with the pedal boosters, he had to arch his feet to reach them. "I'm gonna become sterile riding this Goddamn thing, you know that, don't you? Or get ball cancer, like Lance Armstrong.

Shadaisy gave a little hop, swung her leg over the seat, settled her off foot on the right pedal and pushed with the other. "Come on, Lance, let's go meet the wild west." Tristan wobbled after her.

CHAPTER SEVEN

Steve Getz stood in the middle of Josie's kitchen. He had knocked on her door and without waiting for an answer, walked in holding a pie. "There is a wolf sitting in the bathtub next to your door," he said. His mouth was so dry his words sounded furry.

"That's my dog," Josie said, staring at the pie. "She's a Siberian husky. They sometimes look like wolves."

"Are you sure? That thing looks exactly like the pictures of wolves I've seen. Are you, um… are you okay?"

"Yes, of course, why wouldn't I be? It's cause she's mostly gray. All over. Most huskies are more clearly marked." Josie pulled her sweater around her chest. She was wearing a shapeless black cardigan with stains down the front, a white, ankle-length flimsy nightgown, and no shoes. Strands of hair from a ponytail framed her face. There were dirt stains on the knee area of her nightgown, dirt under her fingernails, and her feet were filthy. She noted the look on Steve's face. "I've been working in the garden," she said.

In order not to spend the day under the covers, she had put her feet on the floor the minute she woke. It was a nice morning, not too cold, so Josie let momentum carry her outside where she began pulling up growth the weed wacker had missed. She worked until dizziness forced her to stop.

She leaned over with her hands on her knees and hung her head. When the whirling ceased, she went inside for a glass of water. Now, the sight of the pie made her sick. She walked to the door and called to Rambles, who jumped out of the tub and trotted into the kitchen, wagging her tail.

Steve's eyes followed the dog as she nosed over the floor looking for a tidbit, then he turned to Josie. "I brought you a pie. It's strawberry rhubarb. I got it at that Amish store on the way out here."

Josie nodded. She could see the bright red juice from the fruit leaking through the vents in the crust and around the edges. Definitely not blueberry. She wondered if Getz had known he couldn't possibly bring a blueberry pie out here or if he simply got lucky. "I was just making tea," she said. She made the tea and opened a cupboard, retrieved two plates, and put them on the table across from each other. It took her a while to find a cutting knife, but when she did, she cut two pieces from the pie. The inside was a gelatinous, bright red. Josie stared at it. "Strawberry rhubarb," she said. She put the slices on plates, indicated to Steve that he should sit down, rummaged in a drawer until she found two forks, poured the brewed tea into cups, sat across from Steve, and forked a piece of her pie into her mouth which filled with saliva. Josie swallowed; afraid she might throw up. She leaned against the back of her chair. "Um, why are you here?"

A blush spread across Steve's face.

Josie lowered her eyes. "I'm sorry. That wasn't very nice."

Steve smiled uncertainly. His well-ordered life didn't allow for women in nightgowns and uncombed hair, sitting barefoot in kitchens at eleven in the morning. "I've come with a question. No one has heard from Will since he left town with that girl, and we wanted to know if you had had any contact with him." Steve waited for Josie to reply. When she didn't, he hesitated, gazed out the window over the sink, at the door to the living room, lifted his eyes to the ceiling where there was a water stain, then dropped them to the floor where the dog was still looking for crumbs. He whistled to her. "Here, pooch, you want a piece of crust?" Rambles ignored him.

"Her name is Rambles."

"Here, Rambles." Steve broke off a piece of pie crust and held it toward the dog. She glanced up at him and went over and sat next to Josie. The man sat holding the crust prissily in mid-air, smiling what he hoped was a friendly smile, then eventually sighed and ate it himself. "Look, Josie," he said, "have you heard from Will?"

"No, I haven't heard from Will. Why would I?"

"No one has. The Winstons, the Albrights, the Wonderliks. They have all tried to get in touch with him. His cell is turned off and the letters come back 'return to sender.' Emails go into the ether with no response. It seems he vanished..."

"I can't help that." Josie felt her heart beating against her ribs.

Steve shifted in his chair. "I'm sure he's fine. Busy with..."

Josie stared at him.

"A lot of people in town feel badly about his going off with that girl the way he did. Leaving you alone."

"It wasn't his fault. He had every right to leave. Of course, he left. Who wouldn't? And the girl—he needed someone, he..." Josie's voice trailed off. She looked around the kitchen as though surprised to find herself there.

"No one blames you. It was a tragedy, that's..."

"But you blame Will for leaving. That's wrong. I'd have left me too, if I could. And Jess, Jaylene's husband? I bet no one knows where he is either."

"I suppose not but..."

"And that's the way they want it. Do you think they want anyone calling them or texting or emailing? Reminding them of what happened. Tell your friends in town to leave them alone."

Getz leaned forward, his hand almost touching hers. "Josie, why don't you come for Sunday dinner? Martha always roasts a chicken. Come eat with us. It would please..."

"I can't do that!" Josie sat up straight in her chair.

"Josie, Josie. Don't wall yourself off like this. I worry about you out here alone. We all do. "Getz regarded the room. "I shouldn't have shown you this property."

"It was what I wanted. I would have been mad if you hadn't."

"You should be in town where people can watch out for you."

"You don't know what I need. You don't know me that well."

Steve raised his hand. "Sorry. "We care about you, that's all."

"Who's we?"

"Like I said, the Albrights, the Wunderliks. All your friends."

Josie said nothing.

"Don't get mad at me, Josie. I'm coming back soon. To check on you."

"Erik comes every day," she lied.

"He does? That's good." Steve moved his hand infinitesimally closer to Josie's, which was so pale and thin it appeared translucent.

The wolf/dog rose to all fours and gave out a sharp yelp. Her tail wasn't wagging and her hackles bristled.

Steve pushed his chair back and stood up from the table. "Is your phone working?"

"Of course," Josie said, even though she hadn't charged it since she talked to Erik.

"I'll call you," he said. "If that's okay?"

"You can call if you want, but I'm okay. Really."

As soon as Getz was out the door, Josie flopped onto the couch and dropped her forearm over her eyes. Erik would arrive in the early afternoon, and she had promised him dinner. The thought of the pork forced into links waiting for her in the refrigerator made her feel sick. She would have to slit the casings and push out the sausage out into the Dutch oven. She considered canceling, but who knew when Erik would make this offer again. She drew a deep breath, held it, then let it slip out slowly. After repeating this three times, her stomach settled enough to think about the sausage browning in the pan.

After emptying the meat, Josie returned to the couch, leaving the pork to brown on its own, sizzling in the pan. She did some more deep breathing before going into the kitchen to dice an onion. Josie dropped the pieces in with the meat, along with two cloves of garlic still in their skins. Back to the couch for a few more deep breaths. Next, Josie poured in her favorite jarred pasta sauce and spices. She turned the flame under the pot as low as it would go, flopped onto the couch, and stayed there for over an hour until the sauce was done.

When Erik arrived, she was sitting on the steps outside of the kitchen.

"Why are you still in your nightgown?"

"I don't know. Maybe cause Steve Getz brought me a pie. You can take it home with you."

Erik watched her, his face thoughtful, then he seemed to decide to let go of whatever he was thinking and rubbed his hands together. "Let's get started. This is going to take a while."

He wrestled with the rototiller for over three hours. Josie found the noise frightening with its uneven rumble, grinding and roaring as it struggled with something that sounded like it could destroy it, then dropping into the purr of a well-oiled machine only to roar and screech again. By five o'clock, Erik was drenched in sweat, his shirt sticking flat against his torso. The garden had turned into a series of rich, dark clumps of sod. "You'll have to break these clumps up by hand," he said. "You have the tools?"

"Yes."

"Good. I'm starved. Let me take a bath, then let's eat."

Josie placed the Dutch oven full of pasta and sauce in front of her brother who helped himself. He was a surprisingly dainty eater, rolling the noodles against the side of his bowl until they were secure before he placed them in his mouth, not spilling a drop. He brought this same fastidiousness to his half of the baguette, breaking off a piece and spreading butter on it as though he were painting. Once the bowl was empty, he pushed his chair sideways to the table and crossed his legs. It looked as though he might light a cigar, but he'd given up smoking years ago. '"I see you haven't eaten a thing."

"I had some."

"I'm not going to lecture you. Others might, but not me." He bounced his foot up and down.

Josie looked down at her plate, her hands folded in her lap. A few tears dripped into the Bolognese.

"I lost a sister, too." Erik leaned back against the chair, gazed at his sister, and misread her silence completely. "This will cheer you up. One night, when you and Jaylene were seventeen, you had a really bad strep throat. High fever, headache, sore throat, the works. You were out of it. It was Friday night; Jaylene and I were bored so we went to the Dew Drop Inn."

The Dew Drop Inn was a dingy, popular bar in Chatham, fifteen miles away, where the Whitts, in all likelihood, would escape recognition. "I swear," he went on, "when we walked in the door, every head swiveled to look at Jaylene. I put some money in the jukebox, and we began to dance. The men never took their eyes off her. We danced two dances and were heading to the bar when the place erupted with applause. Everyone shouted, 'More, more.' So, we went back onto the dance floor. Man, could Jaylene dance. I'm good but she was better. When she twirled, all that black hair flew around her head. When she slid, she went right between my legs and never missed a beat. We must have danced seven, eight, ten dances in a row. Finally, Jaylene put her forehead on my shoulder and said, 'I'm whipped.' So, I took her home. I'll never forget that night. She was on fire."

Josie was surprised by how much his words hurt. Not only had they gone without her, Jaylene never told her about it. Even worse, Erik had no idea how much this story was bound to hurt her. She wanted to say to him, *she wasn't your twin*. She wanted to say to him, *you weren't the one who killed her*, but she couldn't.

CHAPTER EIGHT

Despite Tristan's objections and their rusted, dirty frames, the Dutch bikes with their slim elegance, slipped through the atmosphere with the exquisite balance of a hawk. Other than Tristan's seat bones, the bicycles produced no soreness in their riders. Shadaisy rode in front while Tristan drafted behind her. They couldn't talk, so they rode in solitary wonderment. Neither had ever imagined a landscape so empty. They rode for stretches without seeing another human, though the locals complained bitterly about the encroachment of the posh people who were crowding the land, the roads, the shops not only with their persons, but with their opinions. But to Shadaisy, this felt like a different planet, barely inhabited. "We're on Mars," she shouted to the wind.

The youngsters took Route 9 to 9G with the Hudson River on their left. They didn't have much of a plan except to veer onto back roads before reaching the city of Hudson. The sun was warm, the air cool, and their bodies young and strong. They ate up the miles. When the light faded enough to form a flimsy cover, Shadaisy brought her bike to a stop. Tristan rolled up beside her. She said, "Let's take the next small road to the right. If we turn left, we'll end up in the mighty Hudson."

The day had left Tristan in a trance. The emptiness, the exercise, the clean air, the newness of everything, and his now empty stomach had put his mind in an altered state where it was hard to focus, even on Shadaisy. Obedient, he nodded an okay. Without saying any more, the girl put a foot on a pedal and pushed off with the other.

After riding ten more minutes, Shadaisy turned onto an unmarked macadam road boarded by rolling lawns with old, formal houses sitting well back. The evening light turned the air blue, creating long, dark shadows and highlighting the pale new leaves uncurling along their branches. The sky showed streaks of crimson. The two kept riding until the houses became scarcer and the lawns turned into fields, some with rows of fruit trees, their tight blossoms poised to bloom. Eventually, Shadaisy spotted a large barn behind one of these orchards. It was nearly hidden by the trees, but the twilight turned the barn so dark and solid that for a few moments it stood out as a solid mass against the twisting trees. There wasn't another building in sight. She pointed to it, and they rode a dirt path to the entrance.

Inside, bales of hay were stacked to a few feet below the rafters. Tristan looked at Shadaisy in disbelief. He rolled his bike behind randomly stacked bales near the rear of the barn and climbed the mass of bales placed one atop the other until he reached the last row. He held his arms out wide. "Is this perfect or what?" he called down.

Shadaisy joined him.

Together, without talking, they pulled and shoved bales to build a small fort. They yanked hay loose from its twine and fluffed it into piles inside this nest, making soft warm beds and pillows. It didn't take long, and when they were satisfied, they sat cross legged facing each other and grinning. Tristan said, "We've died and gone to heaven." Shadaisy laughed and reached for her backpack. They had stopped at a small, dirty country store smelling of rancid meat and bought Doritos, Snickers, and Cokes. The man behind the counter didn't even look at them when they put down their money, just palmed it, turned to the cash register, put the change on the counter, and returned to his magazine.

Shadaisy and Tristan ate their supper, leaning back among the fragrant bales. Neither could keep from smiling. "You know," Tristan said, "the country might not be so bad after all. Are you warm enough?" He had dropped the idea of sleeping bags in his haste to leave Rhinebeck.

"Warm as toast," Shadaisy said. "In fact, maybe even a little too warm."

Tristan stretched out his legs and closed his eyes. "I think it feels wonderful." He scrunched his bottom into the loose hay. After a companionable silence, he opened his eyes and looked at Shadaisy. "Hey, Shadrack, have you kidnapped me?"

"What are you talking about?"

"You're seventeen, right? You can choose not to go to school, but I'm only fifteen, so by law I have to go. I'm obviously not going. And I'm here with you. Breaking the law. I mean, of course, I came willingly, but, you know, our ages… have you kidnapped me?"

Shadaisy thought this over for a moment. "Look, Mouse, it's almost summer. School will be out. And I intend to be in the city by Thanksgiving. So, you're not missing that much school. And don't think for a minute that I don't intend to graduate from high school. I'm not going to be some jumped-up, bitter waitress like we met today. I intend to do things with my life."

"Like what?"

"I don't know. Maybe work for the FBI."

"Um, Shads, you're a felon."

"Not yet. I'm not a felon until I've been arrested and convicted."

"The FBI does extensive background checks."

Shadaisy picked up a stalk of hay and put it in her mouth. "So, you think my history in foster care will work against me?" she said.

"Not according to 'Bones.' She was in foster care."

"Anyway," Shadaisy said, "maybe I'll become a personal trainer. No background checks there. What about you?"

"Plants. Not a farmer. That would be awful. But own my own greenhouse. Or get into landscaping."

"Do the landscaping first. Work hard, live in your truck, and save enough money to start a greenhouse. Or build your own landscaping business until all you have to do is drive around in your Beemer and tell your staff what to do."

The sun shone through the narrow spaces between the old barn's shrunken boards, spreading tiny stripes across the hay and Shadaisy's eyes. She moaned and opened them.

Tristan, already awake, had piled bales on top of each other and now stood on them, his arms overhead and fingertips touching the peaked roof. "I heart this barn," he crowed before scrambling down to their nest where he rummaged through his backpack. Retrieving the last Snickers bar, he held it out to Shadaisy.

She shook her head. "I'm not hungry. You eat it."

"Let's stay here forever."

"You know we can't."

"Where are we going to settle?"

Shadaisy put her arms behind her head and looked at the ceiling. "Farther away from the city, for one thing. Near a very small town. One that has a grocery store and maybe a drug store and an orchard nearby. We can pick fruit all summer. Farmers don't ask for any ID. They hire illegals so they can pay crappy wages. That's okay. We'll get by. We need to find an empty building somewhere. Abandoned. With no one around."

"There's no one around here." Tristan bit into the Snickers bar.

"This hay didn't crawl in here by itself. Someone is using this barn. They'll come by sooner or later."

"But I heart this barn. It's so cozy."

"How's your ass, by the way?"

"It hurts a little, but the rest of me is fine."

"I'm sore."

"We should stay here and rest a day or two."

"Let's ride until we find a place for breakfast."

After dismantling their nest and putting the bales back where they found them, Tristan and Shadaisy got on the road, staying parallel to the

Hudson River. They passed orchards with their buds just beginning to show their flowers. The few houses they saw sat far from the road. Around ten o'clock, Tristan pulled next to Shadaisy and shouted, "I'm starving."

"I haven't seen a McDonald's or Burger King or nothing like it," she shouted.

"Let's go to a greasy spoon."

Shadaisy dropped her head, her eyes staring at the road beneath the bike's front wheel. "I haven't seen one of those either," she muttered.

"What?"

Shadaisy looked over at Tristan. "You go ahead, let me draft behind you. If you see a place to eat, pull over."

They rode steadily on, the girl focusing on Tristan's back wheel and her feet pushing the pedals round and round. She lost all sense of time and nearly ran into him when he stopped and pointed at a small, yellow and red wooden building with a giant ice cream cone on the roof.

He turned his bike onto the gravel parking lot, bouncing over the pebbles until he came to rest in front of the building's door, which had Country Cone ineptly painted above the lintel. He hopped off his bike. "This place looks great."

Shadaisy was breathing hard. "What will we do with the bikes?"

"Look around you, Shadrack. There isn't a car in sight. We can sit in that booth next to the window and keep an eye on them."

They stood their bikes near the window and went inside. They were the only customers. A waitress came out from the kitchen and smiled broadly at them as they sat in the booth. "What can I get for you?" She took a pad out of her pale green uniform pocket, continuing to smile.

Tristan ordered "the farmer's special." Shadaisy asked for tea and toast. He leaned toward her over the table and whispered, "Hey, did you see these prices? Can you believe it? All that food for five ninety-nine. Why'd you only get toast? You worried about money?"

Shadaisy smiled and shook her head.

After breakfast, the two fell into a rhythm, concentrating on the road, paying little attention to their surroundings, eating up the miles in a forward motion that left them unaware of their bodies until Shadaisy noticed the light had changed and the sun no longer warmed her shoulders. She shuddered. They rode for another hour and there was nothing. No barns, no outbuildings of any kind. Still drafting behind Tristan, she started to shiver. She was becoming desperate, afraid they would have to bed down in a field when she noticed on their right a dilapidated building, little more than a shed. There was nothing else around it. She shouted to Tristan to stop and pointed.

The shed stored hay, but it wasn't sweet smelling like in the barn of last night. These bales stank of dust and mold and weren't stacked neatly but thrown here and there. A loft about two yards below the roof protruded over a third of the dirt floor. Using hay bales, they climbed onto it. They made another nest, this one more musty than cozy. They had stocked up on candy bars, cupcakes, and Coke from the Country Cone. Shadaisy ate a few bites of chocolate cupcake, drank two cans of Coke, burped mightily and said, "I'm pooped. Wake me in the morning."

She woke to pitch black, her head pounding. Her limbs felt like water. As she laid very still, she became aware of the bones in her body, the throbbing pain they radiated, the way they tied into her joints, which hurt so much she felt sick. She moaned, pushed a hay bale aside, leaned over the loft and threw up on the dirt floor. She retched until there was only stomach fluid left, then flopped onto her back and flung an arm across Tristan's chest.

He sat up and rubbed his eyes. "Shadrack? Are you all right?"

"No, I'm not all right. I think I have food poisoning."

"From toast?"

"No, from that bitch in Rhinebeck. I bet she put something in my food."

"Wouldn't you have gotten sick sooner?"

Shadaisy was something of an expert on food poisoning, having had it several times in her various foster homes. She knew that there were basically two types: the kind when the bacteria were young and viable and kept their poisons to themselves a day or two or the other kind when the bacteria were dying, releasing toxins into your stomach as soon as you ate them. You might as well be drinking poison, a friendly doctor had told her. She didn't have the strength to tell Tristan any of this, even though after vomiting she did feel better. She drifted to sleep for about half an hour then sat bolt upright, jumped to the ground, ran out the shed door into the bushes, where she managed to yank down her pants and squat before exploding. Cramps and dry heaves shook her for what seemed like forever. Eventually, she fell over on her side. With the expulsions over, sleep overwhelmed her. She came to with Tristan shaking her shoulder.

"Oh, Mouse," she moaned.

"Whew," he said. "You're sick." He helped her to the shed and covered her with loose hay, placed his palm on her forehead. "You're burning up."

"I'm dying."

"Don't say that. Do you want some Coke?"

"Yes, please."

Tristan was more alarmed by the "please" than anything else. He held her head in the crook of his arm as she sipped a drop. She pushed his hand away and rolled onto her side, groaning.

Five more times that night she ran outside, and five more times Tristan helped her back to their nest. He held her against him when her teeth chattered and pushed all the hay away when she flailed and cried, "I'm burning up." By the time dawn arrived, Shadaisy was a limp, searing bundle. Tristan couldn't wake her. He smoothed a curl away from her temple. "Don't you die on me," he said. He hunkered down, his bottom resting on his calves, and continued stroking her hair. He wondered if he should go for help. But where?

His mother had been sick like this before she died. What would he do if Shadaisy didn't make it? Would he pedal to Rhinecliff and take the train to New York? And then what? Turn up at Social Services? How could he possibly return to his old life without Shadrack in it? "Don't you dare leave me," he whispered, his voice husky with tears. He placed his palm on a flaming cheek. It didn't seem possible a person could be so hot and still be alive. "Shadrack," he whispered over and over again with no hope of a response.

A movement breaking the light coming in through the shed's door caught his eye. A wolf stood watching him, cheerfully wagging its tail. Having caught his eye, it flattened its ears in greeting, smiled a friendly wolf smile, trotted toward him, and raised onto its hind legs, resting its front paws on the hay right next to Shadaisy's head. Tristan's instinct was to leap into the air and run like hell, but he couldn't leave Shadaisy unprotected, so he turned to stone instead.

Rambles sniffed the girl's damp curls, assessing the situation. When satisfied, the dog jumped up onto the bales of hay and straddled Shadaisy's inert body. She licked a burning cheek. Tristan jumped to his feet, threw his arms in the air and yelled, "Get out of here! Get out, goddamn it." Rambles lifted her head, looked at him calmly, and wagged her tail. She howled deep in her throat, a low, lilting, friendly sound, and jumped down into the aisle where she continued to hold Tristan's eye and wag her tail encouragingly. A moment passed while Tristan's breathing slowed, and Rambles maintained her cheerful vigil. Eventually, she turned and trotted to the doorway, stopped and looked over her shoulder at the boy and howled again, this time ending with a sharp yelp.

Tristan followed her along a thin dirt path. It was like walking through a tunnel of tall weeds and grass. When the path made a right-angle turn, he saw a small, single-story dwelling sitting amidst the wild growth. Next to it, a white witch stood in a cleared patch of ground. She wielded a hoe, lifting it high over her head and swinging it to the earth and smashing the dirt so swiftly that her body moved all in a piece, surging in a continuous frantic motion. Totally focused, she was unaware of anything going on around her. Before he had a chance to think about it, Tristan called out hello. The woman froze with the hoe over her head. She had blond hair that fell in long-tangled disarray down her back and wore a thin nightgown to her ankles. Staring straight ahead, she seemed to have turned to stone.

"My name is Tristan."

The woman turned and looked at the boy, surprising him with her young face. Her eyes were the blue of arctic shadows. He took a step back and began talking so fast Josie found it hard to understand what he was saying. Eventually, she made out he wasn't alone, that he and his sister had spent the night in the shed, and that she was very sick. Finally, he slowed himself down and said very distinctly, "Can you help us, please." He looked to be about twelve, unkempt and under fed.

"Where did you come from?"

"I'll tell you later. You have to help us. I can't wake her up."

"But who are you?"

"Are you deaf?" the boy shouted. "I think Shadrack is dying." He took a few steps toward Josie, his hands balled into fists.

Josie dropped the hoe and followed him.

CHAPTER NINE

The girl was flat on her back with one arm flung out to the side and the other above her head. She appeared to be about the same age as the boy. "What's her name?" Josie asked.

"Shadaisy."

Josie placed the inside of her wrist against Shadaisy's forehead then carefully shook her shoulder. The girl made no response. Her face was a grayish white, with crimson splotches on the cheeks, and her eyelids were so lavender it looked as though she had put makeup on them. Her head lolled from side to side. Josie took hold of her hand, pinched a piece of skin on the back, and watched as it slowly returned to its place. She glanced at the boy. "Your sister is dehydrated." She sat back on her haunches, knowing she should call 911. But the memory of the siren's wail, the unit careening over the road, the medics jumping out with all their equipment while she wandered around, her mind whirling, unable to stop it, to formulate any coherent thought, was unbearable.

Driving the girl to the hospital herself was out of the question. Columbia Memorial was where the medics had taken Josie to be treated for shock.

"I'll get the car. Wait here." Josie ran to the cottage, leapt into the SUV, spun it in a wide circle, bounced over the dirt path and overgrown fields and slammed on the brakes, jolting her forward as she came to an abrupt stop in front of the shed.

With Josie holding her shoulders and Tristan her legs, they carried Shadaisy to the Jeep. Being hauled down off the hay roused the girl. She moaned and weakly tried to struggle free. Josie placed one arm under Shadaisy's shoulders and one under her knees while Tristan opened the back seat doors. He crawled through the far side, took hold of Shadaisy's ankles, and pulled her toward him onto the seat. "What the hell," she groaned.

Together, Josie and Tristan inched the girl into the car. When they reached the cottage door, Josie slid out of the car, ran into her house and into the bathroom. Fortunately, her cardboard box of medicines sat alone on the floor away from the chaos of opened boxes in the other rooms. A quick rummage through it produced a thermometer.

Shadaisy had fallen into a fevered sleep, her mouth open and breath shallow. When Josie put the thermometer behind the girl's ear she woke, reached up, and batted Josie's hand away. It was awkward leaning over the girl's body, halfway into the car. Her back hurt and her hair fell into her face. She held the thermometer in front of her eyes. One hundred and five degrees. Josie backed out of the vehicle. "We have to get her fever down."

In the house she attached the hose to the sink faucet, adjusted the water to tepid, and ran back outside. She dropped the nozzle in the tub. "Help me," she said. She grabbed Shadaisy under the arms and unceremoniously dragged her out of the car. When the girl's bottom hit the ground, Tristan grabbed her legs. "What are we doing?

"Help me get her in the tub."

The boy hesitated but did as he was told.

When the water flowed over her, Shadaisy cried out and flailed her arms against the enamel sides. Josie knelt and tried to hold her still. Shadaisy kicked and slapped at Josie while screaming profanities. She opened her eyes and glared at Tristan in a way that started him crying again.

"Run inside and check the clock on the stove. Now!" Josie shouted. She was holding Shadaisy down by her shoulders.

Tristan dragged himself away from the scene and dashed into the house. He was back practically before he left. "Eight ten," he gasped.

"Help me." Josie was soaking wet by now. The longer Shadaisy stayed in the cooling water, the stronger she became, thrashing about with her hands, feet, and legs while screaming oaths. Tristan cried silently as he tried to hold her knees down. A lifetime passed. Tristan closed his eyes. Then he heard Josie say, "Go check the time again."

"Eight-twenty-three."

"Help me get her out, and we'll put her to bed."

Shadaisy was able to stagger inside with Tristan and Josie holding onto both arms. Once in the kitchen, Josie leaned the girl against Tristan, who continued to hold her, as Josie began pulling off the girl's jeans. Shadaisy tried to push her away.

"Don't be an idiot." Josie continued to yank at the clinging denim. "You want to sleep in these wet clothes?"

Shadaisy went boneless, letting Tristan support her weight, while he blushed to his hair roots and did his best to keep his eyes averted.

After pulling her t-shirt over her head and wrapping her in a towel, Josie helped the girl into her bed, straightening the covers under her chin. "I want to take your temperature. Is that okay?"

Shadaisy nodded.

The thermometer read 103. "Better. My name is Josie. You spent the night in my shed. You're very sick, but your temperature has come down. You're dehydrated. I'm going to make some tea for you." In the kitchen Josie boiled water, made the tea, and poured sugar into it. Somewhere she had heard this helped prevent shock.

But Shadaisy wouldn't let her get the liquid near her lips. She slapped at Josie's hands, tossed her head back and forth, and finally buried her head in the pillow.

Josie asked Tristan to help, but he backed up when she did, and shook his head. "I can't."

"Okay, let her sleep. We'll try later. Now you, Tristan, come with me and tell me what the hell is going on." The boy followed her back to the kitchen.

Josie's legs felt wobbly, and she was dizzy again. She sank slowly into a kitchen chair. Tristan sat in the other one. Josie stared blankly in front of her for a while before turning her full attention on Tristan. He was an odd-looking boy. His dark eyes were as round as marbles; he had big ears and a small nose. "Tristan," Josie said, "we have to call your parents. They need to know how sick your sister is."

"Sister?"

"Yes, your sister. That's what you called her, anyway."

Tristan straightened in his chair. "Yes, that's right. My sister."

"What's their phone number?"

"We don't have parents."

This didn't surprise Josie. Finding a strange boy in her garden and a strange, half-dead girl in her shed, followed by the battle in the bathtub, had used up her ability to be surprised.

"We've been in foster care all our lives."

"Then we need to call your foster parents."

"No. Oh, no. You can't do that." Tristan leaned toward Josie. "They were horrible. That's why we ran away. We had to. It was unbearable."

"From where?"

"What?"

"Where were you in foster care?"

Tristan sat against the back of his chair and squared his small shoulders. "Ohio." He had known a boy who had lived in Akron, Ohio until his parents moved to New York City, where he was placed in foster care when his parents took up residence in a crack house.

Josie looked Tristan up and down. She didn't believe what he was saying, at least not all of it, but he appeared so harmless and distressed sitting in front of her, actually quivering like a frightened dog, she couldn't be mad. "How old are you?"

"Fifteen."

Josie sighed. Fifteen or twelve, he was still underage. She was sure the law required her to inform the authorities about these minors showing up at her place. As soon as the thought crossed her mind, she dismissed it. What a brouhaha that would make.

A silence fell between them that lasted so long Tristan squirmed in his chair until he finally asked, "Do you think Shadaisy will be all right?"

"I think so. Her temperature is down," Josie answered in a flat voice. Her gaze strayed from the boy to the floor. He was still there. And the girl was still in her bedroom. She sat for several moments with her shoulders slumped. Eventually, she roused herself. "We need to find her something easy to keep down. Every time she vomits, she loses more fluid."

"I can go on my bike."

"No. Not yet. We'll try the sweet tea again. That usually works. Right now, she needs to sleep."

Tristan stood. "I'll go stay with her."

Josie followed him into her bedroom. Shadaisy laid on her side, one hand hanging off the edge of the bed. She was asleep, her mouth open and her breathing steady but shallow. Tristan dragged a cardboard box close to the side of the bed and sat on it. He must be worn out, Josie thought. "I'll find you some blankets so you can lie down." It took her a while. After going through all the boxes in her bedroom, Josie went into the second bedroom and was almost finished digging through the boxes there when she found the blankets in the far corner.

After giving the blankets to the boy, she went back to the kitchen and stood with her arms crossed under her chest. Shadaisy's clothes were in a heap on the floor. She put them in the washing machine, which was in a closet off the kitchen, poured in laundry detergent and bleach, and went out into the garden.

While waiting for the clothes to go through the cycle, she picked up the hoe from where she'd dropped it and began breaking up the rest of the large lumps. Next, she used the spade, followed by the three-pronged claw and finally her hands, rubbing and sifting the soil through her fingers until it was a fine meal. She didn't think about the children in her bedroom. She focused on the task in front of her and refused to let her mind go anywhere else. Periodically, like the cycles in her washing machine, her mind shifted to a new job. Then she would leave the garden to check on Shadaisy, who had fallen into a deep though rousable sleep. Josie took her temperature each time she checked on her. It remained at 103 until four o'clock when it registered 104.5. Josie leaned over and said, "Daisy, I'm going to bring you some sweet tea, is that okay?'

"Shadaisy," Tristan corrected her.

"Right. Shadaisy."

Josie supported the girl's head in the crook of her arm and held the cup to her lip. "Slowly, now. Sip it slowly."

Shadaisy sipped, wrinkled her nose, and tried to push Josie's hand away.

"Just a few more sips, for now. That's good."

Josie touched Tristan on the shoulder, motioned him to follow her out of the room. "You hungry?" The boy appeared on the verge of collapse. She made three peanut butter sandwiches, one for her and two for Tristan. They washed them down with water. When they finished, Tristan returned to the bedroom and Josie poured a glass of juice, carried it to the kitchen stoop and sat sipping it while watching the light change from yellow to orange to lavender and finally to blue. She went inside and found two pillows in a box in the living room. She took Shadaisy's temperature again. 103. This time the girl didn't fight the sweet tea. When she was finished, she looked at Josie with half-closed eyes and said, "Who are you?"

"I'm Josie, and this is my place."

Having grown up in foster care, Shadaisy was used to waking up to strangers. "Thanks," she said, and closed her eyes.

Josie gathered two more blankets and gave one plus a pillow to Tristan and settled herself on the couch with the other. That night, she dreamt of her sister relentlessly turning into a blueberry pie while Josie ran around in circles unable to stop and help her. She woke to Erik standing over her, his hands on his hips. Daylight flooded the room.

"Do you know that Goldilocks is sleeping in your bed? And she has someone with her."

Josie sat up, holding the blanket around her. "Erik, why are you here?"

"Just checking up, and it seems it was the right thing to do."

Josie told him the whole story. Erik sat next to her and listened without interrupting, staring so intently into her face it made her uncomfortable. She stood and walked into the kitchen. He followed her and sat at the table.

Josie filled a pan with water and put it on the stove. "Do you want some tea?"

"No, I had coffee on the way out." Erik crossed his legs. "Now, I'm not saying there's anything strange about what you just told me. Stranger things have happened, God knows. But I wonder if these two might be felons planning to kill you in your sleep and take everything you own."

"They're just kids."

"Kids have been known to do just this sort of thing. Think of Lizzy Borden. And they were her parents."

"That's not the same thing at all."

Josie poured tea into her cup with the roses painted on it and brought it to the table. "The girl is too sick to travel, and her brother won't leave her side. I can't kick them out now."

Erik sat in a brown study while Josie blew over the steaming liquid. "Your garden looks nice," he finally said.

"Uh huh."

"Ready to plant, I would say. Do you have any fertilizer?"

"No."

"Always good to give them a little boost when you plant. You could make your own mixture with bone meal and green fertilizer, or you could just go to Lowes and buy Miracle Grow."

In fact, Josie and Jaylene had had their own mixture they used when they planted. It had bone meal, peat moss, and dried grass clippings. Josie stared at her brother without seeing him. Instead, she saw herself carrying a tray of tomato plants, balancing them carefully so they wouldn't spill as she walked through the trees and crossed the road on her way to Jaylene's, two twisted thin lanes spread like a ribbon of molten lava dropped into the copes of trees burning so cleanly that no space existed between the macadam and the forest. As dense and thick with fallen leaves and debris as the woods were, it was still the quickest way from one house to the other. She and Jaylene never used the driveways when they visited back and forth on foot. They walked out of the trees and crossed that road two, three times a day, often without checking left or right, so rarely did cars drive by.

Erik waited for a response and when he didn't get one, said, "Tell you what. I think I have some of my own mixture left over from last year. I'll go get it." He put his hands on his thighs, pushed himself to his feet, and turned toward the door.

Josie looked up and followed him with her eyes. "Are you leaving?"

"Sure. To get the fertilizer."

"Today?"

"Why not? It's a beautiful day. Might as well get started. It's supposed to rain tonight, which would be perfect." He opened the door and closed it gently behind him, gone before she could answer him.

Josie continued to sit, her hands in her lap and her eyes focused on the door for several minutes, then she rose and crept back to the bedroom and peeked in. Tristan had put his pillow and blankets on the floor right beside Shadaisy. They were both sleeping, so she shut the door and laid back down on the couch and this time fell into a deep dreamless sleep that lasted until Erik's van coming up the driveway two hours later woke her. She scrambled off the couch and met him coming inside.

"I've got the fertilizer. Shall we get started?"

Outside, Erik looked over the plants Josie had placed under the oak trees. "I see you're sticking with the old favorites."

"What?" Josie leaned on the upright handle of the hoe, pressing it into the ground.

"These are all Big Boys. No better tomato for sandwiches no matter how many hybrids they come up with."

Josie had simply emptied the shelf in front of her at Lowes without checking the labels.

Erik dropped to his knees and, using the trowel, dug deeply into the dark, ready soil. "You've got some good land here. Great topsoil." He scooped about a tablespoon of his mixture into the hole, removed the bottom leaves of the plant, and coiled the stem into it. In the meantime, Josie joined him and began preparing the earth for the next plant. She didn't want to plant tomato plants today or ever again. Or any other vegetable. She didn't want to garden. She wanted Jaylene. She wanted to be able to love Will again. What had she been thinking, buying all these plants?

"Do you ever plan to change that nightgown?" Erik asked.

Josie glanced at herself. The white material was turning gray, and the knees and hem were a chestnut brown.

Before the accident, Josie had always had a touch of whimsy about her. For example, she loved the early 1900s, when women's clothing made the dramatic change from instruments of torture to garments so loose, they barely touched the skin. "I was born in the wrong era," she used to say. Around twelve, she started wearing nightgowns made of white, thin cotton and continued doing so all through her years at Pratt and her marriage. Will laughed at her and called her "Your Majesty." Jaylene said she wouldn't be caught dead in one of those old lady nightgowns. She wore boxers and t-shirts to bed.

Now there was nothing whimsical about Josie's nightgowns. She tried to think of an answer to Erik's question that wouldn't sound like whining or an excuse but couldn't, so she said nothing.

"Did you get any?"

Josie looked over her shoulder, frowning. "Any what?"

"Poison ivy."

She sat up and considered at her hands. "I think I've got some on my hands. There're blisters between my fingers, and they itch."

"You'd better be careful with that. Could get infected. An infection in your hand is a nasty piece of work. Hard to treat. You could end up in the hospital on IV antibiotics. Or even need surgery. An artist needs their hands, Josie. You're planning to get back to work at some point, aren't you?"

Josie leaned back on her heels. "Don't you have a show you should be getting ready for?"

"Not for a few weeks. I just finished a painting and need a few days off to clear my head."

They continued working in silence. The sun rose overhead then made its descent toward the horizon. Josie, dripping with sweat, felt the dizziness return. She straightened and put her hands on the small of her back. The kitchen door opened and shut. Tristan called from the stoop, "Shadaisy's in the kitchen. I gave her some tea, but she threw it up."

Inside, Shadaisy stood wrapped in a bed sheet, which pooled around her feet. Her skin appeared translucent, a waxy white with lavender smudged around her sunken eyes. She glanced from Josie to Erik, where her gaze rested a beat too long.

Josie glanced at her brother, who was focusing on his hands while he pulled off his gardening gloves. She hadn't noticed he was wearing them. He went to the sink to wash up. "Whew, what's this mess?" he said, wrinkling his nose at a wadded-up dish towel.

"I cleaned up Shadaisy's puke," Tristan said.

Erik waited while his sister picked up the wet cloth and, holding it between her thumb and index finger, carried it to the washing machine where she added it to the jeans and t-shirt and set the machine back to start. It wouldn't hurt to wash Shadaisy's clothes again. Erik sprayed water over the enamel bottom of the sink, picked up the bar of soap on the counter, and washed his hands. He dried them on his jeans. "You'd better wash yours, Josie. Like I said. Don't want to risk infection."

Shadaisy took hold of the back of a chair and slowly sank onto the seat. She watched Josie walk to the sink then shifted her focus back to Erik, who pulled out another chair and sat across from her. "I'm Erik, Josie's brother. I saw you and *your* brother while you were sleeping in Josie's bedroom."

"Brother?"

Tristan moved to the table. "I explained to Josie that we're brother and sister."

"Oh. Yeah. Right."

Finished with cleaning her hands, Josie pulled a chair from the living room into the kitchen and sat at the head of the table. "Erik, this is Shadaisy and Tristan. Tristan, Shadaisy, this is Erik, my brother."

Shadaisy let the sheet slip off her shoulder. Josie reached over and put it back against her neck. "Tristan said you threw up again."

"I hate that sweet tea."

"Is there something else you would like? You need to drink something."

"I'd kill for an Orange Crush."

"Orange Crush? Do they even make that anymore? How about a Coke?"

"I threw up gallons of Coke last night."

Josie leaned back in her chair. The thought of driving to supermarkets or tracking down small mom and pop stores scattered along back roads, trying drug stores, gas stations, and specialty shops was nightmarish. She never wanted to drive a car anywhere again, let alone hunting all over the place for something as obscure as Orange Crush.

Erik pushed his chair back and rose to his feet. "I'll go look for some."

After he left, Shadaisy slumped in her chair, her head lolling as if too heavy to hold up.

"You're white as that sheet, Shadaisy. Go back to bed."

The girl shuffled through the kitchen and living room, holding the sheet under her arms.

When the t-shirt, jeans, and dish cloth had completed the cycle, Josie took them outside and hung them on tree branches to dry. Then she walked back to her bedroom, where Shadaisy was sitting up in bed, the covers pulled to her neck. Josie retrieved a t-shirt and jeans from her dresser, folded them, and placed them at the bottom of the bed near Shadaisy's feet. "You can wear these. Your clothes are washed and hanging to dry."

Shadaisy bent at the middle and pulled the clothes close to her. "You're the best," she said, her voice listless. "I hate not having any clothes on. Makes me feel weak." Shadaisy pulled the t-shirt over her head. It fit her like a short dress, the sleeves hanging below her elbows. She slid out of bed to pull on the jeans. The bottom of the legs ended well beyond her feet. She rolled them up. "When do you think Erik will be back?"

"Not soon. He'll probably have to drive all over the county to find that stuff, if he can find it all. Where are you going?"

Shadaisy was heading out of the bedroom. In the kitchen, she settled herself at the table to wait.

Josie and Tristan followed her. "He could be gone a long time," Josie said. "Wouldn't you be more comfortable lying down?"

"I'll wait."

She didn't have long. Erik was back in less than an hour, holding a small paper bag.

"That was fast," Josie said.

"There's this horrible country store not too far from here. Disgusting. The man behind the counter was boiling something on a hot plate that could have been a skunk and people were actually eating bowls of it. I couldn't get out of there fast enough, but I saw this on a shelf, big as life." He handed the paper bag to Josie. "The top is still sealed so it might be okay."

Josie pulled out a glass bottle containing an unnaturally orange liquid. Wondering if soda ever went bad, she took a can opener out of a drawer and pushed back the metal top. Tiny bubbles of fizz escaped. A good sign.

She tipped her head and sniffed at the opening. Nothing strange there, so she retrieved an ice tray from the freezer, twisted some cubes into a glass, and poured the Orange Crush over them. It bubbled and popped. Josie noticed the same fake bits of pulp she remembered from many years ago.

Shadaisy, whose eyes had been riveted on the bottle, whispered, "Holy crap, you found it."

Josie handed the glass to the girl but kept a firm hold on it while Shadaisy tried to up end it and gulp all the soda as fast as she could. Josie held firm, so she could only sip.

When she finished, the girl closed her eyes, sighed, and turned to Erik with her best smile. "That was awesome."

Erik leaned against the door to the outside. "Glad to help," he said while pulling his gloves out of his pocket. He separated them, turned them over, and examined them. He looked around for a waste basket, finally found one under the sink into which he shook the dirt off the gloves. Once again, Josie was struck by how little she knew her brother.

"I'm going now," he said. "I should have been home hours ago. You can do the rest of the plants, right? Aren't that many."

"I can plant them," said Tristan.

The other three stared at him.

"I worked for a professional gardener for years. He said I have a gift."

That night, Josie slept on the couch again and dreamt of her sister dancing on the stage with Will, Jess, and Erik while the audience became more and more hysterical until they climbed on the stage in a mob, Josie leading the pack, ready to tear the four of them apart. She woke the next morning confused as to where she was and why. Slowly, the memory of the past two days came back to her. I can't do this, she thought. She turned her face into the back of the couch. The house was silent and finally, curiosity got the best of her. She sat up, stumbled across the hall, and opened the bedroom door. The girl slept curled on her side, looking like an angel. There was no sign of Tristan.

Josie wandered outside. Tristan was in the garden. He had lain the tomato plants in rows and was measuring the distance between them with his feet. When he heard the kitchen door close, he stopped. "If you want them to thrive, tomato plants need to be three feet apart." Josie went down the steps and walked over to where the boy stood and stared at the first row of plants.

"You can trust him about that. He knows his stuff. Learned from the best."

Tristan and Josie turned and looked up. Shadaisy stood in the doorway, hanging onto the frame. "Let's go to the shed, Mouse. I need fresh air." The two youngsters, without saying another word, walked down the dirt path, almost, but not quite shoulder to shoulder. Josie continued to plant until the light grew too dim, then she took the sheets off her bed and put them in the washing machine. She didn't know if the kids were planning on coming back to the cottage that night, but if they did, Shadaisy could sleep on the couch. She appeared to have turned the corner and, as far as Josie knew, had not thrown the soda back up. Anyway, Tristan would come get Josie if needed. They might even decide to leave Willow Bark tonight. Might already be gone. Josie didn't wait for the sheets to finish washing. She wasn't going to hang them on the trees tonight. She pulled the blanket off the couch, sank with exhaustion onto her bed, and pulled the blanket around herself. There's a special hell, she thought, for people who sleep on a bare mattress.

It was mid-day when Tristan and Shadaisy came looking for Josie. They found her in the garden on her hands and knees, patting soil around the last of the tomato plants which stood, obediently, three feet away from its neighbor.

"I would have done that for you," said Tristan, sounding hurt. Josie rocked back on her feet and met their gaze. She felt a surprising clang of unease go off inside her. Shadaisy's skin had lost its sickly pallor and, in fact, except for her hair, which lay matted against her head in some spots and stood up in sweat crusted cork screws in others, she looked good as new.

As though reading her mind, Shadaisy said, "Can I wash my hair in your bathroom sink?"

"Of course." Josie wanted to ask them how long they would be staying, but discovered she was afraid to. An awkward silence followed. Finally, she said, "Are you hungry? Do you think you can eat something?"

Tristan said, "Yes please," and the three went inside. The kids sat at the table while Josie went through the cupboard and refrigerator searching for food. She found half a loaf of bread, a jar of peanut butter, and a bowl of soup with green spots floating on the top. "Sorry I can't offer you more. I need to go to the grocery store. You should go easy, Shadaisy. I don't have any soda, but ginger ale would be good for you. I can pick some up, I guess. If you're staying." She went to the sink to fill two glasses with water when Shadaisy said, "I could go to the store for you. You could make me a list."

Josie slowly shut off the faucet and turned around. She could feel her muscle fibers uncurling, the easing of the tendons in her neck, her torso, letting go of their tight grip on her spine, the small of her back releasing her hip bones. She looked at Shadaisy carefully. "You're old enough to drive?"

"Of course."

"You have a license?"

"Sure."

It was a lie. One of her foster care placements had been on Staten Island in a moderately rundown neighborhood with no grocery stores nearby. Her foster mother, Mrs. Hatch, rose at noon, fixed herself a large mug of coffee with rum, and settled in front of the television. When the coffee was gone, she switched to vodka and orange juice and returned to the TV, where she stayed until midnight eating chips and cookies and drinking steadily. Her husband returned from work around five. As soon as he said hello to whoever was in the house and kissed his wife on the top of her head, he went into the bedroom and changed into pajamas and a ratty bathrobe. Next, he invariably went to the refrigerator, took out whatever food might be in there. and brought it cold to the couch, along with plates and silverware for himself and his wife. Before settling in beside her for the night, he put a six pack of beer on the coffee table. They sat in a companionable fog watching TV until they fell asleep. When their snores became too loud, they bumbled off to bed.

It wasn't a bad placement. Shadaisy's foster parents weren't mean drunks. No one went hungry. They had delivery pizza and Chinese four or five nights a week and the other nights, whatever Shadaisy chose from the store. As the oldest, she was given the job of driving the car to pick up food, cigarettes, and any other sundries. She was thirteen.

Mr. Hatch had taught her to drive in one weekend. He showed her the lights, the windshield wipers, the brakes, the gear shift, the window switches, the door locks, and the gas pedal. Then he settled himself against the seat and dozed off, waking only when Shadaisy jerked the car left or right or another driver honked their horn at the girl for cutting him off. Shadaisy was a quick study and by the end of the weekend could drive well enough not to bring attention to herself.

Josie placed her hand on the back of a chair and leaned on it. She was mulling over whether she should come right out and ask these strange children to live with her a while so Shadaisy could run errands for her, when the phone rang. It was Erik. "I was planning to grill a steak tonight, and I wondered if you'd like some too. You can bring those kids if you want."

CHAPTER TEN

Josie eased gingerly into the passenger's seat. His eyes round and dark, Tristan sat in the back, staring straight ahead.

Shadaisy stepped lightly on the gas pedal and the SUV rolled forward smoothly out of the driveway and onto the road. They could have picked up the state highway 9G a few miles from the cottage, but Josie decided for this test drive the back roads would be best. This one was a typical country lane, unfurling like a ribbon on the ground with gentle twists and long loops.

The speed limit was forty-five miles per hour on the gravel roads. Having only driven on Staten Island going from her foster home to the grocery store with a few exploratory excursions on the side, Shadaisy had never gone faster than thirty-five miles per hour. Her eyes jumped from the speedometer to the road. She kept the needle exactly on the forty-five marker. She glanced over at Josie, who was in her normal trance, her facial muscles flat.

Shadaisy eased to a halt in front of a stop sign. She waited, her eyes on the road. She waited some more. Tristan cleared his throat. Josie stared out the front window. After a long moment, she said, "Turn right."

They continued in this manner for eight miles. Shadaisy's hands went slick with sweat, Tristan was quiet as a mouse, and Josie stared out the side window at the trees. They grew thickly down to the road, but not as thick as along the road separating Jaylene's property from hers. Here, you at least could see oncoming traffic from inside the woods. Yet even with this difference, a picture of a pie flying high in the air and Jaylene under it with her arms stretching skywards formed clear and sharp as though shot from a professional's camera. Josie snapped her eyes away and closed them. Tilting her head down, she stared at the tiny warp and weave in the fabric of her jeans. She hated jeans. They were cold in the winter, hot in the summer, and no matter what the style or size, they cut into your waist when you sat down. Why were they so popular? Pondering this made her think of Erik, who, except when he was at a show, lived in jeans. His were worn and washed so many times the fabric had lost any hint of shape and hung loosely around his legs. The naturally torn knees made the jeans look comfortable for the summer weather. He wore them just below his navel. His stomach was so concave, Josie decided the waist band didn't cut into him there but must pinch and grab him around his hips. Thinking of Erik, her constant low-grade nausea ratcheted up a notch. She wondered how she was going to hide the fact she wasn't eating from him. He'd been so helpful lately, she didn't want to appear ungrateful. It was over a year since she'd been to his place and then it had been with Will, Jaylene, and Jess.

The car rolled to a stop, and Shadaisy said, "Which way?"

Josie had forgotten she meant to observe the girl's driving skills on the way to Erik's. They must be good if they'd gotten this far so seamlessly. That was something, anyway. "Turn left. It's only a few miles more."

The road turned to macadam and lawns replaced the trees, the houses set as far back as possible. Josie instructed Shadaisy to pull into a wide driveway with a large Dutch barn at the end. The gabled roof curved gracefully downward. The eighteenth-century structure had originally been a carriage house with space enough for a coach and six stalls for the horses, a hay loft above the ground floor, and above that a space for ventilation. In the front were two sliding barn doors, each ten feet wide.

"Wow," Tristan said.

One of the sliding doors moved slowly to the left. Erik appeared in the opening. He smiled and waved.

Shadaisy bounced out of the SUV, followed by Tristan and then Josie, who managed a smile.

Erik smiled back. "Come on in."

Inside, they stood in the middle of a vast space. Floor-to-ceiling windows filled the place with light. There were no walls, only columns supporting the stories above. A seven-foot easel dominated the middle of the room. It was a work of art on its own, with its three long legs, graceful triangle shape and perfect proportions. The edged wooden bar meant to hold a canvas was empty. Erik saw Josie noticing this. "I'm starting a new painting tomorrow," he said. A bar stool with a table next to it faced the easel. On the table, mason jars filled with all sizes of meticulously cleaned brushes lined up in neat rows. Surrounding the easel were apple crates stacked on top of each other to form cabinets. Most of the crates contained tubes of paint arranged by color. Shades of gray, blue, green, gold, red, burnt sienna along with large tubes of white. A few of the crates held cans of turpentine, linseed oil, and gesso. The air was redolent with the smell of oil paints. Here and there canvases covered in old sheets leaned against posts. Shadaisy stepped toward the largest one. "Can we see your paintings?"

Erik walked around, pulling off the sheets. He never said anything when he showed someone his paintings. His face expressionless, he would stand still and watch them as they walked around. It made people nervous, as though they were the ones being judged.

Tristan glanced around before standing in front of the only painting with bright colors. Red, scarlet, orange, and yellow painted in horizontal lines bled into each other, covering the entire front of the canvass and over onto the sides. "This is my favorite," he said.

Shadaisy took her time perusing the rest, which were realistic, painted in subtle hues of pale green, gray, blue, ochre, and amber with an occasional splash of color. "They make me sad," she said. "I don't know why, but they make me sad. Maybe it's the colors. I think I like them though."

Erik said, "Let's go upstairs."

At the top of the stairs to the left, jewel-colored fabric hung in front of a door. Erik pulled it aside with one hand and with the other waved his three guests into a bedroom. The room was spare, utilitarian except for a huge arched plexi-glass window facing the bed. Outside, navy-blue mountains filled the horizon. On the right, the view was filled with wild bush roses and on the left, the ground was covered with straight emerald-green plants, their thin, pointed leaves reflecting the sunlight. There was a moment of silence while everyone looked at the view. Tristan walked up to the window and stood so close his nose almost touched it.

"Get back from there," Shadaisy said. "You'll smudge the glass."

Josie said, "Imagine waking up to that view every day."

"It does rain sometimes," Erik said.

"Even that would be beautiful."

"You get to take a bath in the great outdoors. I would be arrested if I did that here."

The second floor was as wide open as the first and appeared even more vast due to the scarcity of furniture. The living room contained a futon, two fruit crates turned upside down that served as a coffee table, two stuffed chairs, and a dining room table that looked like driftwood surrounded by mismatched chairs.

The kitchen lined the back wall of the open floor plan. It consisted of steel runners on the wall, steel shelves, steel counters, steel stove, and refrigerator. Off the kitchen was a wooden deck where Erik kept his two Weber domed grills, one filled with cherry wood, the other with charcoal. "The wood is ready. I'll put the steaks on" He carried a platter with four New York strip steaks at least two inches thick outside.

In the kitchen, Josie set the table with plain white pottery plates and mismatched silverware. Erik had cut up a canvas drop cloth for napkins. She peered into the oven to see what smelled so good and saw four jumbo-sized russet potatoes. She found coleslaw from the village deli in the refrigerator. There was a huge chocolate cake from Amy's bakery on the counter. "Help yourself to wine," Erik called from the porch. "Or beer. There's vodka in the freezer."

Josie retrieved a bottle of Coors from the refrigerator and twisted off the cap. Before raising the bottle to her mouth, she turned to Shadaisy, who was already sitting at the table. "You want one?" she asked.

"Ummm, sure. I guess." Shadaisy didn't drink. She didn't do drugs either. She had seen what those substances had done to her mother. "Actually, I'd rather have a soda if there is one."

Josie rummaged around in the fridge until she found a Coke. "I'm afraid there's no Orange Crush. Will this be okay? You said it made you sick."

"It's funny. Nothing else but Orange Crush would do at that moment, but now I couldn't care less about it. Coke's fine."

Josie put the potatoes, wrapped in a dish towel, in a basket on the table. The potatoes burned her fingers when she took them out of the oven. She added butter and sour cream to the table then brought a Coors outdoors for her brother and a Coke for Tristan, who watched Erik's every move. "I swear one day this porch is going to fall right off the house," she said, handing her brother a beer. Erik took a long, satisfied swallow, pushed the middle of a steak with his fingertip, and said, "These steaks are almost done. Can you bring me a platter?"

There wasn't much conversation during dinner. Josie fluffed her potato with a fork, moved her coleslaw into a mound to make it look like some of it was gone, and tried a bite of steak. It tasted heavenly, but after a few more bites her stomach closed. Shadaisy and Tristan went after their food like starving wolves, and Erik ate with his usual fastidiousness. When he finished his cake, he placed his knife and fork across his plate and looked at Shadaisy's, which was wiped clean. "Ah, the resiliency of youth. You must be feeling better."

"Yes, I am."

"So, how long are you two staying with my sister?"

Tristan looked up from his cake.

Shadaisy didn't skip a beat. "If Josie will let us, we thought we would stay the summer, get a job picking apples. We'd help Josie with errands, of course, and Tristan could take care of the garden."

Tristan stared at her.

"You won't be picking apples till fall. But the cherries should be ready soon," Erik said.

"Cherries then."

Problem solved. Josie felt the same relief flow through her as when she'd learned the girl could drive.

Tristan switched his gaze to Josie. "Really?"

"We can try it for a few weeks. I guess."

Tristan pushed away from the table and started taking dishes to the sink. The others followed, and when the dishwasher was full, Tristan asked if he could go walk around outside.

"I guess so. Sure," Erik said.

Tristan burst through the door onto the porch and ran down the stairs.

"Well," Josie said.

"Come on, let's sit in the living room." Erik carried two more Coors and a Coke into the living area where he settled on the couch. Josie sat next to him, and Shadaisy curled her legs underneath her on a chair opposite them. "Are there many farms around here?"

"I'm not sure about where Josie is, but there are plenty all around Hollandtown. The Hudson River Valley is still farming country though it's changed. People in the city come here and buy up places, thinking they're going to make a killing by going organic or turning the land into a vineyard. Or a company buys adjacent farms, bulldozes the houses and barns and use refrigerated semis to drive the fruit directly to the city. It's all done from a distance. They make money, but the tree huggers and wine makers don't last much more than five years, if that." He looked and sounded angry. Josie could tell he was already into his next painting, forming composition, colors, proportions. It was time to go.

Erik put Josie's leftovers in plastic containers, which he placed in a paper bag and handed to her. "This should last you about a week."

"I really appreciate this. The cupboards at Willow Bark are pretty bare."

Outside, Tristan leaned against the SUV with his arms crossed. Apparently, he was ready to go as well. Shadaisy gave him a looking over before she climbed into the driver's seat. She made a nice three-point turn then headed out the driveway.

"We can take 9G part of the way home. That way I can see how you handle traffic."

At first, Shadaisy didn't think she would survive driving sixty-five miles an hour. But the natural riskiness of youth clicked in, and the speed changed from terrifying to exhilarating. If Josie hadn't been in the car, she would have happily pushed it to eighty.

In what seemed like no time at all, they were in Josie's driveway. Shadaisy parked the SUV next to the cottage. Tristan was out of it and heading to the shed the minute the wheels stopped rolling.

"Wait up," Shadaisy shouted after him.

Tristan stopped and slowly turned around.

Shadaisy handed the keys to Josie and caught up to him. She scowled. She continued scowling and looking at him sideways as they made their way to the shed. Once inside, she turned to face him, hands on her hips and looked him up and down. "What the hell is going on underneath your shirt?"

CHAPTER ELEVEN

The last of the evening sun hit the shed, came through the door, and landed on Tristan. "Nothing," he said, his eyes round and eager.

"The hell. Take it off."

Tristan raised his t-shirt above his waist. Roots as fine as filaments and covered in dirt slid free.

Shadaisy raised an eyebrow.

Tristan lifted his shirt some more, revealing a row of stiff green stems circling his waist. He pulled his shirt away from his body with one hand and taking hold of one of the stems with the other, lifted it gently downward and outward. Leaves appeared, followed by a full bright green plant standing straight up, aggressive in its vitality. He laid it gently on the ground. He continued until all the plants were lined in a row on the shed's dirt floor. He straightened, squared his shoulders, and lifted his chin ever so slightly.

Shadaisy stared at the display in front of her.

Tristan waited. Finally, he said, "Do you know what this is?"

"Of course, I know what this is."

"Well?"

"Well, what? What do you plan to do with them?"

"Plant them in the garden."

Shadaisy shook her head. "Honestly, Mouse, you've had some crazy ideas, but this takes the prize. Here we have a place to stay, a safe, comfortable place, away from prying eyes and a chance to make money, and you steal marijuana plants from Erik?"

Tristan leaned down and picked up a plant. He caressed one of the leaves. "It'll be fine. I have it all figured out. We'll get more tomato plants, pole beans, and sunflowers, make the garden bigger, plant the marijuana in the middle and the other plants all around them. No one will see them. Josie wouldn't know what they were anyway, and no one ever comes here."

"Except Erik."

"He won't be able to see them."

"Don't be too sure."

"Erik only notices Erik."

"Do you even know how to grow it?"

"Remember the guy I used to work for, you know, the gardener I was talking about? He grew pot. He grew it inside with grow lights. It didn't take up all that much space. He didn't show me how to take care of it or even anything really. But how hard can it be?"

"Pretty damn hard, I expect. And you don't think Erik will notice some of his weed is missing?"

"No, there's so much he needs to thin it out. I'm doing him a favor, really."

Shadaisy sat on a bale of hay. Tristan's look caught and held her. It said that he knew he needed her help, that she would have to drive Josie's SUV to get the plants, then help him hide the weed until they could plant it, probably at night. It also said she would have to help him explain the extra vegetable plants to Josie. He would freeze if he tried. Now he said, "We can make this work. If Josie gets mad or Erik does or both, I'll throw myself on their mercy and swear you had nothing to do with it."

"Right. Like who is going to do the driving? How you going to convince her I didn't know you were loading up the SUV with more vegetable plants? And sunflowers?"

In the end, when Josie handed Shadaisy the keys, she told her Tristan would have to stay here at Willow Bark. All three knew the reason why. Shadaisy would never drive away for good without taking Tristan with her.

"You have the list," Josie said. "Look it over one more time to make sure you understand exactly what I want. Two percent milk, not whole. Plain Cheerios, not sugared. Canned peas, not frozen, and Dawn dish soap. Be sure to get all the things listed. I know it's a lot, but the cupboards are bare. Are you sure you don't have any questions?"

"I got it." Shadaisy didn't need to look at Tristan to know he was thinking the same thing: Be sure to get all the plants I need.

Tristan and Shadaisy started planting before sunrise, their only light coming from a full moon. They planted the marijuana first then surrounded it with the vegetables. Shadaisy had even managed to find sunflower plants. They had just started planting them when Josie wandered outside in a clean nightgown with her tea and sat on the grass next to the garden. Rambles settled down next to her. For a while, woman and dog watched the kids going about their work. Josie sat cross legged, blowing on the steaming liquid. Tristan sneaked a look at her over his shoulder. She appeared as vacant as ever.

"Where'd you get the pot?" she asked.

Tristan straightened and looked at Josie helplessly.

"Looks like what Erik grows."

"It is Erik's. I stole it from him." The skin on Tristan's face had tightened and stretched.

Josie sipped her tea. "He's got too much of it anyway. Needs to be thinned. He's not really into gardening. He's good at growing weed, knows his stuff and is all enthusiasm in the beginning, but then he starts a painting and that's it." Josie said this as casually as she might have said he ought to fix his porch. She sipped some more tea, ran her hand over

Rambles' head, scratched her behind an ear. "It looks like it's going to be another nice day," she said to no one in particular, the fact of marijuana growing in her garden evidently forgotten.

Tristan and Shadaisy exchanged a glance. Very slowly, Tristan moved on to the next sunflower, put it into the hole he had prepared, and sifted the well-tilled dirt around the roots. Josie watched for a few more minutes, rose, and wandered into the house. "Come on Rambles, let's get your breakfast."

Two days later, when the youngsters walked up from the shed, Erik stood staring at the garden with his hands in his pockets.

"Well, shit," Shadaisy said.

"You go talk to him," Tristan said.

"Why me?"

"Cause he thinks you're cute."

"No, he doesn't! I've tried the whole flirty thing and he doesn't pay any attention."

"Doesn't matter. Guys are guys."

"You're just a coward, that's all."

Shadaisy and Tristan approached Erik slowly and stood on either side of him. There was nothing to do but see what happened next.

"Is that my weed?"

"I don't know," Tristan said.

"You don't really have enough to do much with it. And you've got some males mixed in with females. They'll pollinate them and give you an inferior product. You should get rid of them. Just plant females. This is the Chronic strain. Very hardy. Popular with most people. Calms you down. I'll bring you more females in my van. You're going to need more tilled land. I wouldn't put it here where people park. That's a little too blatant, even for around here. There's a nice spot behind Josie's house. Flat. Lots of sun. You should get some Prowl. It's a thick, yellow substance. A lot of people use it for their tomato plants. You put it around the base. Never put anything on the plant itself. Makes the product taste funny. Do you know anything about growing weed?"

"Not so much."

"I'll bring you some females to get you a good start. Have to keep enough for my home boys, though. I mean, there aren't many jobs around here, none that pay well. What are my guys supposed to do? They aren't gifted like me. They have to find some way to support themselves. So, they grow some crop and sell it in the city. They make enough to get by. But there's plenty at my place. You can have enough to supply a few of the locals. No problem. A little extra change above picking fruit. It'll be a steep learning curve, but you'll get it. I'm going inside to see my sister. She in the house?"

"I guess so."

Erik found Josie in the bedroom under the covers, holding onto her teacup and staring at the wall. Rambles lay beside her. He shoved his hands in his pockets and squared up his feet in line with his shoulders. "You need to get out of bed."

"Why?"

"Because it's not healthy lying around all the time."

Josie said nothing.

Erik sat on the edge of the mattress. "Are you doing any painting?"

"Not at the moment."

Erik took the teacup, looked inside it, bent to sniff then put it on the chair next to the bed. "Look. I'm not going to give you a pep talk or any platitudes. What happened is as bad as it gets." He waited then continued. "Do you ever hear from Will?"

"No."

"Do you miss him?"

"I miss everything. All of it. But I can't think about it. If I did, I'd lose my mind." She ran her hand along Ramble's back. "Actually, it might be a good thing… losing my mind. A total psychotic break."

"Have you thought about calling him?"

"Why would I do that? I wouldn't want to be married to me. Why should I expect him to? Why is everyone so interested in Will, anyway? Even if he did come back, it wouldn't change anything. My life is…"

"Over? Do not say 'my life is over.'"

Josie touched her brother's thigh with her toe under the covers. "Thanks, but no one, not even Will, can fix this."

Erik turned and watched his sister's face for a while. "When all else fails, turn to your art," he said, his voice low and serious.

"I can't right now."

"If you wait too long, you'll get afraid of it, and you won't be able to go back."

Josie's eyes were at half-mast. For some reason, since the accident, she hadn't been able to open them all the way, giving her a look of eternal exhaustion. She had no answer for Erik. He turned away. "So, the kiddies are going to grow marijuana."

"It appears so."

Shadaisy appeared in the doorway. "I've brought you some money. For our share of the groceries." She reached in her pocket and put a hundred dollars on the bureau.

"Are you sure?" Josie pushed her hair away from her face.

"I told you we're not free loaders. We've got some money."

"You did? I don't remember you saying that, but okay."

Shadaisy said, "So, keep the money. We don't want to be beholden." She waited a long moment, and when Josie didn't respond, she said, "I'll be going now."

"That's fine." Beholden? Josie thought. Where would this girl get the word beholden?

"Bye." Shadaisy turned, looked over her shoulder, and briefly waved as she left.

Erik said, "Well, well."

CHAPTER TWELVE

Shadaisy and Tristan ventured forth to look for cherry farms. Not wanting to push their luck by borrowing the SUV too often, they rode their bicycles.

The Dutch arrived in the fertile Hudson River Valley in the 1600s. The land produced a good living back then. Fruit trees liked the well-drained earth, which was a result of the many hills and shaly soil. Farms were passed from generation to generation. Over the centuries, this changed. The many hills made using large equipment difficult. No one wanted to be the farmer who lost the family land, but small farms found it harder and harder to compete against the flat land of the Midwest and the fruit it produced which was trucked east in huge semis. People who hung on found themselves barely able to make a subsistence living and were kept going by pride and just enough money to hang on for another year. Already taciturn, they often turned bitter, shut off, at war with the world.

This was the world Shadaisy and Tristan headed into. Josie couldn't tell the teenagers where the nearest farm was, so they decided to follow their noses. They turned right at the end of the driveway, a direction they hadn't taken before, and rode with the sun warm on their backs and the air fresh and clean in their lungs. They had only gone five miles when Tristan pointed to a clapboard farmhouse with a steep hill behind it. Rows of similar looking, gnarled trees spiraled horizontally upwards to and across the hilltop. The house sat close to the road.

Tristan stopped pedaling and put his foot down. "Does that look like a farm to you?"

Shadaisy cupped her hand over her eyes to block the sun. "I guess. Those trees are kinda strange looking though. Old like."

"The house looks old too. Do you think we should go knock on the door?"

"I suppose. That's what we're here for."

When they knocked on the faded white surface, a woman in a faded dress with a rip under one arm answered.

"We're here looking for work as cherry pickers," Shadaisy said.

The woman told them they would have to speak with her husband, who was out in the orchard spraying. "It'll be hard though," she said, "with the roar of the tractor and sprayer, he might not hear you. Dangerous, too. He might not see you, so be sure to stay out of his way."

Tristan and Shadaisy wandering among the gnarled trees were drawn to the raw sound of struggling machinery. They heard the rumble of a diesel engine and quickened their pace. The tractor came toward them, pulling a large milky white plastic cone, which sprayed a white liquid into the branches of trees. They waved their arms and called out, but it drove past them, around to the other side of the hill and out of sight. The man, humped over the wheel, never looked their way. When the tractor came back into sight, Shadaisy jumped in front of it, dragging Tristan with her. She jumped up and down, waving her arms as the machinery made its slow way toward them. When the tractor was ten yards away, it shuddered to a stop though the motor kept running. Still humped over the wheel, the man shouted, "What are you doing in my orchard?"

"We're looking for work picking cherries," Shadaisy shouted.

"I don't need no pickers. I got a man stays here full time. That's all the help I need. Now I got work to do, so you'd best get out of here. This spray is poison." He stepped on the pedals; the tractor rumbled and shook and started forward. The attachment behind spewed a fan of nasty smelling mist. The kids ran between the trees until, panting, they reached the road. Tristan, leaning over with his hands on his knees, said, "How come that man isn't dead, if he's spraying poison?"

"Who knows," said Shadaisy, distracted. She was looking down at her body, twisting this way and that, running her hands down her arms and legs, checking herself all over. Satisfied, she turned to Tristan, straightened him with a hand on his shoulder and slowly rotated him, looking for drops of poison.

"Maybe that's why he's so mean," Tristan said while Shadaisy inspected him. "Gone to his brain. Like rabies."

She shook her head and laughed. "You're such a goof. Come on, let's get going."

They rode until the sun was high and they were both sweating. The next orchard sat on rolling land and, as before, a farmhouse stood between the trees and the road. The woman who answered the door wore jeans and a flannel shirt. When Shadaisy inquired about work, the woman directed her and Tristan into the kitchen. The large room was bursting with furniture, brooms, mops, milk jugs, hen crates, packing crates and people. Numerous children of varying sizes sat at a rectangular table. A man looking to be in his fifties sat with them. Plates filled with eggs, hash brown potatoes and toast lined the table. Tristan felt saliva fill his mouth. In their haste to begin their quest, the two adventurers had forgotten to pack food. Again, Shadaisy produced her best smile and offered their services.

"I got all the pickers I need sitting right here at the table," the man said, not unkindly. "We been up since dawn, checking the orchards. Came in for breakfast." He looked with pride at his family. Using a piece of toast, he pushed some scrambled eggs onto his fork. "Bob Raymond hires for the season. He's four or five miles straight down this road. You can't miss him."

Raymond's farm turned out to be more like ten miles down the road, but the man at the table had been right about one thing. You couldn't miss it. Tristan stopped pedaling and planted his feet on the asphalt. "Oh my God," he said.

Trees, in neat rows, grew right down to the edge of the road, so laden with blossoms they looked like something out of a fairy tale. Delicate pink and white petals touched and entwined and grew in such a way that you couldn't tell one blossom from another. To Tristan, they looked like pink cotton candy or scoops of scarlet and white sherbet. "This must be Oz," he said, for the air was redolent with an intoxicating scent.

"Hey there," came a voice from above.

The teenagers looked up. "And that must be the tin woodman," Shadaisy said.

A man in washed-out overalls stood on a ladder at the top of a large tree. "Can I help you?" he asked.

Shadaisy held her hand over her eyes as she gazed upward. "We're looking for work as pickers," she said.

The man began a carefully thought-out descent down the ladder. Tristan and Shadaisy watched as, careful rung by careful rung, he made his way to the ground. "I'm not as young as I used to be," he said when, finally, he came to earth and walked, slightly bent over, toward them. "As you can see, I'm not picking right now, but in a few weeks, I may need some help. Give me your number and I'll call you."

"Um, we don't have phones," Shadaisy said, blushing. Everyone had a cell phone these days.

If the man was surprised by the teens lack of devices, he didn't show it. He reached into a pocket in his overalls and produced a pen. "Hold out your hand," he said to Tristan. "Come on now," he continued when Tristan hesitated. Tristan held out his hand and the farmer turned it so the palm faced down and wrote a number on the back. "Call me in a few weeks and we'll see what's what."

Tristan and Shadaisy arrived at Willow Bark around dusk, tired, dirty, and sweaty. "I'm so hungry I could eat a bear," Tristan said, throwing his bike on the ground. Inside, the cottage was quiet as the grave. Shadaisy went looking for Josie and found her in bed, staring out the window, a book open in her lap. Rambles lay beside her.

"Do you mind if we make PB and J sandwiches?" Shadaisy asked.

Josie shifted her eyes in the girl's direction. "No, of course not."

"Do you want anything?"

"No, I'm okay."

Shadaisy wondered if Josie had been in bed all day. "Look," she said, "how about a cup of tea with honey?".

"Do we have honey?"

"Yes. It was on the list. Remember?"

In the kitchen, Tristan was already finishing the sandwiches. "She in bed?"

"Yes." Shadaisy put on the tea kettle.

"You know there is something seriously wrong with her." Tristan sat at the table with his food. Shadaisy took Josie her tea before she joined him.

"What's she doing in there?" Tristan asked around a mouthful of food.

"Nothing. Reading a book maybe. Staring out the window." Shadaisy bit into her sandwich. "Thanks for making these."

Tristan took a long drink of milk. "She must be crazy just staying in bed all the time. I mean, that's what crazy people do, right?"

Shadaisy thought for a minute. "I think something awful happened and she's broken. All that emptiness on the outside, I think, is a shell protecting what's going on inside."

"That's profound."

"No. I mean, she can function when she has to. I just think maybe she's got a lot of broken pieces trying to find their way back together again."

"Maybe. I just think she'd want to stay busy. She should work with me in the garden. She was the one who started it."

"Maybe *she* just needs to be quiet now."

"Why don't you ask her what happened?"

"You ask her if you're so interested. I think it's none of our business."

After supper, Tristan hooked the hose to the sink faucet and filled the tub with water. With the help of a large bath towel, he managed to undress without disclosing what he had spent most of his childhood hiding from the world. With the towel wrapped around his waist, he delicately tested the water with his toe. Satisfied, he climbed in, still wrapped in the towel, and bent his knees. Only when his bottom was an inch above the water did he snap off his covering and drop it on the ground as he lowered himself below the surface. Getting out, he reached over the tub, wrapped the terry cloth around his chest, and lowered it as he stood up. Using the same awkward measures to get dressed as he had to undress, he then topped off the water in the tub until it ran over the sides. "Your turn," he called to Shadaisy. "I'm going to the shed."

Unlike most teenage girls, Shadaisy didn't like spending time in front of a mirror. She wasn't interested in her looks except as a tool when needed. She preferred to be invisible. As she grew older and accidentally caught her image coming out of the shower or changing clothes, she was startled by the new curves, confused by a mixture of pride and fear of where that satin skin might land her. She had preferred it when either a boy or girl could have been under those Walmart t-shirts and jeans. She was nearly as fastidious as Tristan when taking a bath.

Tristan had spread out the sleeping bags by the time Shadaisy made it to the shed. The evening was still too warm to zip them up, and the amber inside cloth stood out in the flashlight's beam. Josie had told Shadaisy to buy a heavy-duty one since there was no electricity in the old shed and they would need a source of light. Tristan had changed into a clean t-shirt and jeans from his backpack and sat on his bed, eager to talk about the day. The beds, formed out of hay, faced each other for easy conversation. Loosely mounded hay formed pillows, and in the evenings the two leaned against them, their legs stretched out in front, their feet a foot apart. Shadaisy changed into clean clothes in a dark corner and then joined Tristan in the loft. She rutched around on her bed until she was comfortable. "So, it looks like we might have a job in a few weeks."

"You mean with the tin woodman?"

"Yeah. I mean, did you see those blossoms? If half of them turn into cherries, we'll be set." Shadaisy sat up straight. "Did you write down that number before you took your bath?"

"Of course. It's on my t-shirt."

"Don't let Josie wash it before you write it someplace you can keep it."

Tristan rolled his eyes. "I'm not stupid. Anyway, why do you think she's got that tub in the yard? She's got a washer in the house. Why not the bathtub? That's just bizarre."

"I like taking a bath outside. It's completely different. Makes you feel part of nature."

"I didn't know you were such a nature lover."

Shadaisy relaxed into a semi-prone position. "It's nice watching the sun go down."

"As long as no one is watching you."

The two were silent for a while then Tristan shifted into a more upright position. "I've been thinking," he said.

"About?"

"Maybe we should concentrate on growing bud. Maybe we could make more money doing that."

"And hang around here all day? I don't think so."

"It's a long ride to that farm. And standing on a ladder all day, picking cherries and riding home possibly in the dark. I don't know."

"What's the matter with you? You're strong enough. And there might be a shortcut. We'll ask Josie."

"I'm going to put a garden behind the house. I'm starting tomorrow so it'll be ready when Erik brings us more plants. I'm serious, Shadrack, I'm getting into the business." In the shadows, Tristan's eyes were huge and his expression so earnest, Shadaisy laughed. "Okay, I believe you," she said. "But do you even know when it will be ready to harvest? Seems like a lot of work for a short-term thing."

"Short-term?"

Shadaisy put a piece of hay in her mouth. "We're going to the city by Thanksgiving, remember?"

Tristan leaned against his mound of hay and said nothing.

"Don't tell me you're thinking of staying here?"

"It's a pretty good gig, you have to admit."

"No. I don't. Out here in the middle of east Jesus. No, siree. I'm getting to the city as soon as things settle down."

After the first few days, neither of them had mentioned the shooting. Tristan put the images so far in the recesses of his mind he had almost forgotten them. Shadaisy, on the other hand, felt the kick and the noise of the shotgun at least once a day. Every morning as she first came awake, she wondered if the man was dead, or had he survived to continue having a go at her mother. To her surprise, both possibilities upset her. She took the blade of hay out of her mouth, examined it, and threw it aside and selected a fresh one to chew on. "Mouse?" she said.

"Yeah?"

"I'm never getting married."

"You've told me that before."

"I'm never even going to be with a man. I can't stand the thought of a man doing to me what that creep did to my mother."

"Not all men are like him."

"Doesn't matter. I can't unsee it. I'll never get those images out of my mind. Never. The thought of anyone touching me that way makes me want to vomit."

"You might change your mind someday," Tristan said.

"When you say that it makes me think you don't understand."

Tristan sat perfectly still. The silence between them became thick. Finally, Shadaisy said, "It's okay. You're still my family. I know that. You think you'll ever get married?"

"I hope so."

"Tell me why."

"I want a family. Kids. Home. You know, a regular life."

"Without me."

"No. Never without you. You'll always be my best friend."

Shadaisy pulled the sleeping bag loosely around her, scooched down into a prone position, and turned onto her side. "You'll change once you're married. You might think you won't, but you will."

"No, I won't. I won't change, just like you won't. I swear." He waited for a response, but none came, so he turned off the flashlight and tried to settle into sleep. "Anyway," he whispered to himself, "I'm only fifteen."

CHAPTER THIRTEEN

Josie rummaged under her bed for her art material. She couldn't even think about painting at the moment, but lately she had been feeling a niggling concern about the condition of her oils. She loved her oil paints. She loved the luscious feel of them in the tube and on her brushes, the way they smelled, the colors you could find nowhere else; vermillion, cadmium, cerulean; the way they appeared on her palette, thick and unctuous with just the slightest ooze of oil. It would be a shame if they dried out.

Finally, shoved to the almost unreachable middle under the bed, she came across a box. She pulled it out. The label said, "brushes and things." There were the brushes, held together by a rubber band. Graceful wooden handles, each topped with different bristles, soft and slender, rough and thick, wide and generous, the textures unique. Josie hated to be a snob, but if the truth be told, the sables were her favorite. They held the paint so perfectly, caressed it onto the canvas so smoothly, held their form faithfully despite being so soft. "I prefer sable," she would say whenever she'd had the chance, back before the world ended. The brushes were all in good shape due to having been cleaned thoroughly before being put away. And there were the cans of turpentine, of linseed oil. Josie inhaled their aroma deeply. She lifted a cloth gift bag out of the box. Inside were her oils. She gently squeezed the large tube of white, which gave to the fingers exactly as it should. The smaller black one was stiff. The nearly full cadmium red gave to her pressure with just the right amount of sensual resistance. Josie unscrewed the top and there it was, the reddest red in the world, so beautiful it was tempting to lick it.

Josie leaned back on her heels. Maybe she could start again. Maybe she could lose herself in the paint. She could start with no thought as to what forms she would create on the canvas, merely allow herself to feel the way the paint moved. She sniffed the open tube, touched it with a fingertip. Her fingerprint popped into a crimson view. She rubbed her thumb against it. She was looking at the whorls in the skin on both thumb and finger when there came a knock on the door.

What the hell? Who could be after her out here? Certainly not a neighbor stopping to call. The knock sounded again, this time slightly louder.

It's probably Jehovah's Witnesses, Josie thought. They could find you anywhere. Even here, hidden among the weeds. She screwed the top on the tube, shutting away its brilliant promise, climbed over the other boxes and rounded into the living room, planning what she would say. Before they could open their mouths or hand her one of those hatefully joyful pamphlets she would say, "May the Lord Jesus Christ forgive you your sins." She yanked open the door. Steve Getz stood on the other side of the threshold holding a loaf of bread.

"I come bearing gifts," he said. "Gosh, Josie, I didn't mean to scare you."

She had gasped when she saw him. "Oh, no, it's just I thought you were Jehovah's Witnesses, that's all." They both stayed where they were, not knowing what to do next. Finally, Steve waved his hand toward the kitchen. "May I come in?"

Josie moved out of the way. "All you need is a cheap, black suit and a bible."

Steve placed the bread on the table and gave it a gentle pat. "Man lives by bread alone. Isn't that what the bible says?" He pulled out a chair and sat.

"I think it says, man doesn't live by bread alone," Josie answered with an edge to her voice. She was thinking she was glad she had put clothes on today and she didn't want to think that way. She didn't want to worry about looking presentable for company. She didn't want company. That was why she was out here. The only reason she was wearing clothes was because her nightgowns were all dirty.

"Homemade," Steve went on. "Made by the Amish. Absolutely delicious. How have you been, Josie? I haven't seen you since I was last here. Do you ever go to town?"

Josie sat opposite him. "Sure, I do."

"I see you hired someone to help you."

Josie looked confused.

"That boy working in the back."

"Oh, yeah, him."

"Glad to see you're planting a garden. Keep you busy. Good for the soul."

"Yeah."

"What are you planting?"

"Squash."

"Doesn't look like any squash I've ever seen."

"Beans. Pole beans."

"Really?"

There was a silence.

Eventually, Steve said, "Where does that boy come from? I don't think I've ever seen him before. Hollandtown?"

"No, Ohio."

"How did you find him all the way in Ohio?"

Jesus Christ. Couldn't people just let her live or not live her own life?

"Actually, I have a friend. Lives in Ohio. He's her boy."

"I didn't know you had a friend from Ohio."

Josie rose from her chair.

Steve hadn't become a successful realtor without being able to read people. "I'm sorry. Just being nosy. It's none of my business. You have to be careful living alone out here, that's all. Just watching out for you. How about I go out and be friendly and introduce myself?"

Since Josie practically lived on tea and toast, she automatically filled the kettle with water and put it on the stove. She set the table with her mother's porcelain. She sliced the bread which had things in it, possibly nuts or raisins, who knew what with the Amish. Could be sunflower seeds or barley. Anyway, she refused to take the time to toast it.

Steve brought Tristan with him when he returned from the garden. The boy's round eyes stood out in his face. When the three of them were settled at the table, Steve said in a too casual tone, "Tristan tells me he has a sister. That she lives here with him. She's out running errands now. Driving your car. You must know her very well. Letting her take your car. His mother lives in Hudson, right? That's what he said." He caught Josie's gaze and held it. She felt her chest tighten, knowing if she said anything, her voice would shake.

Though he looked like he might flee at any second, Josie could see that Tristan was trying with all his will to appear casual. He looked at her, silently apologizing for the new lie. It seemed as though he reached down to the marrow of his bones to stay calm and said, "Yeah, that's right. We're here for the summer. Mama doesn't have a car and it's too far to ride our bikes here every day. So, we're just staying with 'Auntie' for the summer to help her out." He smiled a sweet smile at his "aunt" radiating all the filial love anyone could ask for.

"*Auntie?*" Steve raised an eyebrow. "I thought you said that he was from Ohio."

Josie turned her teacup around on its saucer. "He is. Originally. But his mom and the kids moved to Hudson recently."

"And he calls you 'auntie.'"

"It's a term of endearment," Josie said quickly and stepped on Tristan's foot under the table. What the hell was the matter with him? Why did he have to go and tell a different story to Steve? Hudson? Where did he come up with that? And why?

Steve gave the boy his complete attention for what, in polite company, would be a rude amount of time. "Where did you learn to garden?" he asked finally.

Tristan stuffed a piece of bread in his mouth, mumbled around it, "My dad," then slid out of his chair and out the door, his ability to channel Shadaisy evidently drained.

"Huh," Steve said.

Josie raised her teacup daintily to her lips, pinky extended. She rolled her head back until every drop was gone, lowered the china to its saucer, opened her mouth and allowed a resounding belch to escape. "I do know those children very well," she said. "Apparently, that is something that escaped your notice. Before. They are a great help to me. I trust them completely. Your concern for me is touching but unneeded."

Steve left shortly thereafter. When he rounded the first bend in the road, he pulled off to the side. He might wear his hair short, button-down shirts and laser-creased khakis now, but he had been no boy scout growing up. He knew marijuana when he saw it. He pulled his cell phone out of his slacks' pocket and dialed Sheriff Dobbs.

Tristan might have a sharp learning curve when it came to growing marijuana, but both he and Shadaisy had just as sharp a one regarding how life at Willow Bark would be. They had been wrong about Josie's reaction to the pot. They had been wrong about Erik. They also knew nothing about a realtor named Steve Getz, who appeared whenever he liked. They didn't know he was a man of principle, a man who took his civic duties seriously, who belonged to Rotary, went to church every Sunday, and sat on the town council. They didn't know he was a man who believed in following the rules.

CHAPTER FOURTEEN

Having neither watches nor cell phones to tell them the time, Shadaisy and Tristan were on their bikes just as a slit of morning sun turned the air from black to gray. Their normal start time would be seven o'clock but today being the first day, Mr. Raymond wanted them there at 6:45 to receive a brief tutorial. They were determined not to be late.

Arriving at the Raymond's orchard, the two walked their bikes up the long gravel driveway and stopped just where the lawn began. They kicked out their bike stands and sat on the lawn. The sun now spread brilliant yellow stripes along the emerald grass. This was the time of year in the Hudson River Valley when the humidity hadn't gathered yet and the air was so clear the colors could dazzle. There were lights on in the house but not a soul outside.

"I wonder what time it is," Tristan said. The two sat in silence for a while, then turning his head from left to right, Tristan added, "It's beautiful here. Look at these colors. I've never seen colors like these."

"I guess."

"You nervous?"

Shadaisy thought for a minute. "I guess."

"I've never climbed a tree before." Tristan was picking blades of grass, putting them in his mouth, chewing them then spitting them out.

Eventually, they heard the rattle and bang of an old truck approaching. It had a make-shift wooden bed with slats for sides. When it stopped at the bottom of the driveway, four teenagers jumped out of the back. They walked slowly up the hill and stopped in front of Tristan and Shadaisy. The group consisted of three boys and a girl, all of whom were brown with black, black hair. The boys looked shyly at the ground. The girl did her best to meet Shadaisy's eyes. Tristan nudged his friend with an elbow.

She stirred and said, "I'm Shadaisy and this is Mouse."

Tristan slit his eyes at her.

The girl had a round, sweet face and a sweeter smile. "I'm Lucia. These are my brothers, Julio, Pedro, and George."

Shadaisy shifted her gaze to the others. The boys nodded without looking at the two white children. Lack of social graces rendered all six mute, and the silence hung heavy and miserable around them. Finally, a door banged, and Mr. Raymond gimped across the yard. "Good morning, folks," he said. "Hope you're ready for a good day's work."

The tutorial consisted of teaching the pickers how to set a ladder against a tree so that it wouldn't move, how to sling their canvas bags over their shoulders and most importantly, if they remembered nothing else, the thing that would determine if they kept their jobs or not important, was how to place the cherries in the bag so they would *not* bruise. "Treat them like they are newborn babies," said Mr. Raymond, "and *don't* crowd them."

Tristan was three feet up the ladder when he suspected this wasn't the job for him. By the time he reached the place where the cherries grew along the branches, he was sure of it. Each picker had been allotted their own tree so he couldn't see how the other five were doing. He stripped all the branches he could reach without moving off the ladder. Soon there was not another cherry to be had without moving the damn thing or climbing out on a branch. Since he wasn't even sure he could place the ladder the way he had been shown, he reached over his head and grabbed onto a branch and placed a sneakered foot on the nearest one below him. It was still wet with dew and his shoe had lost its tread long ago and before he had time to grasp what was happening, his foot flew off the slippery branch. He lost his grip on the limb above him and plummeted toward the ground. Sprigs, twigs, leaves, berries, a rush of air, and the earth came flying up to meet him and slam him in the back.

When he opened his eyes, Mr. Raymond was staring down at him. Tristan tried to say help, but nothing came out. He flailed his arms but could not breathe. Mr. Raymond put a gentle foot on the boy's flailing thin wrist. "Easy there, youngster, you've knocked the wind out of yourself, that's all. You'll be fine soon."

Shadaisy climbed down off her ladder and sat beside Tristan and held his other arm.

"There now, girl," said Mr. Raymond. "Rub his belly softly just under his ribs. I'd do it myself but, if I got down, I wouldn't be able to get up."

Shadaisy lifted Tristan's shirt and made circular motions on his pale skin. The boy soon stopped struggling and shortly after that his chest rose and fell.

"There now. See, you're fine. Except you've turned half a bag of cherries into jam. It's your first day, so I'll forgive you, but next time you're fired. Pedro, you share a tree with Tom here and see he doesn't go too far out on a limb, pun intended." Raymond smiled.

Tristan leaned forward and rested on his elbows. "It's Tristan. Not Tom."

"Tristan. That's a funny name. Doubt I'll remember it. How about Tim?"

"You can call him Mouse," Shadaisy said.

"Mouse. Now that's a funny name too, but it kinda suits him."

Tristan shot Shadaisy a murderous look. She grinned, took hold of his shoulder and pulled so she could see his back and burst out laughing. "Holy Christ, you like you've been gunned down by the mob."

"Here now, Daisy, we'll have no profanity." Mr. Raymond reached for the boy's hand and lifted him to his feet. "That bag will need to be washed before it can be used again. I brought some extras just in case. Go fetch one and let's get to work."

The pickers worked until seven, when the old truck rattled to the end of the driveway and stopped. The brown youngsters piled their ladders against a single tree, climbed into the vehicle, and were gone.

Tristan moaned and whined the whole way home.

"Isn't it a beautiful day?" Shadaisy said as they pedaled through the blue evening light.

"I don't know. Can't lift my head up. It hurts too much."

"Maybe you should go see the doctor."

"Shut up. You could give me a back rub when we get home."

"A nice hot bath will help."

"Yeah, with Josie sittin' in that chair right next to me."

They rode in silence until Tristan said, "Look, I have to stop. I can't go any farther."

"We're almost there. If you stop, you'll never start again."

Tristan moaned, "I'm dying." Then a few minutes later, "I think I broke something."

Shadaisy, humming a soft tune, pulled in front of him to draft him.

Josie was sitting in the chair beside the front garden watching the vegetables grow when the teenagers returned. Tristan dropped his bicycle on the grass, too sore to do anything else. "Mind if I get something to drink?" he asked Josie.

"You know I don't." She raised her eyes toward him as he passed by. "My God," she gasped. The back of his shirt was covered in dark red turning brown. She struggled to raise herself from her chair. Adrenaline shot through her with such force that her hands and feet tingled. Sweat promptly dampened her hair and her mouth turned to sand. "What?" was all she managed to say.

Shadaisy stood her bike up. "Tristan fell out of a tree his first time up. Squashed half a bag of cherries. Mr. Raymond wasn't that mad at him. I'll wash his shirt if you want me to. Looks like he's been shot, doesn't it?"

Cherries, blueberries. Josie slid into her chair and put her head in her hands. Shadaisy touched her shoulder. "You okay? You're shaking like a leaf."

Josie shook her head, her face still covered.

"He's gonna be fine, Josie. Just sore. Bruised a little. He'll be right as rain in a few days. Do you have any aspirin? That should help. And a hot bath."

Josie lifted her head, her face ashen, waved her hand vaguely toward the cottage and whispered, "Bathroom."

Shadaisy told Tristan to go look and Josie to stay put.

Though Josie rarely drank hard liquor, she kept a bottle of vodka in the freezer for Erik, who occasionally liked a very dry martini. Shadaisy made three orange blossoms and passed one to Tristan when he came into the kitchen with the aspirin. She carried hers and Josie's outside, handed one to Josie who accepted it without question, sipped, recognized the vodka, and emptied the drink in four swallows. She leaned over and threw up.

"Jesus," Tristan said.

Rambles came trotting out of the tall weeds, approached Josie, shook herself from nose to tail, getting rid of the debris and whined deep in her throat. She stretched with her front legs out, bowed her head over them and yawned a giant yawn, baring her teeth. She snapped them shut and nipped Josie's big toe, something she had never done before.

Josie gazed at the dog. Rambles wagged her tail and trotted into the cottage. Josie rose, a ghost in her floating white gown, and drifted into the cottage, Rambles behind her.

Tristan stared at the undigested vodka and orange juice. "What the hell was that all about?"

"I don't know. Maybe she doesn't drink."

"So, why did she now? You know what? Erik said something to me about Josie running her sister over with her car. Her sister was carrying a blueberry pie. Guess I sort of reminded her. Bits of fruit mixed in a bloody sauce."

"Jesus." Shadaisy blinked. "Jesus," she said again.

The bath and the aspirin, the vodka and his youth did the trick for Tristan. The next day, the bicycle ride to the Raymond's was enough to loosen him up. When they reached the orchard, Mr. Raymond told the pickers this was a bumper crop. The best crop he'd had in years, the best since he could remember even. His face crinkled into a smile. "Course the weather still could ruin everything."

They worked from seven to seven for seven days straight. Tristan went grimly about his work, saying very little. At Raymond's instructions, Pedro continued to work the same tree with him. On the eighth morning, as the sun was filling the shed with enough light to see by, Tristan pulled a thin blanket under his chin and said, "The gardens are going to ruin. The tomatoes are crawling all over the ground, covered in grubs, the squash needs straw under it or it will rot, the beans are coming on, and there's weeds everywhere. Something has to be done."

Shadaisy, who had been getting dressed, poked her head over the loft and looked Tristan in the eye. "Like what?"

"I'm staying home today."

CHAPTER FIFTEEN

The day after Tristan came home covered in gore, Josie woke as she always did, trembling uncontrollably. Paradoxically, other than the shakes, she was unable to move. Her muscles refused the idea of getting out of bed. She always woke with the same thought: how is it possible I am still alive? She knew what terrified her but wouldn't allow the words to form in her head. How could she possibly enter into a world where Jaylene didn't exist? If she stayed in bed, she avoided that terrible place. If she gazed outside the window on a cloudy day, the gray seemed to suck the color out of everything; if sunny, the world filled with yellow. When it rained, there was a protective curtain between her and everything else. The problem was, after two hours of lying in bed, she would look at the clock and five minutes had gone by. This glacial passing of time was unbearable.

Today, as she waited for the trembling to stop and her body to uncoil, a thought occurred to her. It took forever to starve to death but dying from dehydration took only two to four days. She knew it was a horrible death but going on like this was equally horrible. When the trembling stopped and her limbs unfroze, she stretched onto her stomach, her face turned just enough to breathe. She waited, wondering how bad a mess her leaking, dying body would make on the bed. Rambles jumped onto her back, her four feet feeling like rebar digging into Josie's body. Josie didn't move. Eventually, Rambles plunked her bottom onto Josie and brushed her thighs with her wagging tail. When Josie didn't react, Rambles hopped onto the floor, grabbed Josie's nightgown in her teeth and growling deeply in her throat, gave it the death shake. The thin material ripped in half. Josie still didn't move. Rambles took hold of what was left of the nightgown and backed up, pulling the fabric along with her.

"Jesus." Josie rolled over. She hated clothes. It felt like she had lost her skin and all her nerves were exposed to the world. Even though they hung on her, she could still feel the waist band of her jeans, the inseams. The collar of her t-shirt nearly drove her mad. At least her nightgowns left her alone. Now this one was destroyed. Rambles jumped, landing on Josie's belly. The dog sat, stretched out her legs, and placed her front paws on Josie's eye sockets. Immobilized and blind, Josie noticed for the first time it was raining. She wondered if the kids would be home early. Her eyes began to sting. "Get off," she said and tried to shove the dog away. Rambles lay down full length, her paws still on Josie's eyes.

"All right. I give up." Josie sat up, tumbling Rambles to the middle of the bed. "I can't keep doing this. Come on, let's get up." The dog thumped her tail.

The rain pounded on the roof. A sudden memory struck. Josie's mother always had a rain barrel. When she was home, she washed her hair in it. "Nothing better than good, pure rainwater to create beautiful hair," she'd told her daughter. Her mother's hair was beautiful, like a lion, tawny, thick and coarse, standing away and framing her face with the force of its vitality. Josie's hair couldn't have been more different and was the bane of her existence as a teenager. Stick straight, so fair that in strong sunlight it appeared colorless, it hung to her chin like the picture of the Dutch boy on a can of paint. Ashamed of her vanity, Josie snuck out to the rain barrel whenever no one else was close by. As she scrubbed, she couldn't help picturing her mother doing the same thing, her hair still thick and lush even though it was wet. Once Jaylene caught her bending over the barrel, her hair full of shampoo, and laughed. "You get the hair you're born with.

All the rainwater in the world won't make a difference."

Today another image formed. Her mother used to wash her exotic, hand-sewn delicates in the rain barrel as well. Most women hung their clothes in the backyard where they couldn't be seen from the road. Mrs. Whitt's clothesline ran from an attachment on the side of the house, across the lawn to a stand of maples. You could see her laundry as you came down the road, tiny rainbow-colored flags. Josie had always wanted to paint them, to capture their delicate beauty. She used to take them off the line before her mother could, just to feel the weightless fabric float between her fingers.

Josie slid out of bed and with Rambles at her heels and wearing what was left of her nightgown, made her barefoot, awkward way to the shed, ignoring the rain. She found what she was looking for. In a cobwebbed corner was a large, black garbage can, the kind used for leaves and gardening debris. She dragged it bumping behind her to the front of the cottage and placed it under a gutter that had come loose from the roof and dangled precariously along a corner. The can would take forever to fill with rainwater so, even though it was cheating, she retrieved the hose from where it lay curled in the tub, dragged the nozzle end into the kitchen, attached it to the faucet, turned on the water and filled the rain barrel more than half full. The rain had stopped, but clouds still hung in the sky. Nature could do the rest. Josie turned the nozzle to off and stared at the shadows on the surface of the water. This was New York. The rain barrel would freeze by Christmas, if not before. But it would also snow. It always snowed in the Hudson River Valley. She pictured herself disturbing the perfect mound of white fluff topping the barrel, pushing it with her hands into a bucket. By the time it melted in the house, there wouldn't be enough to wash her face, let alone her hair. Winter was far away. She'd cross that bridge when she came to it.

Delicates. Josie had only one nightgown left. However, she had sheets in a box somewhere in the second bedroom. They were easy to find, as was her sewing kit. The first set of sheets had been washed enough times, but the other two were new, 600 count, stiff Egyptian cotton. They wouldn't be soft as gossamer for years.

Josie tucked her sewing kit under her arm and dragged the worn sheets outside to the chair by the front garden. She cut two same sized rectangles out of the cloth, threaded a needle with white thread, and began sewing them together by hand. She was still sewing when the kids came home that evening from work.

Tristan approached and watched her making tiny stitches, the fabric draped over her knee. "You makin' a scarecrow?"

Josie looked up from her work, her eyes red from strain. "You might say that." She turned her head. "Shadaisy, I want you to do me a favor. Take the car and go to Walmart. Buy several yards of soft white cotton." She held out the material to the girl. "It has to be as soft as this. Or softer. Like my night gowns."

"What if they don't have it?

"Then get it in blue. The most important thing is it has to be soft. Like my nightgown. If they don't have it in white… or blue…. um, get it in blue and white…"

Shadaisy stepped forward. "Josie?"

"Stripes. Blue and white stripes. Oh, you know what? Right before you get to the real fabrics, they have flour sacking and muslin. Or maybe it's in the back of the store. Look for it and bring some of that home too. There is some of my nightgown on the floor in the bedroom. Take that with you. It has to be that soft."

"Okay." Shadaisy looked at Tristan, who shrugged.

"There's money in my purse. Take that."

"Okay."

"I think it's in the kitchen. My purse."

"Okay." Shadaisy turned to go, but Josie said. "You haven't said anything about my new project."

Tristan and Shadaisy looked at each other.

"The rain barrel. See, right there. I filled it from the hose, which is cheating, but I won't do it again. That was just to get it started. It rained a little today but not much. It will more, though."

That night, rain thundered on the roof.

CHAPTER SIXTEEN

Straight out of Mayberry, the sheriff's well proportioned, sunlit office with posters on the walls of mountain peaks and lakes could have been a travel agency instead of a place of correction. The only giveaway was a single iron cell in one corner, and even that had an old-fashioned, nostalgic air about it.

Sheriff Robert Dobbs was a different matter. He had the tall, lean body of a cowboy in a Western. His eyes were the kind that appeared transparent, showing only a blue background. They caught the light and reflected it back, giving his thin face an inscrutable quality. Most people were afraid of him. Until he smiled. Then his wide full lips lit up his entire face, and it was impossible not to feel he was a jolly guy to be around.

He rarely smiled.

John Bond, his deputy of one month, was no Barney Fife out of Mayberry, either. Twenty-one years old, he had a full head of black hair, flawless skin, broad shoulders, a buff body and standing at six-feet-five inches, he looked more like superman.

Pulling into the parking lot the sheriff's office shared with three other municipal buildings, Steve Getz wondered if he shouldn't have gone to the state boys with his discovery. But he felt that would somehow be disrespectful to the local authorities. Besides, he liked Dobbs, and it would be hard to find a more conscientious, honest man.

The door to Dobb's office faced the parking lot. Steve knocked on it and without waiting for an answer walked straight in, calling out, "Hey, Robert." He hesitated when he saw John Bond.

Dobbs waved a hand in his deputy's direction. "Hey, Steve. This is my new deputy, John." Having heard way too many jokes about the last name, the sheriff no longer used it. The young man was simply John.

Steve offered John his hand, trying hard not to show his admiration when the young man stood to shake it. "Steve Getz, local realtor," he said. "Crime must be on the rise."

Dobbs raised his eyebrows.

"You've never had a deputy before."

"No, crime's about the same as always. The position's been in the budget for years and the county just this month got around to approving it. I think they figured they'd better now that I'm past my prime." He was thirty. "What can I do for you, Steve," he said. "Or did you come here just to chat?"

"Much as I'd love to spend an hour or two shooting the breeze, I do have a reason to be here other than entertainment. I called you. Remember? About the Whitt woman? The one who ran over her pregnant sister? I told you she's growing pot at her place."

"Oh. Right. I do remember."

John looked up from his paperwork.

"I was out to her house a couple of days ago." Steve paused for effect.

Dobbs said nothing; continued watching the realtor quietly.

"I sold her that place, and I like to check on her from time to time. Place is a dump. I tried to talk her out of it, but she's gotten a little strange after the accident. But who wouldn't? Awful. Anyway, there's a kid living with her. She says it's her nephew. And he has a sister. She wasn't there at the time. Maybe they're a friend's kids. Can't remember exactly. I've never seen him before. Comes from Hudson, supposedly."

"How old is he?"

"Twelve, thirteen, fifteen somewhere around there."

"You think he's dangerous?"

"He sure doesn't look dangerous. Pip squeaky little thing. Funny looking. But you never know, do you? That patch of marijuana growing out there. It's pretty big, Sheriff."

Dobbs leaned his chair back, nodding slowly. "How big?"

"Well, I don't know for sure, but I'd say at least half an acre. Maybe three quarters." As a realtor, Steve was good at sizing up parcels of property. He was pretty sure the plot was at least a quarter of an acre. He was also sure it was more than enough for one or two people.

"Steve, half the people around here grow their own weed."

Steve uncrossed his arms and ran his hands along his thighs. "Really? I didn't know that. But that much? That's more than for personal use only. That's enough to sell."

"Maybe. If it's really as much as you say. And growing pot isn't likely to hurt her. Probably die when winter comes, anyway."

"I don't know, Robert. Seems like more than just for personal use. And that kid has something to do with it. And where did she get the plants? I think you should look into it. We don't want to be one of those towns on the news that becomes famous for its opiate production."

"I doubt that will happen. Most small towns in New York have a healthy amount of marijuana growing."

"This doesn't sound like you, Robert."

"What would you have me do?"

"Investigate. Make some arrests, maybe. At least burn the crops."

"I'd have to set half the county on fire. If I investigated every small-time grower around here, I'd spend my time doing nothing but chasing my tail."

"Should I call the state boys?"

"You can if you want. I doubt they'd do anything, either. And do you really want to cause that poor woman any more trouble?"

"She's causing her own trouble. Growing pot is against the law. I'm sure she knows that. I don't care if everyone and their grandmother are growing it." Steve's voice rose slightly.

Dobbs had been leaning the back of his chair at a forty-five-degree angle. Now he leaned forward. He put his elbows on his desk and folded his hands. "I remember when those Whitt twins were girls. One so dark, the other so fair. What a sight they were. Practically raised themselves. Their parents always traveling. And good girls too, considering how much attention they got from the other kids. Bells of the ball they were. But they didn't let it go to their heads. Didn't go wild with it. Went to college, came home and married their high school sweethearts. Josie didn't just lose her sister, Steve. No. She lost half of herself. And then her husband leaves. I'd say if she wants to smoke a little dope, I'll roll the joint for her."

"We aren't talking about a joint or two or five or ten. I keep telling you there's a lot of marijuana growing out there. And it's going to get someone hurt."

Dobbs sighed. Steve was a nice guy. A little too pleased with himself at times, a little too sure he was in the right. But a good man. A God-fearing man. He'd go to the state-police for sure if Dobbs didn't give him satisfaction. That's the last thing Josie needed. Sour faced men in uptight uniforms flashing badges, invading her privacy. Standing with their hands in their pockets, staring at the crop. They'd make threatening noises. Try to scare her, then drive back to wherever they came from and forget the whole business. He straightened, rolled his shoulders. "Okay, Steve, I'll go out there if it makes you happy. See what's going on and who this kid is."

The realtor reached in his pocket, retrieved a business card, wrote Josie's address on the back, and placed it on the desk directly in front of Dobbs.

When he left, John said, "Wow… that's some story." Born and raised only eleven miles away in Hudson, this country town was still foreign to him. "I guess it was an accident… her running over her sister. That's as bad as it gets."

"Yeah, you'd be right about that."

John stared into the middle distance for a long while then turned to

Dobbs. "Do they really grow that much pot around here?"

"I might have exaggerated a little."

"I'll go check out that woman's place if you want me to. Were they beautiful? Those girls?"

Fast learner, eager, team player. Maybe. Dobbs hadn't known John all that long. "Yes, they were beautiful and no, thanks for the offer, but I'll handle this myself."

CHAPTER SEVENTEEN

Sheriff Dobbs entered Josie Whitt's address, such as it was, into his GPS: Gravel Road, New York, 12426. Not even the name of a town. He couldn't decide if he was annoyed or relieved that Getz had given him this task. It had been quiet lately and the weather was fine, so he guessed it was all right to be going for a drive, even though he was sure it was pointless. He'd driven about every road in this county, so the obscure address didn't worry him.

People assumed it was always quiet in this small town, but a surprising amount of violence took place out here. Drunk driving, drunken bar brawls, domestic abuse, age-old feuds showing themselves in odd ways: barns burning down, dead dogs, poisoned livestock, even cows with their throats slit. A wall of silence met every investigation. In Dobb's opinion, this was a relatively lawless place, mildly akin to the wild west. People here expected to be left to their own devices, to solve their own problems and disputes. Even if you were the so-called victim, you didn't go running to the authorities. You bided your time and when the opportunity came, you struck back. "It's against the law," held little meaning unless it was a property line dispute that needed an official surveyor and even then, there often was subversive revenge taken by the loser. Dobbs meant it when he said he didn't have time to chase after the small-time users and growers of pot. He much preferred someone lying around home smoking a dooby and munching on Fritos to someone breaking their wife's arm or cutting down a neighbor's fences, letting the cows wander across the highway.

Once he passed the township line, the sheriff drove by what people still called the new development, even though it had been there twenty years. The brick ranch houses with their small yards, no matter how neatly they might be kept, were considered an eyesore by the families who had lived in homes built in the 1700s. Dobbs tended to agree with them. The proximity of the houses, trees no more than ten or twelve feet, garbage cans visible next to garages, the same roof line repeated over and over. All of this looked unnatural compared to most of the county.

Once past the development, the lawns grew. Homes sat discreetly in the back of the property, half hidden by stately shrubs or the gentle roll of a hill. Occasionally a huge cedar or stone-sided home with large windows and roof lines that jutted here and there sat close to the road. Newly built by newcomers from the city, they were considered an abomination by the locals.

Eventually, there were no more houses, only fields, some of them cultivated and some wild. It felt to Dobbs like this patchwork terrain would go on forever when his GPS told him to turn right onto Brewster Lane. Though still macadam, the road was narrower than the one he had turned off. He entered a gloomy stretch of dense woods, giving him a prickly sense of not only being watched but lost. He was glad when, after two miles, he came out into sunlit fields even though there wasn't any sign of cultivation or civilization. The grasses and wildflowers grew as high as a man's waist. Josie Whitt had certainly planted herself in the middle of nowhere. How had she even found the place? Well, Steve Getz found it for her. If he was so concerned about her, why did he bring her out here? Five years older than Getz, Dobbs had known him as a boy and his holier-than-thou attitude didn't fool him.

The GPS spoke up again, telling him to turn onto Gravel Road. Three miles later, after many twists and turns, it ordered him to turn right onto a dirt driveway. He had reached his destination. More wild flora, a small ramshackle shed, a ninety-degree turn in what passed as a driveway, and hidden by the weeds was a worn-out cottage with Josie Whitt in a blue and white stripped nightgown standing next to it, dunking something in and out of a barrel. Sheriff Dobbs became instantly alert. He eased his car to a stop, opened his door, and stepped quietly out. "Hi, Josie, I'm Sheriff Dobbs."

"I know who you are."

They stared at each other, both waiting to hear what would come next. Dobbs knew there was no point in trying to come up with an excuse for why he was there. "I heard you're growing some marijuana along with your vegetables." He'd already noticed the marijuana plants next to the pole beans.

"That would be Getz who told you."

Dobbs felt a wave of relief. She wasn't as crazy as she looked right now. He didn't want to get into the legalities of what she was growing in her garden. Instead, he said, "What are you doing?" and nodded at the barrel.

"This is a rain barrel."

Dobbs waited.

"It's almost full."

Smiling amicably, Dobbs covered the distance between them and glanced inside. "I can see that."

Josie held up something that looked like a white sheet. "I'm washing this. Rainwater is good for everything. Clothes, hair, your skin." She wrung out the cloth fiercely, twisting it in her hands, then holding it by the shoulders, she shook it with such vigor it produced two sharp snaps causing the sheriff to step backward. Josie turned and hung the fabric over the branch of a tree. Returning to the barrel, she bent and picked up a cloth measuring tape, the kind you use in sewing, then she carefully measured the distance from the top of the barrel to the level of the water. "We've had decent rain you know. It pretty much stays at thirteen inches. That's important. I don't want to have to add water from the hose. That would be cheating. But we've had good rain. It's good for the plants, too. Tristan is very pleased."

"Tristan?"

"He lives here. He takes care of the garden. Works at it sunup to sundown."

"May I meet him?"

"He's in the garden."

Dobbs raised his eyebrows in a question.

Josie waved her hand at him to follow her. They turned the corner of the cottage.

"Huh," Dobbs said and put his hands in his pockets. There before him were rows and rows of the best-looking marijuana he had ever seen. Precisely spaced, the plants stood as straight as soldiers, their brilliant green leaves stiff with water and nutrients. A young boy slowly walked along a middle row with his back to them. As he walked, he examined and stroked the leaves gently. He bent and pulled out a few weeds. Coming to the end of the row, he turned and started down the next one. He looked up and saw a man in a law enforcement uniform standing next to Josie, watching him. Surprise, then fear, passed over Tristan's face. He held perfectly still. Dobbs looked at Josie. Her face was as blank and pale as a wax figurine. Only a shadow remained of the girl he had once known, charming the town as she and her sister grew into stunning young women, their sparkle bouncing off each other. He touched her arm. "May I trouble you for a cup of coffee?" he asked. He didn't really want any coffee, but he wanted a chance to observe Josie Whitt a little longer.

Inside, he sat at the kitchen table where he watched the woman take a can of Maxwell House coffee and a filter out of the cupboard. She carefully placed the filter in the Mr. Coffee. Next, she rummaged around in a drawer until she found a spoon. She measured four spoonfuls of the fragrant grind into the filter, filled the carafe with water from the faucet, placed it under the drip lid, and turned on the machine. Her movements were slow and automatic. She stared at the machine until it finished dripping dark liquid into the carafe. There was no way Dobbs was going to question this woman. The boy outside was none of his business. What the boy outside was growing could be his business, but he decided then and there it wasn't. He would keep a look out around the county for an influx of strange cars or strange people heading out this way, but for now, that was all he would do. The crop that kid was growing was plentiful enough to sell, but to whom? He was sure Josie didn't have any contacts. Maybe the kid did, but that was almost as impossible to imagine as Josie slipping around dark alleys, meeting up with thugs. Erik? It was easy enough to imagine Erik mixed up with the wrong people. However, he'd always struck Dobbs as too disorganized to manage subterfuge. And his own crop was hopelessly uncared for.

Dobbs looked up to find Josie staring at him. "Do you want milk or sugar?" she asked.

"Nothing, thank you. Black."

Josie filled a mug and placed it in front of him.

"Aren't you going to join me?"

"I prefer tea." Josie slid into the chair opposite Dobbs, folded her hands on the table and waited.

Dobbs felt a blush spread up his neck to his cheeks.

Josie leaned forward and said, "Just say it. Are you going to arrest me?"

"For what?"

"The marijuana."

"What marijuana?"

Josie leaned against her chair. "Why are you here?"

"Getz asked me to come by."

"I knew it was him. So now what's your plan?"

"I don't have a plan. I want to make sure you're okay."

"I'm not crazy, if that's what you mean." The muscles in Josie's face were slack, her eyelids drooped, and her eyes were focused on something no one else could see.

No, thought Dobbs she's not crazy. Just sad. Sad enough to kill herself?

His gut told him no. But what if she did? After he had seen her, talked to her, and walked away without anything more than, "Are you okay?" He'd have to take a chance. He'd talk to her brother. Ask him to keep an eye on her. He'd come back in a few days. At least there was someone living here with her. Even if he, or rather they, were only kids. One of them with an amazing talent for growing things and the gumption to carry it off. "I know you're not crazy, Josie, but you've had a lot to deal with. An awful lot. Indulge me a little. I'd feel better checking up on you from time to time."

"I'd rather you didn't. I want to be left alone."

"Do you have a phone?"

"Yes, I have a phone."

"May I have your number?"

Josie rose, rummaged around in a different drawer, retrieved a piece of paper and a pencil and wrote on it. She handed it to Dobbs, who glanced at it, thanked her, and put it in his pocket.

"I don't charge it much. Most of the time it's dead."

After leaving Willow Bark, Dobbs drove to Erik's who called out, "Come in" when Dobbs knocked on his door. He didn't turn around when the sheriff walked inside, he didn't even look up from his careful brush strokes. He was painting a solitary tree in what Dobbs thought was a strangely bleak landscape.

"What?" Erik said.

Dobbs looked around for a chair. Finding none, he pulled an empty crate next to where Erik sat on a stool in front of his large canvass. "I'd like to talk to you about your sister."

"Uh huh." Erik dipped his brush into a smooth dollop of creamy green paint and carefully fanned it across the background.

"Do you visit her?"

"Normally."

"Normally?"

"I'm getting ready for a huge show in the city. I've been a little busy, as you can see. So, I haven't seen her in a while."

"What's a while?"

Obviously annoyed, Erik turned toward Dobbs. "I don't know exactly. What's this all about?"

"Concern, that's all. She appears really depressed."

Erik turned back to his work. "Yeah. I guess she is."

"Do you think she would hurt herself?"

"No." Erik picked a different brush out of his jar of turpentine and dabbed it in a silver color on his palette.

"Are you sure?"

There was a silence while Erik applied streaks of silver to the trunk of the tree. Eventually, he said, "No, I'm not sure. Can anybody be sure of something like that? And why is it your business?"

"Suicide is against the law."

"Jesus." Erik flung his brush into the turpentine, snapped his head toward the sheriff. "Haven't you got anything better to do?" His breathing had changed. He looked like he might start shouting or hit something. Instead, he picked up his brush and wiped it with a paint-stained cloth. He heaved a sigh. "Leave her alone."

"Will you check on her?"

"I'll be gone for at least two weeks. After that, I'll check on her. Anyway, she's got these kids staying with her. They'll keep an eye on her."

Outside, Dobbs walked behind the barn. Erik's crop was its usual tangled mess; marijuana fighting for space among the weeds. It was large enough to produce product for Erik and maybe a few friends, but that was it. There was no way the same person who kept this patch gave any assistance to the boy with the magnificent rows of glorious plants the sheriff had just witnessed.

CHAPTER EIGHTEEN

Unlike Tristan, Shadaisy found freedom in the branches of the apple trees. Short, slight, she could climb to the near edge of a branch and stretch to harvest the farthest cherries. She discovered that by leaning forward and grabbing hold of the next limb, she was able to swing herself through the trees barely needing a ladder. Carrying three burlap bags on her shoulders, she set herself a goal of finishing a tree without having to touch the ground.

When she did alight, Mr. Raymond limped over to her. "Let me see your bags."

Shadaisy handed him the first one, the one that would have the most damaged fruit if there was damaged fruit. Raymond picked through it, cherry by cherry. He held out his hand for the second bag and finally the third.

"You're not regular," he said. "Never seen someone who could do this. You have a rare talent. I may even give you a raise. Picker like you can go anywhere. But I'd like it if you'd always give me first dibs."

Shadaisy moved her ladder to the next tree, picked up new bags and began again, Mr. Raymond's words hanging in her mind. She liked the physicality of moving through the branches, the sense of power and flight but truthfully the thought of making a career of picking fruit made her sick.

She spent her mornings telling herself this was temporary; she would return to the city in the fall, but the fall felt very far away.

The mornings were bearable because eventually they ended, and she could sit and talk for an hour with Lucia. The boys always sat apart from the two girls.

Lucia was polite to the point of timidity. There was a secret to this quiet girl, something so different, Shadaisy mistook it for serenity. She could use some serenity herself, that was for sure. Leaping about in trees took the edge off somewhat, but there existed inside her a restlessness so strong it was painful. She tried not to rush her questions.

Over time, Lucia revealed that she and her family were from Mexico, where there was no work. They had visas which allowed them to travel up the eastern states, following the seasons. The Vegases had been working for Raymond three years now. Yes, he was a good boss. When the pears were finished in the fall, the Vegases traveled south following the jobs. They traveled all the way to New York because of the wages, which could be two or sometimes three times more than the southern states paid.

Each day, Lucia brought the same lunch. A burrito stuffed with rice and other things that Shadaisy couldn't quite make out. She longed to taste it. She'd had plenty of Mexican food in the city, but she was sure none of it was the real deal. Finally, she blurted out, "Your burrito looks fabulous."

"Here. Do you want some?"

"Oh, no." Shadaisy's cheeks pinked.

"I don't mind."

"No, that's your lunch."

"Why don't you come for dinner tomorrow? I'll tell my mom."

Shadaisy's mouth opened. She breathed in. She couldn't believe her good luck. She hadn't been fishing for this invitation. It never occurred to her she would be invited to the Vegases' home. "I'd love to," she said. "Are you sure it's okay with your mom? She won't mind? I don't want to impose. But I'd love to. Thanks, thanks so much." Stop gushing, she told herself.

Lucia smiled shyly. "No, of course. My mama wouldn't mind. Why should she?"

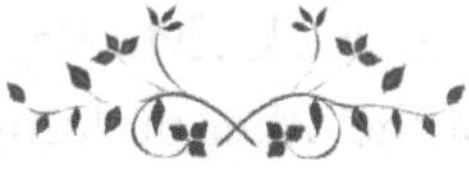

The next evening, the familiar old truck stopped in front of the Raymond driveway. The same man who had driven it every morning and evening was behind the wheel. Shadaisy had had no interest in this person until now.

Lucia noticed her friend looking at the driver. "That's my papa," she said. They climbed into the back of the truck. "He works at another farm then comes here to get us. He's a foreman at the other place. It's really big." She blushed and ducked her head.

The three brothers bounded down the hill to join the girls, creating a great deal of noise and energy as they jumped into the truck and stirred around, picking their spots. Once they sat, there occurred a second of silence, then George jumped up, bounced off the tailgate, and loaded Shadaisy's bicycle into the pick-up. Mr. Vegas turned the key. The engine growled then stopped. Mr. Vegas tried again, then again. On the fourth attempt the engine, unmuffled, roared to life, smoke puffed from the tail pipe, the truck shuddered and started down the road. Once they reached fifty miles per hour, a thrill ran through Shadaisy like none other. The truck, bouncing and swaying, sped down the road, knocking its passengers around. She had never ridden in the back of a pick-up before. Her hair bounced around her face. The wind slit her eyes. She grinned at Lucia, who smiled back. Imagine! This girl and her brothers got to do this twice a day, every day. As Shadaisy settled into analyzing the exquisite nature of this new experience, the truck slowed and made a left onto a dirt one-lane road.

The condition of this driveway was so bad that they couldn't go more than twenty miles per hour. The air stopped flying by, and the jolts were more painful. They stopped in the middle of a small village of wooden shacks. Shadaisy thought instantly of slave quarters. She glanced at her new friends. All sat impassively, their expressions unreadable. As if on cue, they jumped out, and George helped Shadaisy down before all three ran ahead and into one of the shacks. Mr. Vegas eased out of the cab and walked off into the midst of the other buildings.

"He's going to his second job. He helps with repairs around here," said Lucia. "He'll come by later."

The two girls walked toward a square dwelling, about twenty by twenty, made of rough-hewn lumber, with two cinder blocks leading to what Shadaisy assumed was the front door. She had seen plenty of ghetto housing, but even if the buildings were strewn with litter, broken bottles, fast food bags and worse, it was obvious at some point someone had made a pretense at respectability. The paint might be chipped, peeling, faded and cracked but there was paint on the siding. The windows might be rusted and broken but there were windows. As far as Shadaisy could tell, this box in front of her was windowless. Lucia opened the door for her. Inside, stripes of fading sunlight shone through the gaps between the boards. That and a bare light bulb hanging from a cord and one window facing onto what looked like a back porch provided the only light. Four bare mattresses strewn with blankets and pillows lined one side wall. A stove, refrigerator, and a sink stood in a corner, and a plain wooden table filled the center of the room.

The boys were busy hugging and kissing a short, plump, black-haired woman who batted at them with a wooden spoon. "Ah, ow, you're hurting me Mamacita," they mocked while trying to snatch bits of whatever was in the large black kettle on the stove.

"Go sit down. You know the rules." Mamacita did not sound amused. The boys moved away and roamed around the table.

"Mama," Lucia said, "this is Shadaisy. I told you about her. The girl who picks with me. You remember. She flies through the trees like Tarzan."

The woman turned around, wiped her hand on her apron and held it out to Shadaisy, who shook it a little too enthusiastically.

"Lucia, take this bowl to the table for your friend before the boys grab all the places." The woman handed her daughter a chipped, blue and white enamel bowl.

That came all the way from Mexico, Shadaisy thought with satisfaction.

"You sit here at the head of the table." Lucia, with a hand on Shadaisy's shoulder, guided her to a chair. "You get the place of honor cause you're the guest." She placed the bowl in front of her friend and sat to her left. The two bigger boys, fast as cats, slid into the two remaining seats.

Mrs. Vegas served them and then handed George a bowl. "You. Out on the sleeping porch."

She had been pretty once. Shadaisy could see that. Still was, only somewhat faded. Shadaisy imagined her as she would have looked as a young woman: sultry dark eyes, red lips, bosomy with a round, high bottom. She took her stare away from Mrs. Vegas and looked with high anticipation into her bowl, eager for the real deal Mexican food. Mrs. Vegas placed a smaller blue and white bowl in front of her guest. It contained coarsely chopped onions. Lucia leaned toward Shadaisy and whispered, "That's cause you're here. They're special for you."

A lumpy, thick, grayish-brown substance lay on top of white rice. The words "mystery meat" floated through Shadaisy's head. Undaunted, she lifted a generous spoonful. She was struck by an odd odor. She hesitated. Perhaps it was cilantro. She didn't like cilantro, but it was too late now. She popped the food into her mouth. She recognized none of the flavors and the texture was unfamiliar as well. She chewed and swallowed. "Um, Lucia, what kind of meat is in this?"

"No meat." Lucia smiled. "Just beans.

"I love beans." Shadaisy spooned onions into her bowl. She wasn't a fan of raw onions but still. The second bite had a definite "off" element to it, which the onions couldn't hide. Since there was no meat, it couldn't be protein gone bad. The third spoonful was much smaller and mostly onions. Even so, Shadaisy could taste something musky, with an acrid edge and the texture now felt slimy in her mouth. She glanced at Lucia, who ate slowly and steadily. The boys practically gulped the food down.

Shadaisy tried another bite, and this time she had to fight a gag reflex. Lucia was almost finished with her meal, and the two boys bolted from the table, tossing their bowls clattering into the sink before running out the front door. While keeping an eye on Lucia to make sure she didn't notice, Shadaisy used her spoon to push the food to the sides of the bowl, making it look like she had eaten more than she had. The second Lucia was finished, Shadaisy was on her feet. "That was delicious. Thank you," she addressed Mrs. Vegas, who was washing dishes.

"But you didn't finish," Lucia said.

Shadaisy patted her stomach. "I'm really full. Small me. Small stomach."

Lucia said no more even though she had seen her friend put away two PB and J sandwiches in under five minutes.

"Thank you," Shadaisy said again to the woman's back.

"You're welcome. I hope you liked it," Mrs. Vegas answered without turning around. "Lucia, take your friend onto the porch and send George in here."

Another mattress lay on the floor where George reclined against the wooden wall, his legs straight out in front of him while he licked his blue and white bowl.

"Mama wants you inside."

Once George was gone, limp with relief at being away from the food, Shadaisy sank onto the mattress. "It's nice here." She slid her gaze around the three sides of screening to see if this was true. In fact, it was. The gentle evening light gave everything a blue hue and softened the grassless spaces between huts. Lucia sat across from her. "Do you like it here, Lucia?"

"Yes, I do. The washrooms are close, and the water is always hot at least until ten o'clock. The toilets are clean, and the garbage is picked up twice a week. New York is our favorite place to work. The farther south you go, the worse it gets. In Georgia, the toilets are always stopped up, there's no hot water, and garbage everywhere. Disgusting."

Shadaisy realized for the first time this little house had no bathroom. She had slipped out of the shed during the night to pee in the grass more times than she could count, but she couldn't imagine Lucia doing that with all these other homes so close.

"Are they nearby?"

"What?"

"The restrooms."

"Oh, yes. I sleep out here, so it's no problem. No waking anyone in the middle of the night when I have to… relieve myself. Mama doesn't want me sleeping in the same room as the boys." She patted the faded pink and green comforter.

Struck by her friend's delicate assurance that decency was honored in this home, Shadaisy felt tears sting her eyes. She ran her own hand over the quilt, whose stuffing had thinned over years of use. "But what if you get cold?"

"I run inside and get another blanket. We got more. It doesn't get cold much here in the summer, though."

Shadaisy nodded before climbing to her feet. "I have to go now. It'll be dark soon."

"I can go find Papa and ask him to drive you home."

"God no. I wouldn't dream of it. He's busy."

Calling another thank you to Mrs. Vegas, Shadaisy hurried through the front door. She yanked her bike off the truck bed. Knowing it was a risk but needing to do it anyway, she kissed Lucia on the cheek. "See you tomorrow. Thanks for everything," she said as she slung her leg over her bike.

As the light faded, Shadaisy pedaled faster and faster. She had never been afraid on the city streets, but figures formed behind and around the trees and looking down the road, there was nothing but emptiness.

In the near dark, Tristan pounded posts around the tomatoes. "Look at these," he said as Shadaisy leaned her bike against the SUV. "This soil is awesome. I can barely keep up with these plants. Look at the way they're twisting and sending out new vines. And they even have flowers already. Look there."

"You really love this, don't you?"

At Shadaisy's tone, Tristan turned his back to her. "Yeah, I do."

Shadaisy leaned against the SUV, crossed one ankle over the other. She watched Tristan work in silence. Eventually, she said, "Do you ever think about going back to the city?"

The moon was up and only dark shapes were visible. He can't possibly see what he's doing, Shadaisy thought.

Still, he worked on, not facing her. Finally, he said, "No, Shadrack, I don't. Do you?"

"Yeah, Mouse, I do."

CHAPTER NINETEEN

It had been a busy week for Sheriff Dobbs and Deputy John Bond. There was a nasty brawl at a bar located off Route 9, popular with a certain set of locals. Some college boys from the city had decided to slum it in the rural Hudson Valley. They chose the Dew Drop Inn because of its neon sign and fake log cabin siding. The fight started when a local kid tapped a college boy on the shoulder and cold cocked him as he turned around. A scene from the old west ensued: young men leaping across the bar, glasses and liquor flying, chairs and tables over-turned, two broken noses and several broken ribs, and finally a call to the sheriff's office. That was Saturday.

Sunday, Dobbs and Bond were called to a domestic, and the sheriff missed getting hit by a flying can of baked beans by inches.

Monday, an out-of-towner robbed the local liquor store. Fortunately for Dobbs and his deputy, the perpetrator's car stalled in the middle of Main Street. He was apprehended, a sad sack from New Jersey coming off a heroin high.

Tuesday, a farmer's pig broke through a fence, tore up his neighbor's prized roses, and ran off into the woods. The neighbor held a gun on the farmer, insisting he pay him two thousand dollars in reparations for a lifetime's work. It took most of the day to get the gun away from him and take him to Hudson for lock up. No way was Dobbs having him sit around in his one cell waiting for arraignment.

Today—Wednesday—had been quiet so far. The two men sat at their desks, catching up on paperwork in welcome silence. Sheriff Dobbs leaned back and stretched his arms over his head, and before he could resume his work, the bell his mother had insisted on placing over the door tinkled. He glanced up and there was Wilson Elliot, of all people. Josie Whitt's husband. Maybe. Dobbs couldn't remember if they had actually gotten a divorce or not. Wilson smiled at him. "Guess I'm the last person you expected to walk through that door."

Wilson Elliott was not just another pretty face. John Bond, with his superman persona, was a handsome man, but his shoulders were a touch too square, his neck too rigid and his back a little too straight. On the other hand, Wilson, known as Will, sometimes Wills, never Willie, had something more than lovely features. He had a quality often attributed to the Duke of Windsor, who abdicated to marry the love of his life after going through girlfriends like Grant through Richmond. You wanted to reach out and touch him. Blond hair falling over his forehead, navy-blue eyes, he stood an easy six foot one and could have been a model for the perfect mesomorph. But more than any of these physical blessings, it was the grace with which he carried himself. He was a man completely at ease in his own skin, aware of and happy, even joyful with his body. It was easy to imagine him lying naked on a beach, spread eagle to receive the sun, having sex behind a sand dune, or on pine needles in a dark wood.

Will, Josie, and Jaylene had found each other and become inseparable when they were fifteen. Teenagers and adults alike wondered what the Whitt twins and the Elliott boy were up to when no one was looking, and given the senior Whitt's lifestyle, there were long periods when no one was looking.

Josie's grandparents had owned and managed a glass company which made them, if not very rich, very well off. Upon their retirement, they gave the business to their son Harold, Josie's father. A year later, he sold it and bought a travel agency. When his father heard about this from a friend—Harold didn't want to endure the scene that would take place if he told his parents directly—Mr. Whitt stormed into his son's house without bothering to knock and strode into the kitchen, where Harold was pouring syrup over his pancakes. A more or less one-sided conversation ensued with phrases like, "What were you thinking, nobody uses a travel agency these days, after all the work your mother and I put into it, when were you planning to tell me?" comprising the bulk of it. When the tirade finally wound down, Mr. Whitt said rather plaintively, "I don't understand you at all." And he didn't. No one did. Until over time it became obvious the reason Harold and his wife, Rose, had bought a travel agency was because they loved to travel. Harold used to say that his agency was *crème de la crème* because if he told you a hotel was charming and clean, the hotel was charming and clean. If he said you'd love a certain obscure town in Italy, Spain, Cambodia, Australia, or anywhere, really, you would love it. He even recommended the choicest, off-the-beaten-path restaurants, most not found in guidebooks. He could do this because he and Rose had been to all the places he spoke of. They had been to hotels, towns, and restaurants all over the world.

Josie and Jaylene were ten and Erik fifteen when their parents began going away for long stretches of time. When their neighbors and friends noticed the Whitt children alone and unsupervised most of the time, they began a subversive vigil. Cars drove by the house at odd hours, casseroles appeared on the kitchen table with no note. If one of the Whitt children missed school, the teacher asked a neighbor to check on them. Every Sunday, some adult offered to take them to church. Being Hudson Valley New Yorkers, the locals never spoke of the situation, just shook their heads and did what they could. This lasted five years. When the twins turned fifteen, the vigil stopped. At fifteen, a person's character was formed as far as the valley people were concerned. They had raised the Whitt children as best they could and now their job was done. When Will Elliott slipped between Josie and Jaylene as easily as a hot knife through butter, they raised an eyebrow or two, shook their heads, but did not interfere. Not even when Will's car appeared more than once outside the Whitt house at sunrise. And besides, it wasn't that surprising. The twins were stunning, Jaylene dark and voluptuous, Josie willowy and fair. Will was the town's golden boy. It was natural that the three found each another. The town got used to seeing them together and even nicknamed them "The Trio."

That is, until, as startling as a falling star, Jess Hart, a tall, whip-thin, black-haired boy with a merry smile came to town. Everyone in Hollandtown sat up and took notice. He played guitar, bass, and piano so well he performed with various bands at bars, weddings, graduation parties, dances, and concerts. When Josie and Jaylene met him, his circle was beginning to widen, taking him to places like Albany, Schenectady, and Troy. Once, when the second guitar /vocalist of a hot new band got sick, Jess took his place playing in a trendy bar in The Village. As it turned out, he had the kind of voice that drove teenagers crazy.

In August, Jess played lead guitar and vocalist at the state fair for the headliners White Thunder. Josie, Jaylene, and Will went to watch him the last night. There was a huge crowd. The stage was outside, and Josie couldn't see to the end of the audience. No matter how good he is, she thought, he can't be up to this kind of attention.

He was magical.

No need for screeching, no need for blood dripping from black lips or a heavy cross hanging from his neck on a tractor chain. Bent over his guitar, his shoulder-length black hair swaying, the intensity of his joy made the girls scream and the boys fantasize about what they could do.

After that night, the four of them were inseparable. For a while the nickname "The trio" was dropped and replaced by "The Quartet." Jess, with his quick wit and merry, quixotic demeanor, intimidated Josie. His mind was so agile, his mood so mercurial, she thought of him as quick silver, had the feeling he could disappear at any moment, which he often did, leaving to play at some venue or other.

It wasn't too long before Jaylene started disappearing with him. At first it was now and then, but soon it turned into every night he had a gig until inevitably the two were gone for the whole weekend. When Jaylene returned after midnight on Sunday, she slid into bed next to Josie, hugged her and caroled she was "in love, in love, in love, and Jess loves her too." Wasn't that amazing?

Josie felt a clang of fear. They were seventeen. The future stretching out before her turned, in that instant, uncertain. She had never imagined life without Jaylene.

The summer dragged. The quartet dissolved into two sets of duets. Jaylene and Jess were rarely seen. Josie and Will passed their time in a desultory repetition of the usual activities: swimming, using fake IDs to get into bars, hanging out at the diner or Josie's house. Will came around less and less and was seen on several occasions with other girls. Josie's whimsical interest in going to Pratt Institute of Art in the city solidified into a grim determination to get away. What was once a delightful fantasy turned into a frightening need to escape that kept her awake at night. At two in the morning, she lay staring at the ceiling wondering if she had what it took to leave the safety of Hollandtown for one of the scariest cities in the world when Jaylene and Jess came into her room and sat crossed legged on her bed. Jess announced he was tired of being on the road, and Jaylene asked if it would be okay if they went with Josie to the city.

The three lived a happy bohemian life in wretched apartments while Jess tried and mostly failed to support them with his music. Once Josie graduated, they decided they were tired of being hungry and dirty and returned to Hollandtown. Jess's grandmother died, leaving him enough money to marry Jaylene, buy a small farm, and start a bicycle business. He was sick of being out all night and splitting the kitty with at least four other people.

In the meantime, Will stayed in Hollandtown running his father's Ford dealerships and accruing a considerable amount of money. As soon as he heard Josie was home from Pratt, he called her. Sometimes he called three times a week. Other times, he'd wait three weeks between calls. Either way, Josie always sounded surprised to hear from him, making him wonder if she cared as much about him as all his other women did. Still, when they were together, she was enthusiastic and even bought him a book of Kama Sutra. When she began cheerfully and apologetically refusing more and more invitations due to her commitment to her painting and her increasing trips to the city to see her agent, Will proposed.

Now, he slid into the only spare chair in Sheriff Dobbs' office, sat slightly slouched, his legs apart and crossed at the ankles.

"You're right," said Sheriff Dobbs. "You are about the last person I expected to see here today."

Will continued smiling.

"Okay, I'll bite. Why are you here?"

John Bond swiveled his chair.

Dobbs waved a hand in his direction. "Oh, sorry. This is my deputy, John Bond."

Will turned, and still smiling, said, "John Bond? Seriously?"

John did not return the smile, and he didn't answer the question.

"Anyway, it's nice to see the sheriff finally has some backup. Welcome to Hollandtown."

"I'm not sure how you welcome someone to a town you don't live in." Dobbs said. "So, go ahead. Tell us why you're here."

"I need to see Josie, but I can't find her. She doesn't answer her cell. No one knows where she lives. I assume she's still here, but where is a mystery. I couldn't even get hold of her brother. I was hoping you could help."

Dobbs linked his fingers over his belt buckle, pushed his chair to a slight recline. He gazed at Elliott, who stared back at him.

Finally, Will said, "Can you? Can you tell me where she is?"

"I know where she is living. Yes." Dobbs said no more. John looked over at him. Silence hung around the three men until the bell tinkled again and Steve Getz walked through the door.

"It really is you. I was coming out of the café when I saw a Lexus I didn't recognize and a man getting out of it who looked an awful lot like Will Elliott, of all people. And here you are." Getz held out his hand. Will took it, his smile returning.

"I thought I might never see you again. How long are you staying? Any chance you're moving here?"

"I'm here to see Josie. But I can't find her. No one knows where she lives."

"I know exactly where she's living," Getz said, crossing the room to John's desk and sitting his backside on it.

Dobbs noticed the expression crossing over John's face as his deputy rose and took his six foot five strongly built frame across the room to lean on the opposite wall, arms crossed over his chest, eyes on Getz who continued addressing Will. "As a matter of fact, I sold her the property. Not the kind of place I would have picked for her. Truly isolated. A little run down. Well, a lot run down, to tell the truth. I tried to talk her out of it but…"

Will leaned forward. "You know where she is?"

"As we speak."

Will sat up straight. "Give me the directions. I'll go right now."

"It's really isolated, like I said. Lots of back roads. Middle of nowhere. I don't think it's even on a map. I'll take you. You'd never find it on your own."

"That's not such a good idea," said Sheriff Dobbs.

All three men looked at him.

"She's had a really hard time of it. Very fragile at the moment. You, Will, showing up out of the blue. Bound to be a shock."

"We'll call her. Let's call her right now," Will said.

"Easier said than done. If she has a cell phone, she never turns it on. I can't remember if she has a land line, but if she does, the number certainly isn't in any directory."

"We could Google it."

"You could try."

"I'll go with you, Will," Getz said.

"If anyone goes with him, it will be me."

"Why?"

"Because I said so."

Getz lifted his behind off the desk and sat in John Bond's chair. "Last time I checked, this is a free country." He said this in a tone that could be taken as playful.

"And trespassing is trespassing," said the sheriff, his tone not playful at all. "No one is going out to Josie's private property without her knowledge unless it's me."

Getz slid out of Bond's chair. "I think you're being more than a little silly, but have it your way." He walked across the room, bent forward, and shook Will's hand again. "Come by and see me any time. And good luck with Josie. She needs all the friends she can find right now."

"Will doesn't exactly fit into the category of friend."

Getz turned to look at Dobbs as though to say something but only shook his head.

Once the door firmly shut behind him, the sheriff said, "Come on, Will. You can come with me." He opened a drawer and took out a set of keys. "We'll take the cruiser."

Will tried to memorize the twists and turns they made as they traveled farther and farther onto back roads. Finally, he asked, "How isolated is this place?"

"It's not too much longer."

"Why did she move here? It's the end of bum-fuck nowhere."

"She's grieving, Will."

"I get that, but why move away from everyone? Steve said the place was run down. I left her with plenty of money. No need to live like a pauper. I don't get it. Makes me look bad." When Dobbs didn't respond, he went on. "You know, before all this happened the only time Josie and I had a real fight was when she refused to take my last name. Would not budge. That made me look bad too."

"Jaylene did the same thing."

Will stared at Dobbs, who kept his eyes on the road.

Eventually the sheriff said, "Josie's real fragile now. Some people would say strange. I don't, but some people would."

"Like how?"

"Lives off the grid. Never goes to town. Never has anyone out. She needs time. She's got two kids living with her. She says they're relatives or a friend's kids. Something like that. Not really sure."

"Two kids. I don't remember two kids in her life. How old are they?"

"Middle teens, I'd say."

Will leaned his head against his seat. "This just gets stranger and stranger."

"So why now? Why do you need to see Josie now?"

"I'm getting married. I wanted to tell her myself. Face to face."

Dobbs shook his head. "Poor Josie."

"Poor Josie, my ass."

Dobbs swiveled his head toward Will then to the road again. He didn't say another word until they reached Willow Bark.

CHAPTER TWENTY

When Will asked Josie to marry him, she was so surprised she told him she needed time. She loved him, had for years, but wasn't in love with him. Not the way Jaylene seemed to be with Jess.

When those two moved into their farm, they were extra solicitous of Josie, telling her at every opportunity she was welcome anytime. Whenever she left after a visit, she felt waves of relief at getting away from the barely hidden unmitigated joy the two shared in their love nest. Her own emptiness left her limp.

In New York, Jess had been gone most nights and slept during the day. Jaylene stayed busy keeping the roaches and mold away while Josie entered the world of learning about form and color. Now, regular hours and enough leisure allowed Jess and Jaylene's physical desire for each other to become almost palpable.

Then, as though answering her helpless need, the house and land right across the road became available. Completely aware of her less than pure motives, Josie said yes to Will and the two bought the property and moved next to her twin. A deep wood grew between the houses, so it was impossible to look across the land and see each other's dwelling, but it was a short enough distance to walk.

Josie and Will's house sat on a knoll with a large space of cleared land filled with tall grass and flowers. Will bought a tractor and began clearing away the wild growth to make a lawn. Josie put in a kitchen garden, which she tended in the late afternoons and evenings when the light was no longer good for painting. She and Jaylene saw each other at least once a day, generally two or three times.

After living there for only a few weeks, Josie's feelings for Will changed. Insidious at first, these feelings grew until he filled her head more and more, increasing to a point that frightened her. What if her fixation intruded into her painting, confusing or distorting her work? But as much as it frightened her, it seduced her as well.

She lingered in the bedroom in the morning, so she could watch him coming out of the shower, letting the damp towel slip to the floor. She loved the way he carefully buttoned the cuffs of his pressed shirt, sat on the edge of the bed, leaned over to tie his shoes. Once she noticed him cutting down a tree and was enthralled by the way his white t-shirt stretched across his shoulders. The image of him sprawled on a chaise lounge with his hair freshly washed and combed stayed with her for days.

He was the first thing she thought of every morning. They always made love before getting out of bed and often before falling asleep. Josie couldn't believe what she had been missing. Embarrassed, she thought of herself as insatiable. If she'd been disturbed by the physical affection Jaylene and Jess couldn't hide, she and Will were worse. She couldn't stop touching him. Any pretext would do: handing him a plate, walking past him, putting a hand on his shoulder, around his arm. He consumed her. When he left for work, every minute was filled with waiting for his return.

She spoke to Jaylene about this once, saying she didn't understand what was happening. As teenagers, the three had known what the town thought of them and laughed with the knowledge that, while they did a lot of experimenting, they never consummated their relationships. Back then, she never felt the need or desire to go farther. Now she couldn't imagine being able to stop. When she said this, Jaylene turned away with a slight smile and said, "So, he's that good, is he?"

CHAPTER TWENTY-ONE

J**osie was dunking a piece** of fabric up and down in the rain barrel when the two men arrived. Dobbs turned off the engine the instant the car stopped, and in a moment was out and standing next to it. Elliott followed more slowly, closing the door precisely and straightening his jeans. When he looked up, he became still, staring at Josie in disbelief. His ex-wife had always been slender, but the woman in front of him was skeletal. A blue and white striped garment looking suspiciously like flour sacking hung from her boney shoulders to just above her ankles. A light breeze blew her fair hair around a face with deep-set eyes and a sharp-edged jaw.

"Josie?"

"Will. It's you." Josie didn't sound any more surprised to see him than if they had seen each other a few days ago and ran into each other again on Main Street. "How are you?"

"I'm fine, but you look awful. My God, Josie."

Dobbs glanced at Will.

Josie pushed the hair out of her face. "Yeah, I know."

"What are you doing way out here?"

"I think the question is, what are you doing way out here?"

"I came to see you. See how you were doing."

He might as well have been a stranger. A stranger innocent of their lush and sensual history, a history which Josie no longer thought about. He was merely an irritation interfering with her need for solitude. She forced herself not to look at the marijuana plants growing in all their glory right next to her. She couldn't remember if Will had ever seen the stuff before it was harvested and prepared. They had smoked their fair share together and had a good time doing it, but neither had grown their own. Had they known someone who had? Did they sit around smoking and admiring a friend's crop? She had to struggle not to look at Tristan's luscious plants. Finally, she roused herself enough to say innocently, "That's it? Just to check on me? No other reason? You could have called." Josie was aware of but couldn't hide the edge in her tone.

Dobbs looked down at his boots.

An awkward silence followed. She shook the fabric into the air with sharp snaps of the cloth, the water flying in droplets all around her. She moved away from the barrel and prepared to hang the cloth on a branch.

Will took several steps toward her. "I have something to tell you."

Josie turned. "Yes?"

"Should we go inside?" He looked back at Sheriff Dobbs. "It's a little sensitive."

"This is fine, right here."

"Okay, then. I'm getting married."

"And?"

"Um... that's it. In July. Right after the fourth. We figured more people would be able to come if it was around a holiday... I wanted to tell you in person."

"But why? Of course, you're getting married. I'm surprised you aren't already. Is it that woman you left with? I can't remember her name."

"Yes. Lisa Wong."

Josie nodded. "You didn't need to come all this way to tell me. It doesn't matter." She spread another shapeless dress along a leafy branch.

"Let's go inside," said Dobbs, "and sit down."

Josie pointed the men to chairs at the kitchen table. "I have some iced tea." She retrieved a pitcher from the refrigerator, placed it on the table, and sat. Dobbs rose, went to the cabinet, and returned with three glasses. The tea was cold and bitter. The three sipped in unfriendly silence until Will pushed back his chair and said, "I think I'll look around." His tone was just aggressive enough that Josie didn't object. She heard him open both bedroom doors, walk around the rooms, then do the same with the bathroom and living room. He returned and stood squarely in the kitchen. "Why? Just tell me why."

Dobbs stood. "I need to be getting back to the office."

"I need to talk to Josie."

"Not now. You can call her sometime. Or better yet, write her a letter."

The two men stared at each other for a moment before Will let his shoulders relax. "Look, obviously something is going on here, and it isn't good. There's no need for her to be living like this. Money isn't an issue. There's plenty of money. Look at her." He turned to Josie. "Do you ever eat?"

"You don't need to worry about that." She sounded hopeless and tired.

Will addressed the sheriff again. "Let me stay for a while. Talk to her. Find out what I can do to help."

Dobbs put his hands on the back of the chair and leaned forward toward Josie. "What do you want me to do? I can take Will back to town right now if you like."

"Josie can ride me back." Will smiled at her. He turned his chair to face her, sat, placed his forearms on the table and folded his hands. "I know what you've been through. More than anyone else. I *know*. I was there. Remember? You don't need to punish yourself. It was an accident."

"I don't know what you're talking about."

Dobbs said, "Don't go there, Will."

"Do you have any food in the house? And what are you doing in that… thing you're wearing?"

Dobbs, still leaning over the chair, said, "Let it go, Will."

The other man shot him a glance.

Josie looked from one to the other.

Will shook his head. "It's no good hiding out here, living like a lunatic. You need to get out. See people. Get dressed up. Go to some shows. Are you even painting?"

Josie stared at him.

"Get Erik to take you to one of his big deal openings in the city. He still has big deal openings in the city, I assume. Why is he letting you live like this, anyway? He should look after you."

"I don't need looking after."

Will stood up and went to the refrigerator. He yanked the door open and stood, hands on hips, glaring at the inside. Next, he banged around in the cupboards. "Tea bags, pasta, bread, oh, here we go, peanut butter. I guess there is some nutritional value in peanut butter. At least there's plenty of fat. Let's see. Is there anything else? Good God, Josie."

"Stop it."

"Sheriff, isn't there a law against this sort of thing? Starving yourself to death?"

"No."

Will stopped going through Josie's kitchen. He turned and faced her, hands back on his hips, thinking. Suddenly, he brightened. He snapped his fingers. "I know. Let's go out to dinner. Somewhere special. The Bon Appetite. Get dressed up. We're going to town."

The Bon Appetite was the best restaurant in three counties. Even though the owners were from Hudson and spoke with fake French accents, as did the staff, the food was superb and astoundingly expensive.

"Josie doesn't drive much anymore," said Dobbs.

Will looked confused.

Dobbs straightened, rolled his head to loosen his shoulders. "Where are the kids? The girl could go with you. Or both of them. She could drive you home. What's her name again?"

"Shadaisy, but she's not here just now. And Tristan is too young."

"Oh, right," said Will. "I forgot. The kids."

The three looked from one to the other until the sheriff said again, "Josie, you don't have to go."

"Who are these kids, anyway? You never had any kids hanging around when I knew you. Certainly, none that you were close to."

It was unbearable, this poking into her life, pricking her with shards of the past. To stop it, Josie said, "It's all right. I'll go. It'll be fine."

She rummaged through her closet. Not much there: some hanging shirts, jeans tossed on a shelf, a pair of black linen slacks hanging from a clip hanger, a few scattered flip flops and a pair of black Mary Janes. She chose a white linen shirt badly in need of ironing, but moderately clean, the black slacks and, out of respect for Will, the Mary Janes even though they hurt her feet. The slacks hung from her hip bones. She looked around for a belt and finding none, she tore a strip of fabric from the hem of a dress she was working on and used it to hold up the pants. The white linen shirt covered it. In the bathroom, she combed her hair. The rain barrel must be working. Her hair flowed like pale gold around her face. Even so, there was no point putting make-up on those ravaged features.

On the way to the restaurant, Will talked about his new Lexus dealership. He could sell sand in a desert, Josie thought. He didn't seem to notice that she said nothing and even patted her thigh a couple of times. He apparently didn't realize he was a stranger. A stranger innocent of their past, someone not connected to her in any way.

Inside Le Bon Appetite the waiters, dressed in black, pulled out chairs at a private corner table. After draping a white linen napkin across Josie's lap, a waiter opened the black and white menu and held it out for her to take. She started to read the first course items but, feeling slightly sick, closed it. "I already know what I want."

Birthdays, anniversaries, celebrating big sales, hers or Will's, pre-Christmases, and Thanksgivings, Will and Josie always celebrated here, and Josie always had the same thing. Escargot, the beef tornados, potatoes au gratin, a green salad with a vinaigrette and finally, an apple galette drizzled with brandy sauce, all accompanied by bottles of rich, dark burgundy.

The escargot arrived in a metal covered cloche. The waiter, with an elegant sweep of his hand, lifted the lid, releasing a puff of steam redolent with the scent of butter, garlic, and umami. The familiar combination woke the ancient part of Josie's brain and a blessing fell upon her in the form of complete amnesia. She was instantly back to a time before. The time before it all changed. Her hunger stirred, woke, and roared to life, furious at having been starved for so long. Piercing the firm yet giving flesh, she lifted the dark brown, dripping snail to her lips. At the taste, she was overcome. She wanted to go at her food like a lion, had to restrain herself from tearing a hunk off the baguette, slathering it with butter and stuffing it in her mouth. She had to restrain herself from slurping the snails one right after the other and then lifting the bowl to drink the liquid.

When the tornados came, it was all she could do not to pick them up with her hands and take a huge bite out of the rare and still bloody meat; all she could do not to gobble the cognac-soaked toast points and then lick the plate clean. She managed to not quite gulp her wine. She ordered another bottle. Will might as well have been in another zip code.

It was the same with the brandy-soaked apple galette. She did not pick it up in her hands, but she did run her finger around the rim of the dish and licked every trace of brandy-soaked glaze.

Halfway through her second cup of coffee and cream, Josie sat back, her eyes slightly dazed. Will smiled.

"Good for you," he said. "You've even got some color in your cheeks. A few more meals like that and you'll be good as new. I enjoyed watching you eat. Even if you barely noticed me." He said this in the same way a man might tell a woman she had a beautiful ass.

In the parking lot, Josie put her hand on Will's arm. "I'm not feeling very well," she said.

"No wonder. Give it a few minutes. Time for your poor stomach to adjust. You look a little overcome." He laughed. "But don't get me wrong. I loved every minute watching you. You gave me quite the scare when I first saw you. You mustn't do this to yourself, Josie, it was an accident."

"Don't," she said. Her stomach felt like she had swallowed a watermelon.

They settled in the car, Will sat in the driver's seat. He planned to drive to Main Street in Hudson where he had left his Lexus. Josie put her hand on the dashboard. "My head is spinning. I don't think I can drive home. I might be sick." She opened the door, leaned out, but nothing happened. She closed the door, leaned with her head back against her seat, and closed her eyes.

"No problem, Josie, you can stay with me at the Algonquin. Plenty of room."

The Algonquin was the nicest hotel in three counties. Will opened the door to his room with the electronic key. The first and only thing Josie noticed was the bed, which was the size of a pontoon boat. She walked gingerly to it, sat on the edge, kicked off her shoes—her feet were killing her—slipped her slacks over her hips and legs, dropped them on the floor, and rolled onto her side and moaned softly. By the time Will was out of the bathroom, she was sound asleep.

Sometime in the middle of the night she woke feeling worse than ever. She thought about trying to make it to the bathroom but was pretty sure she couldn't. After several slow, deep breaths, Josie glanced at Will. A crack in the drapes let in enough light from the streetlamp to allow her to see him. He slept on his side facing her, the blanket low enough to expose his shoulder's rounded muscles. With his thick lashes and curved lips, he looked like an angel. Josie rolled onto her back and stared at the ceiling. She must have fallen back asleep, for the next thing she knew, sunlight seeped across the bed. The shower was running in the bathroom.

She took note of her condition. Physically, she felt better. Her stomach no longer rolled, and her head no longer spun. Emotionally, however, she was wrecked. Her muscles seemed to jump and twitch. She looked around the room, which attempted to look nineteenth century English and did a pretty good job of it. Heavy dark furniture, mirrors framed in gold, thick floral drapes, peach-colored walls with ornate, sparkling white molding. Everything in perfect condition. Nothing like the shabby chic farmhouse she had shared with Will, or the plain, shabby house Jaylene had shared with Jess. She heard the shower turn off, pictured Will wrapping a towel around his waist. Lying there, she saw images in high-definition roll by like a trailer for a movie: herself barreling along the road between the properties, doing fifty in a thirty-five mile per hour zone. She could feel the car lean into a curve then speed up. And then suddenly there was Jaylene right next to the passenger window, lifting into the air. She remembered her crazy notion that Jaylene had voluntarily thrown herself upward until she heard and felt the thud and saw her twin land on the hood of her car, slide off, and disappear. Lying in that bed in the Algonquin, Josie heard and felt the crunching of bones. She remembered slamming on the gas pedal in a panic thinking it was the brakes, then slamming into reverse to undo what had just happened.

She remembered asking people why Jaylene hadn't heard her car. She asked the medics in the ambulance, the cops in the police station where various men moved her from place to place, finally sitting her down at a long table in a room with no windows. She kept asking and asking until a different man, one who wore a suit, came into the room and sat across from her. "Your sister was wearing headphones," he said. "The police found evidence of headphones at the scene." What he didn't say was that in the midst of the blood, bones, and flesh spread across the road, those pieces of metal and plastic had been hard to find. He didn't say that the rookie cop who found them went into shock and had to be admitted to the hospital. He didn't say those things, but he didn't have to. Josie began to tremble so hard she could hear her teeth chattering. She couldn't speak and finally, after taking her vitals, medics put her back into an ambulance and drove her to the hospital where she was heavily sedated.

Jaylene had been listening to music while she walked over to Josie's, carrying her "world-famous blueberry pie" for their dinner party.

There was an inquest at the hospital. Why had she backed up? Josie couldn't say. Still couldn't speak.

No one seriously thought she'd done it on purpose. She wasn't even indicted. A person who killed her twin and unborn baby was allowed to walk out of the hospital a free woman.

It took only seconds to get out of bed, pull on her slacks, grab her shoes and purse and, barefoot, run out the door, down the stairs and out the lobby doors into a sparkling day. The valet hesitated only a moment glancing at her feet before saying slyly, "You're Josie Whitt, aren't you?"

She didn't answer. He shrugged and brought the SUV around.

Josie nearly screamed when she hit three red lights on her way out of town.

On the back roads, which were nearly empty this early in the morning, she took the turns without slowing down. She drove up the driveway to Willow Bark so fast she was thrown around and hit her head on the car's ceiling.

Tristan sat on the back stoop, his head in his hands. Hearing the SUV, he looked up, jumped down the stairs, and ran to Josie. She rolled down the window.

"Where have you been?" His eyes were rounder than ever.

"It's a long story."

"I thought you were dead. That you killed yourself. You never go away."

"Well, I'm here and I'm not dead."

Tristan stared at her.

"Where's Shadaisy?"

"Gone to work already." Tristan's voice was sharp. "Your car was gone last night, and it was still gone this morning. And Shadaisy stayed late at Lucia's again."

"Did you get any sleep?" Josie hated the idea of the boy lying awake, scared to death.

"Yeah, when Shadrack got home."

"It's okay. I'm here now." Josie patted his hand on the open window. She tried to think of a plausible excuse, but there wasn't one. He was right. She never left the farm. He would know she was lying and telling him the truth was impossible.

He must have seen something in her face because he pulled his hand away and said, "That's okay. You don't need to tell me."

As he turned and walked toward the shed, Josie called after him, "It won't happen again."

CHAPTER TWENTY-TWO

The day after Shadaisy and Tristan had their talk in the garden at twilight, Tristan made a vat of Bolognese sauce. He didn't know how to cook, so he accosted Josie washing her hair at the rain barrel, then in her bedroom, then back at the rain barrel and finally in the chair facing the side garden while she sewed flowing garments in white cotton. He asked her questions, sometimes the same question two and three times, about how much of this or that, what do you start with, how long should this cook, do you drop everything in together, what kind of pot would he need, and on and on. He knew nothing about cooking, not the first thing, and finally Josie told him there might be some cookbooks in a box in the second bedroom. Tristan managed to find a grease smeared, bent eared, multicolored stained Fannie Farmer.

In the kitchen, he scavenged an onion and two carrots from the refrigerator, and a package of ground beef out of the freezer. There were four jars of marinara sauce, two boxes of spaghetti in the top cupboards, and pushed to the back of the bottom shelf of a bottom cupboard, he found a box of herbs and spices that were God knows how old. It took him all afternoon going step by step, reading and rereading the directions to produce enough sauce to feed a garrison of famished soldiers. The sauce looked like what Tristan thought Bolognese sauce should look like, but when he tasted it, all he got was the taste of tomatoes. Canned Chef Boyardee was better. A frantic talk with Josie while she stitched reassured him, but only a little. "It needs to simmer," she said, "for several hours. On a very low flame. If it burns, it's ruined."

Tristan pulled a kitchen chair close to the stove and spent the remaining hours watching the slow blip, blip of the sauce and periodically running to Josie with a spoonful to see if it was okay or on the verge of disaster.

At eight o'clock, when Shadaisy walked through the door, the table was set for two and the kitchen bloomed with a spicy rich, complex, and luscious aroma. Tristen turned from tending his pot and smiled at her. "I thought you might like something other than peanut butter and jelly."

Shadaisy knew instantly what was going on.

"The bathtub is full and steaming."

Shadaisy rubbed the back of her neck. "Yeah, I noticed. That's awesome. I'm so tired I can hardly see straight. What are you cooking?"

"Spaghetti. From scratch."

"Smells good. Did you make it or did Josie?"

"I did all the cooking, but Josie gave some instruction. And this cookbook." He pointed to the Fanny Farmer lying open on the counter, its pages bespectacled with splashes of red sauce.

Shadaisy looked at it uncomfortably, then around the room.

"Take your bath. This Bolognese…" The pride in his voice was unmistakable. "…will wait."

The girl left to fetch her clothes. When she eased into the tub's hot water, she felt the delicious sensation of her muscles giving up the aches and tension of overwork. She leaned her head against the curved enamel. Nothing compared to these old clawfoot tubs. The stars shone delicately in the gloaming. Tears rose in Shadaisy's eyes, spilled over, and trickled down her cheeks.

Tristan had a bowl of sauce and another of spaghetti sitting on the table. Shadaisy filled her plate, swirled a huge amount of food around her fork, open her mouth wide, and after slurping and consuming it, smiled. "It's really good, Mouse."

His smile managed to be both shy and brilliant at the same time. "Thanks. I was thinking. Since tomorrow is Saturday, maybe we could go into Hudson and see a movie when you get home."

"God no. All I want to do tomorrow night is go to bed and sleep for twenty-four hours."

"Maybe a matinee Sunday afternoon."

Shadaisy gave Tristan a dubious look.

"You know. Get off this farm for a while. Do something different. The theater will be air conditioned."

"We'll see."

"How long will those damn cherries be in season?"

"A while. Raymond has several different varieties. They ripen at different times."

"We'll be rolling in money soon."

"Who you going to sell that stuff to?"

"Erik will help."

"Oh, right. Erik."

Shadaisy slept until noon on Sunday. She opened her eyes a slit and seeing Tristan's sleeping bag empty, opened them fully and sat up. She glanced at her new Timex, hoping it was too late to go to a movie. No, they could still make it. She sighed. Tristan was probably in the garden, working on those damn marijuana plants. Maybe he would be so engrossed he wouldn't want to leave them. She slid out of the sleeping bag and down from the loft.

Tristan wasn't in the garden. He was in the kitchen with Josie helping her lay out material for a new dress or whatever you would call it. His clothes were clean and if not what you would call Sunday best, at least they were respectable. His hair was combed. On seeing Shadaisy, he pulled the straight pins out of his mouth and put them on the blue and white striped fabric. "The movie starts at two and then at four forty-five."

"Do you like that material?" Shadaisy asked Josie.

Josie straightened and placed her hand on the small of her back. "Yes, it's fine. You did well. This is the second dress I've made from the same material."

"I'm glad you like it. I wasn't sure when I saw it. I mean, it does look kinda like it should hold potatoes."

"It's fine."

"I saw some patterns for sun dresses you might like."

"This will do."

Tristan put his hands on his hips.

Shadaisy eyed him sideways. "Let's go outside for a minute."

Standing in the driveway, she leaned against the SUV. "I really don't feel like a movie," she said, looking over Tristan's head to the cumulous clouds floating in a blue wash.

Tristan looked at the ground and said nothing.

"I'm not in the mood to sit still for three hours."

"I would think you'd want to sit after climbing trees all week."

"About that."

Tristan snapped his head up and looked at her full on. His heart thumped against his chest so hard he was afraid she could see it.

"I think I might take some time off."

"You're leaving me, aren't you."

"Only for a while."

Tristan opened his mouth to speak but knew he would not be able to control the tremble in his voice, so he said nothing.

"You could come with me. I need to find out what happened. I want to see how my mom is doing. Don't you want to know if we killed that man?"

"No."

"Oh, come on. Don't you care?"

"Not really."

Shadaisy looked away. "You didn't actually shoot him, so I can see why you wouldn't."

"I can't believe you want to go back there. You might get caught."

"No, I won't."

"You might."

"Come with me."

"What for? I've got nothing there." Tristan knew the tremble in his voice was clear for Shadaisy to hear. His cheeks flamed scarlet.

"You've got me."

"Where would we stay?"

"With my mom."

"Are you fucking kidding me?"

"Just for a few days. While we're looking for our own place."

"Our own place! I'm not staying in that goddamn city long enough for 'our own place.'"

"That was the plan, remember? To go after things cooled down. We weren't going to move here, for Christ's sake."

Tristan stared at her.

"We can go check things out. See what happened to that creep. And what my mom is doing. Come on, Tristan, be fair. Let's go for a while."

"How long is a while?"

"I don't know. Couple weeks. A month."

"You can go straight to hell."

Shadaisy reached for Tristan's hand, but he pulled away.

"Don't."

"I just want to see if my mom's okay."

Tristan nodded, stuck his hands in his pockets, and walked off. Shadaisy watched as he retrieved his bike from the shed and rode down the road, standing in the pedals, head bent, not looking into the future.

CHAPTER TWENTY-THREE

Tristan managed to not to say a word to Shadaisy for the next couple days. He didn't come to bed until the sun was completely down and only a half moon lit the way to the shed. He crawled into his sleeping bag and turned his back to the girl, didn't answer her when she said good night.

Shadaisy put up with this for two days and two nights. The first night she had woken, slept, woken, dreamed, and finally rose more tired than when she went to bed. The second night, sleep eluded her completely. Three days ago, barn swallows had moved into the shed, and she had found their busy scratching and rustling as they built their nests charming. Tonight, she wished she had the shotgun she'd shot Mr. Lederer with. She'd blast those birds to kingdom come.

Eventually, the swallow's fussiness stopped, and they fell asleep. Shadaisy listened to Tristan's breathing. If he was so upset, how could he sleep so easily? Anger bloomed, filling her with adrenaline. "Mouse," she said, kicking him in the foot. Tristan's breathing changed but he said nothing.

"I know you're awake, so stop pretending. Get up. We need to talk."

"About what?"

Shadaisy sat up straight. "You know damn well what."

Tristan rolled onto his back, draped a forearm over his forehead.

"This was never meant to be forever."

"I know," said Tristan, his voice dreary.

"Why are you so upset?"

"I didn't expect to like it here so much."

"It's that damn marijuana, isn't it? You wouldn't like it so much if you were picking cherries all day, every day."

"I know that too. I feel bad about you going out there and working your ass off. Can you take some time off?" he asked.

"And do what? Watch you grow marijuana?"

"You could help me."

"No, thank you."

"Once we harvest, we'll have lots of money. What's mine is yours."

Shadaisy turned to face Tristan. "And just what should I spend money on? There's nothing here."

Tristan started to turn away from her, but Shadaisy grabbed his shoulder. "Look at me. We're not going to avoid this any longer. I realized something. Seeing Lucia and her family. They are so close. They may be dirt poor, but no one in that family would ever end up in foster care. Those kids never went through what we did. Family is the difference between us and them." Shadaisy waved her hand through the air, indicating the whole rest of the world whose families were close and stood by each other.

"I thought I was your family."

"You are, but so is my mom. I need to see her. I need to know what happened to her."

"If you see her, will you come back here to stay? You could go to school in the fall."

"School?"

"Yeah. You said you wanted to make something of yourself. That you would never be a waitress."

"Right. And now I'm picking cherries."

"You're being stubborn." He sat up. "You don't want it to work out here." His voice had become strident. "This whole thing was your idea and now you're bailing. Dumping me by the side of the road like trash. Go ahead then. Go to that filthy city. And your mother. Leave me here alone. You said that would never happen. Well, apparently, you lied."

Tristan had never talked much about his own mother who'd died of an overdose of Oxy. His dad had never been in the picture. From what he did say, Shadaisy gathered the woman had been fun loving, affectionate, artistic, and a lover of music. The house had been filled with it. His name was born from an opera. Then his mom fell down the stairs in their apartment building while carrying a load of clothes to wash in the basement and shattered her hip. The doctors let her refill her prescription for pain medicine and then let her refill it again, and then again, and again until she died. Going back to the city would not produce her.

"Mouse, I'm not dumping you like trash. We *are* family. No matter what."

Tristan turned away and laid on his side with his back to her. "I don't want to talk about this anymore. Go. I'll be fine."

Shadaisy slid into her sleeping bag and pulled it up to her chin. "Just don't try to give me the silent treatment because I won't let you."

"Okay, then. When are you going?" Tristan said into his pillow of hay.

"Soon."

"Like…?"

"A few days."

Tristan pulled his sleeping bag over his head.

Shadaisy stared at the lumpy form, the outline of his body under the cloth. He looked so small. Something flip-flopped in her stomach and, for the first time in her life, she felt unsure of herself. She slumped onto her side, her back to the boy. I can go visit my mother if I want to, she thought. There's nothing wrong with that. I've asked him to come with me, and if he doesn't want to… that's his choice. The girl had lost some of her arrogance, however, and found little comfort in these thoughts.

The next morning, as soon as Shadaisy arrived at the orchard, she told Mr. Raymond her mother was sick, and she would have to take some time off. Dismay passed briefly over his face, but then he quickly took her hand and patted it, saying she would always have a place on his farm, she was the best picker he'd ever seen. When she walked into the kitchen after work, Josie was in the kitchen washing dishes. Surprised, Shadaisy considered turning around and slipping outside, but caught herself. It wasn't going to get any easier. She cleared her throat and Josie looked over her shoulder at her.

"Can I talk to you?"

Josie wiped her hands with a dish towel and, leaning against the sink, said, "Go ahead."

"My mom is sick. I need to go see her, so I was wondering if you could take me to the Rhinecliff Station."

Josie brought her eyebrows together. "Your mom. I thought you were in foster care."

So, the woman wasn't as clueless as she appeared. "I was. But I have a real mom, and she's really sick. I need to see her. Social Services said I should."

"I thought you ran away from Social Services. How did they get in touch with you?"

Shadaisy examined Josie's face. Her expression was bland but not blank. Her eyes held steady on hers, waiting patiently but implacably for an answer.

"I'm not sure. Maybe someone told them. Tristan said a sheriff was out here. It must have been him. He must have looked us up somehow. You know how it is with the internet. You can find out anything. He must have tracked us to the city." The words tumbled out of her.

"The city?"

"Yeah, New York City."

"I thought you were from Ohio."

Busted.

Josie pulled a chair out from the kitchen table and sat. She pointed, indicating Shadaisy should do the same. Once she started, the words flowed from her. With the exception of trying to murder her mother's social worker, she told Josie everything: her numerous foster homes, how she and Tristan first met and even though they weren't blood relatives, they were family. She talked about her mother's drug habit, about the nasty pushers who came to the house and the corrupt Social Services system. She described the foster parents, how some of them weren't so bad, but most of them were criminals. When she finally wound down, Josie sat watching her for a long time. Finally, she said, "Is Tristan going with you?"

"No."

"How does he feel about you leaving?"

"He's down with it."

Josie shook her head. "I doubt it."

All three knew there was no point in delaying Shadaisy's departure. They left to catch the commuter train to the city at six a.m. For once, Josie drove. Shadaisy and Tristan rode in the back seat. Josie hoped they would talk to each other, comforting words, plans for the future, promises to stay in touch, reassuring commitments. Instead, they sat hunched in silence.

On the station platform, Shadaisy hugged Tristan, whose arms remained at his side.

CHAPTER TWENTY-FOUR

Josie put Tristan, who appeared dazed, in the passenger seat as they prepared to leave the station. She drove directly to Walmart, not letting herself ponder the reason or what she would have to do once she arrived. The parking lot was nearly empty, it being too early for shoppers. Pulling into the space closest to the vast front door, she turned off the engine. As soon as she did, panic surfaced in her mind, ran down to her stomach, her arms, her legs, even to her hands. It had been so long since she'd been here, she couldn't remember the layout of the store. She would have to ask one of the surly clerks for directions, perhaps even follow him or her across the store while the miserable employee oozed as much hostility as one could muster.

Inside, the place looked even bigger. The store was huge, stuffed to the brim with items that didn't matter, relics from a world that no longer existed for her. There were reminders everywhere: pots, pans, towels, sheets for a king-sized bed—the only size Will would sleep in—and miles and miles of men's and women's clothes.

"What are we doing?" asked Tristan.

"You can't sleep in the shed by yourself. I'm buying you a bed for the second bedroom."

"What… why can't I sleep in the shed?"

"Just trust me, okay? You won't want to when it comes down to it."

Tristan followed Josie to the front of the store where the cash registers were. He had ridden with Shadaisy a few times when she was running errands. He'd never seen anything like Walmart before and had explored aisle by aisle until Shadaisy told him to stay with her, goddamn it, she didn't want to have to go looking for him. Now he asked, "Do they sell beds here? Anyway, I don't need a bed."

Josie stopped and looked around. She couldn't remember if she had ever seen beds in a Walmart. They sold some flimsy pieces of furniture, but beds? Relief replaced the panic. At the end of the mall stood a reasonably sized mattress store. Josie had been in it a few times. Usually glacially empty, with only one overly friendly salesman, it was doable.

The overly friendly salesman, in his thirties, dressed in a white, rumpled button down, tie, no jacket and gray pants, greeted them with a broad smile the minute they walked through the door. However, when Josie told him they were looking for twin beds, his congeniality slipped. "We don't sell many of those anymore. In fact, I'm not sure we have any. Honestly, most parents go straight from the crib to a full size. Sometimes even a queen. Even kids like a big bed these days."

Josie looked around at the flotilla of mattresses on display. They went from big to bigger. Not a twin in sight. A thought occurred to her. "What about bunk beds? It's a small room. A full-sized bed would take up too much space."

At the mention of bunk beds, the salesman brightened and put his hands together. "Well, now, of course. Many parents opt for bunk beds. My boys have them and they love it. Always making forts, wrecked ships, you know. Come with me. We have some back here."

Two sets of bunk beds stood humbly in a back corner, one set made of white curly-cued metal, the other of sturdy, plain as mud oak. Josie turned to Tristan. "What do you think?"

The boy still looked in shock. "Ahh…."

Josie put her hand on the footboard of the oak set. "We'll take this one.

Do you deliver?"

"We can, for a small fee. What is your address?" Josie gave it to him and, still smiling, he entered it into his phone. Several moments passed as he punched here and there on the screen. Finally, smile intact, he said, "Apparently your address isn't listed on the Google search engine. Just give me directions."

Josie tried to describe the way to Willow Bark until finally the salesman fetched a piece of computer paper and a pencil and, as best she could, she drew a map to her place.

Mike, the name on the tag pinned to his shirt, looked at it and said, "We're out that way on Fridays."

"That's too long. We need it tonight." Josie thought a minute. "Can you load one mattress and one box springs in my SUV? You can bring the rest on Friday."

Mike remained cheerful, even though it took several attempts along with Josie's, Tristan's, and his secretary's help to finally shove the mattress and bulky frame far enough into the back of the vehicle to slam the hatch shut.

Once Josie and Tristan arrived home, it was easy to pull the rails to the bottom bunk out onto the ground. It was easy enough to carry them and the head and foot board into the living room. Huffing and groaning, they dragged the box springs through the kitchen, knocking over two chairs, the broom, and a bucket partially full of water. The mattress was even more difficult. Wiggling away from them, refusing to keep its shape, it caught on the bedroom door latch, and they nearly ripped open the cover. When they had it on top of the box springs, Tristan plopped on it and looked at Josie, who sat on a box, exhausted. "Let's just bring the hardware in here and lean it against a wall," she said. "We can assemble it later."

She didn't have any sheets that would fit bunk beds. That meant a trip to Walmart. She considered asking Tristan to do it but dismissed the idea immediately. "I don't have any sheets," she said. "You'll have to use your sleeping bag. We'll just throw it on the mattress till we get some."

"I can sleep in the shed." Tristan felt tears sting his lids. "I don't mind."

"No, you can't. It would be awful for you. You're sleeping here. Tomorrow we can unpack some of these boxes so you have a proper room, but I'm too tired now." She registered his shining eyes. "Friday, Shadaisy's bed will arrive, so we want enough room to set it up. I'll get the man who brings it to help. Which do you want? Top or bottom?"

"What?"

"Which bed do you want? Top or bottom?"

"Ummm. I'm not sure."

"You can let Shadaisy choose when she gets back." Josie hauled herself to her feet. "Right now, I'm going to take a nap."

CHAPTER TWENTY-FIVE

Tristan, lying on his back on the sleeping bag he had thrown on the mattress, stared at the ceiling and wondered if there was no air in the room. Or was it that the air proved too heavy to breathe? Of course, the room had air in it. He knew that. It just didn't move, hung as heavy as wet cotton, soaking him, pushing against his chest, holding him down. Sweat greased the place where his jaw met his neck, trickled under his arms and the back of his knees. The sounds here were all wrong as well. A slight creak, the hum of the refrigerator, the tick of a clock. Empty, lifeless noise. He missed the sound of the swallows settling in for the night—the breeze moving through the leaves outside the shed, the way it slipped in through the door to brush across his forehead, the rustle of the hay when he or Shadrack moved. Shadrack.

How had this happened? How was it that he was lying down for the night inside this room and Shadrack was over a hundred miles away in the city without him? Was she at her mother's house by now? Did they hug and kiss, jump up and down, shout and laugh in their overjoyed greeting? Forgetting him completely? Or were the police waiting for her? Absurd thought. The police wouldn't have any idea she was coming. But did her mother, furious at having her supply cut off, take revenge on her daughter the first time Shadrack turned her back and call them? Anything could be going on while he laid limp and helpless as a rag in this room. Why hadn't he insisted on getting cell phones? Shadrack had said, "no way," those things had GPSs in them and would lead the cops right to them. Tristan wasn't sure the range led all the way to Josie's place, but as usual, he'd given in.

Now he was cut off from her entirely. She might as well be on Mars. Not ever, not in all the years being moved here and there in foster care, had he felt so alone. Even after his mother died, people had swept in, hordes of them it seemed, and told him what to do, where to go, what to wear, shoved him into a room with other kids and told him which cot was his.

Josie had done the same thing, buying this ridiculous bed, making him stay in this airless room. But Josie barely existed. After the confusing hubbub of arranging everything, she had wafted off and disappeared into her usual wisp of floating mist. In foster care, you couldn't get away from people. Here, there was no place in all the world as empty as these four walls.

Tristan slipped out of bed and gathered his sleeping bag under his arm. At least in the shed he would have the swallows. Seeing Josie's bedroom door ajar and without knowing why, the boy peeked inside. She slept on her side, knees bent, and Rambles lay curled into the curve of her body. He was alone here, living with a woman who spooned with a creature that might as well be a wolf. And when she's awake, she either sews rags together or dreams over a rain barrel. How had this happened? Why hadn't he left with Shadaisy when he had the chance?

Carrying his sleeping bag under his arm, Tristan tiptoed out of the house as fast as he could without making any noise, winced when his feet encountered the stones in the driveway, and stopped in front of the marijuana plants. His beloved marijuana. Only now he hated it. Had he really thought these stupid plants could take Shadaisy's place? They were nothing. Weeds. He snorted a bitter laugh. How appropriate that word was. Weed. Yes. Weeds, weeds, weeds. Nothing. Worse than nothing.

Walking across the dew-wet grass soothed his feet. His mood lifted slightly at the thought of the birds snuggled in their nest, the sweet hay, the way the air changed in the shed, cool toward the floor, warm but not too warm under the rafters.

When he slid open the door, the odor that hit him was fecund, smelling of ever-changing vegetation, growing to maturity and beyond. He stood still and listened. There wasn't a sound. The swallows must be fast asleep.

Tristan climbed halfway up the ladder and flung his sleeping bag into the loft where it landed across Shadaisy's. There was just enough light to make out the way both bags lay, hers straight and unused, his tangled and stretched across hers as though holding it down.

"I won't be needing a sleeping bag in the city," she had said in that arrogant tone she sometimes used.

Tristan crushed some hay in a fist. "Oh, damn you," he said. He stepped one rung higher, bent at the waist and laid a cheek on what had been the floor of their bedroom. Until tonight. The hay smelled rich, heavy, familiar, but something was lacking. Damp hair and soap. The scent of a girl. He backed down the ladder.

In the house, Tristan held his breath as he tiptoed through the kitchen, the living room, and into the hall. He pushed Josie's door open and glided silently to the end of her bed. She had rolled onto her back, her arms stretched out on either side. Crucified. Well, she should be crucified. What if Shadaisy was dead? Caught off guard by an enemy because he wasn't there to have her back. He might never even know what happened to her. It wasn't Josie's fault. He knew that, but he wanted to blame someone, and she was there. He slipped closer. Josie's face showed clear in a patch of moonlight. Asleep, she looked ten years younger. The lank hair spread out on the pillow appeared alive, soft and delicate as corn silk. So different from Shadrack's bouncy curls. The boy knew instinctively that when Josie woke, she would put back those ten years and her hair as well as her body would lose its vitality.

The cell phone, along with its charger, lay on top of a book next to the bed. Tristan unplugged it and stole out of the room. He plugged the phone into a socket near his bed, threw his sleeping bag on the mattress and laid on it face down. What would he feel like tomorrow? He hated to think about it.

CHAPTER TWENTY-SIX

The instant Shadaisy stepped down from the train, she felt the beat of the city. It came from the floor through her sneakers, up her shins and thighs, lifting her torso, pushing back her shoulders, straightening her neck. Unable and unwilling to resist, she stepped along to its rhythm. As soon as she walked through the door of Penn Station admitting her to Manhattan, she breathed in the smell of New York City. Though the girl had never been outside of New York State, she knew there was no other place in the world that had that particular scent. She couldn't describe it and didn't want to, didn't want to break the uniqueness into components. It was what it was. Without realizing it, she was smiling.

In the past, she and Tristan had taken the subway to Manhattan three times. Once to gaze at the Metropolitan Opera House, once to marvel at the wonder of Central Park, and once to wander the streets and avenues around Fifth and Madison, two urchins from the Bronx as awed as any tourist by the grandeur of the world's capital. Now she wished Tristan were here with her. She'd have to get him to change his mind somehow. She would think about that later. Now, she ducked into a tiny bagel shop and bought her usual: plain with extra cream cheese. No place in the world made real bagels except this city. Shadaisy closed her eyes as she took a bite and chewed.

Next, she found a subway entrance and sat on an underground bench to finish her breakfast. Satisfied, she stepped into a car. It was crowded, no seats available. That was fine. Hanging onto a strap and swaying to the rhythm of the train, her spirits lifted even more. A man moved closer to her. Automatically, she moved her backpack to her front and held it against her chest with her free arm. Though aware of him, Shadaisy didn't feel frightened. The need to be on guard was as firmly entrenched in her as was the ability to absorb the train's pulse.

Eventually, she arrived at her exit in the Bronx. Before continuing along the familiar streets, Shadaisy stopped at a hot dog stand and bought two hot dogs with mustard, mayo, and relish. Sinking onto a nearby bench, she ate her brunch. No place in the world made real hot dogs except this city. Hot dogs, bagels, and pizza. She would have a slice for dinner. People said it was the water. New York had the best water in the world. Maybe she and her mother would order a whole pie for takeout. There was a great place on the corner. It would be her treat to her mom. Shadaisy sighed. She felt a little sick to her stomach. Whether from nerves or what she'd eaten, she wasn't sure. Hoisting the backpack to her shoulder, she began the trek to her mother's house.

The closer Shadaisy came to the address, the more uncomfortable she became. She was sweating by the time she left the sidewalk to climb the five steps to the metal door. Without taking the time to look around and indulge in nostalgia, she knocked. Nothing. Shadaisy's heart pounded. She knocked again. Still nothing. Well, shit, she thought. She knocked again, much harder this time. Her fist was raised for another aggressive pounding when the door flew open. The woman on the other side raised her own fist. "What the hell you want?" She couldn't have been more than five feet and weighed at least three hundred pounds.

"I'm looking for my mother, Eileen O'Brian."

"Well, she ain't here and get off my steps."

For the first time in her life, Shadaisy went utterly blank. She hadn't allowed herself to imagine that her mother wasn't where she left her.

"Shoo," the obese woman said, waving a plump hand.

"Do you know where she is?"

"Who?"

"Eileen O'Brian."

"No, I don't. Now go away."

"Do you live here?"

"That's none of your business, but yes, I do."

"How long?"

"What?"

"How long have you lived here?"

"By God, you're a cheeky little thing, aren't you?"

Shadaisy smiled, producing her dimples. "Look," she said. "My mother lived in this house forever. I was raised here. I went away for work and now I'm back. I want to see my mother, Eileen O'Brian. If she's not here, do you know where she is?"

The fat woman put her fist on a bulge that could have been a hip. Her body was made up of a series of rolls hanging from her frame. The last ended at her knees. The knees themselves were the size of volleyballs. "I have no idea who what's-her-name is or where she might be."

"Can I come in, please? It hasn't been that long since I've been gone, and Mom may have left a forwarding address or something."

The woman's eyebrows shot up. "Come in my house? Are you nuts?" She slammed the door in Shadaisy's face. The metal rattled against its frame. Shadaisy stared at it. There was no way she could get around the woman even if she managed to yank the door open. She stood still. It had to be hard to move all that flesh around and noisy too, but she heard nothing. The woman must still be just on the other side of the entrance. Shadaisy contemplated going around the side of the house to look in a window, but what would that get her?

"Shadaaaisy. Shadaisy, is that you?" Mrs. Albright was standing on her front porch next door, looking exactly as she had for the past seventeen years. Same white hair neatly waved, same slight build, same ruffled apron. Old but ageless. Shadaisy ran down the steps to what had been her mother's house, across Mrs. Albright's tiny well-kept yard, and onto her porch. "Yes, yes. It's me." Weak with relief, she grabbed onto the little woman and hugged her.

"Oh, my dear," gasped Mrs. Albright. Freeing herself, she opened her front door. "My heavens, girl. Are you all right? Come on in and sit down. I'll get you some water." Mrs. Albright was used to the girl's absences and had never gotten more than a hasty nod or hello from her when she was around.

The house was laid out the same way as Shadaisy's own. Living room, kitchen, bedroom, bathroom. A shotgun house. Mrs. Albright gently pushed the girl into a kitchen chair, ran tap water into a glass, and placed it in front of her. She sat across from her. "Where have you been this time?"

"Where's my mother?"

"You don't know?"

"No, no I don't. I've been away."

"No one told you? Social services didn't tell you?"

"Told me what?"

"Your mother's been arrested."

Shadaisy's eyes popped wide. "For what?" Solicitation, no doubt, she thought, her mind racing. Her mother would need money now that Mr. Lederer was gone. Was he dead? A horrible image of her mother bending into a car window asking a man if he wanted to party formed in Shadaisy's head.

"Arrested for what?" she asked before gulping some water.

"Armed robbery."

"Armed robbery?"

"Yes dear, I'm afraid so." Mrs. Albright reached out to pat Shadaisy's hand. The girl snatched it away. The old woman patted the table instead. "Yes, I'm afraid so," she repeated. "About a month ago."

"Has she been convicted?"

"Oh, yes. Caught red handed by the police. Cut and dried. She's in Rikers Island."

Shadaisy's eyes grew even bigger. "Prison?"

"Yes, of course, prison."

"But how did she get a gun?"

Mrs. Albright tried again to touch Shadaisy. She reached out and took her hand away from the table and held it. "She was with two men. That's all I know."

Shadaisy had spent so much time in foster care she hardly knew what her mother did or whom she knew. The only steady thing when she was at home had been the arrival of Mr. Lederer every two weeks. Instead of pulling away, she held tightly to the woman's hand. "I have to see her. How do I get there?"

Mrs. Albright sat back in her chair, wiggling her fingers loose from the girl's grip. She took in the round, shocked eyes, the angelic face distorted by fear. She placed her hands in her lap, sat up straight, and said, "I can tell you how to get there, but there are certain rules." Mrs. Albright looked Shadaisy up and down. "You're dressed appropriately. They don't allow any provocative clothing. No sharp objects, of course. That's obvious. No belts. No purses, bags of any kind. The backpack will have to go in a locker. And you'll have to have identification."

"Identification? Like what?"

"Do you have a driver's license?"

Sweat broke out along the girl's scalp, making it tingle. "No, I don't have a license."

"What about a state of New York ID card?"

"No. I don't have anything."

"You can get an ID at the DMV."

The DMV. Shadaisy had watched enough TV crime shows to know the DMV was the gateway into anybody's life. Once you registered with the DMV, you could be tracked anywhere. It was an amorphous being just waiting to take you down. Some stranger starring into a computer screen, tap tapping on the keys, could bring up your picture, age, height, weight, eye color, address, and the fact that you'd killed your mother's social worker. Shadaisy drank more water to buy some time. She emptied the glass and put it on the table.

"Would you like some more, dear?"

Shadaisy nodded. When Mrs. Albright was once again seated across from her, Shadaisy's wits were slowly knitting themselves together. "Going to the DMV would take too much time. I have to see my mother. Today. Isn't there any way I can get to see her? She's my mother, for God's sake."

"How old are you, dear?"

Shadaisy did some rapid calculating. If she were eighteen, she would be free of the foster care system, but being an adult could bring with it a longer prison sentence if she was caught. Of course, her real identity and age would be found in the court system anyway, if she landed there. She decided on the truth.

"Seventeen."

"Really? You don't look that old. You could pass for twelve. Easily. Here's the thing, my dear. If you're sixteen or under, you don't need an ID. You do need to be accompanied by an adult, however. I could go with you. It's Thursday, and they only have visiting on Wednesdays and Thursdays." Mrs. Albright had a cousin in Rikers, a fact she consistently failed to mention.

Shadaisy hesitated. Mrs. Albright had been a sliver in her life, pricking her only now and then, but always too friendly, too chipper, too eager. Nosey. Someone to be avoided even if for no other reason than she seemed hungry for connection. She's probably just lonely, Shadaisy thought. Children long gone from the Bronx, husband dead or deserted. Baking cookies in that ridiculous apron for adults and children in the neighborhood. She was harmless, just a white-haired old lady, one amongst the droves of forgotten souls. "Okay," she said. "Yes. That would be great. Please, let's go, let's go now."

Rikers, like New York City, had its own smell, but it did not make

Shadaisy want to dance. Heavy, dense, a mixture of urine, shit, sweat, and other body secretions. Animalistic, Shadaisy thought. But no. It smelled nothing like the organic smells of a zoo. It made the girl want to run from it. The odor held her down, whispered, "Hopeless," in her ear, "All is lost. You are no longer human."

The guards checked Mrs. Albright's ID while listening to her explanation that she was bringing her young neighbor to see her mother. They looked at Shadaisy a moment too long. "Does she have an ID?" one wanted to know.

"Of course not. She's only fifteen."

The guards looked at each other before one shrugged and peeled himself away from his desk to show the girl and the old woman to the lockers, where they could stow everything except their clothes. He led them down a hallway and unhooked a ring of jangling keys from his belt, inserted one of an impressive number into a lock and opened the door to a large room filled with metal tables and chairs.

Sweat ran down Shadaisy's sides from her armpits, down the small of her back into her jeans. She didn't remember ever being so miserable. She found two empty chairs and sat down. Women were brought in by female guards and handcuffed to the tables. Shadaisy began to hope a guard would come up to them and say her mother couldn't see them today. But just as the thought formed, a scrawny wreck was brought to their table and shackled to it. The woman's hair was tangled and filthy, gray at the roots, black on the brittle ends. Her eyes looking out from deep hollows were flat, gray stones, opaque to the world in front of or behind them. She had sores on her face, arms and hands.

"Mom?"

"What you doing here?" The voice sounded as though it had been around a hundred years. The corners of Eileen O'Brian's lips were cracked and one bled bright drops of blood onto her bottom lip.

"I came to see you."

"You took your time about it."

"I've been away."

"Well, yeah." Eileen O'Brian wiped her lips with the back of her hand, noticed the blood and licked the corner of her mouth. "You got any cigarettes?"

"No. I don't smoke. How are you? Are they treating you okay?"

Eileen snorted. "Do I look all right?" She turned to Mrs. Albright. "Why are you here?"

"I brought your daughter."

"Well, aren't you the swell. Do you have any cigarettes?"

"No, I don't smoke either."

Eileen leaned toward the nearest table. "Latisha, you got any cigarettes?"

A black woman reached into the pocket of her jump suit, pulled out a pack of Marlboros, withdrew one, and handed it to a guard who brought it to Shadaisy's mother.

"I owe you." Eileen turned back to her daughter. "So, to what do I owe the honor of this visit?"

"I wanted to see you."

"Well, now you have." Eileen's words were barely intelligible. She turned toward a guard and called to him.

"Don't," said Shadaisy. "I want to talk to you."

"About what?"

Her mother was right. What was there to say? Shadaisy knew the sequence of events that got her mother here, or at least she could guess it. She didn't really want to hear the details. Still, she couldn't stop from asking, "What happened after I left?"

"Mr. Lederer stopped coming round. I needed money. Simple as that. Doesn't get any simpler. You know how it is, girl. And where did you go to? No social worker came looking for you. Not even after I got arrested."

"Yes, they did. Got me from school."

"I didn't hear anything about that." Eileen's eyelids began to droop over the flat gray stones.

Shadaisy knew that look as well as she knew her own face in the mirror.

"You're stoned!"

"Shhhh," Mrs. Albright said.

"She's stoned. How can she be stoned in here?"

"It happens all the time."

"Mom, how are you getting drugs in here?"

"Put money in my account if you want to help me out. You can do it by wire transfer… don't need to come by… wire it to my account." Eileen raised her hand again toward a guard. "Take me back." The guard unhooked her from the table. "Worthless," she murmured as she rose slowly and turned away. "That girl's always been worthless."

CHAPTER TWENTY-SEVEN

Once they had gotten off the ferry that took people back and forth to the island, Shadaisy felt disoriented and wasn't sure where to go, so she followed slightly behind Mrs. Albright. After a few steps, the woman turned to take the girl's arm but stopped when she saw her face. "My goodness, child, you're looking quite shocky. And no wonder. Rikers can do that to you. What you need is a good strong cup of sweet tea. I know just the place to get it." She put her arm around Shadaisy's shoulders and gave her a squeeze. "There's a wonderful little tea shop just around the corner. Been there for ages. Some say it was started by an Irish woman coming here with nothing but the clothes on her back to escape the potato famine. I can't be sure, of course, but that's the rumor."

After two blocks, Mrs. Albright gently guided the girl through a narrow, nondescript door tucked between a nail salon and cigarette store. Inside was a room the size of a suburban bedroom. The air smelled of spices. The shelves contained boxes of teas from all over the world. Every type of teapot, strainer, and other tea paraphernalia lined three walls from floor to ceiling. In front of the fourth wall stood a wooden counter topping a glass case displaying croissants, crumpets, scones, tea cakes, and finger sandwiches. There were four fake wrought-iron tables in the middle of the room, three with seating for two and the fourth with seating for a cramped six. Two young women dressed in black sat at one of the smaller tables, leaning into each other, talking and laughing. An overdressed woman of a certain age sat at another, sipping daintily from her porcelain cup. The largest table was empty.

Ms. Albright pulled out a chair for Shadaisy. "You sit right here, dear, and I'll place our order. Do you have a favorite tea? I think a black tea would be best. Something bracing. Are you hungry? Would you like a croissant? They are divine here." Shadaisy looked at her blankly. "Right, then." Ms. Albright left to go to the counter and talk to the middle-aged woman behind it.

When she returned, she sat, placed her fake leather brown purse in her lap, patted it several times to flatten it as much as possible and said, "Pips." She folded her hands. "Yes, Pips should do the ticket. A good straightforward, hearty English tea."

The Pips arrived in a generous, white with yellow flowers porcelain teapot and two mismatched floral cups and saucers. Ms. Albright poured the dark amber liquid into Shadaisy's cup, scooped in three teaspoons of sugar, stirred and handed it to the girl, who looked down into the dark liquid.

"Go on, now, drink up."

Shadaisy brought the cup to her lips, sipped, and sipped again. The beverage hit her like whiskey would, burning and spreading from her belly outwards.

"There. Don't you feel better?" Ms. Albright poured herself a cup. "Now, dear, I'm sure this has been a terrible day for you. Rikers Island is a terrible place. They're going to tear it down, or so they say. Build a brand-new prison with all the modern conveniences. With the taxpayer's money, of course. Go ahead, now drink some more tea."

Shadaisy looked around. This place was in such sharp contrast to where they had just come from, she felt even more disoriented. I've fallen down the rabbit hole, she thought. And now I'm at the Mad Hatter's tea party.

Where is the Queen of Hearts? The Queen of Hearts who cut off their heads. Shouldn't she be here? No. The Queen of hearts who cut off their heads would be in jail, naturally.

"How long has my mother been in that place?"

"Let's see. A month. Month and a half. She was arrested not too long after you left this last time."

"How long after? Days? Weeks?"

"A couple of weeks, maybe a month. Like I said, they caught her red handed."

"Was she alone? When she did it?"

"No, there were two men with her. I already told you that, I think."

"What did they rob?"

"A bodega."

Shadaisy put a finger in the cup of sweet tea, gathered some undissolved sugar from the bottom and licked it off. Two men? What two men? How long had her mother known these two men? How had she gotten so strung out in a couple of weeks? How did she get a gun? "I didn't even ask how long her sentence was."

"First time. No one killed. I'd say fifteen to twenty. Out in ten if she behaves herself. Officials look the other way when it comes to using in the joint. Now, if you're caught selling, that's a different matter."

"Do you know the men?"

"Good heavens no. Now. Let's stop talking about your mother and let's talk about you for a minute. Where did you go this time? Here in the Bronx? Queens?"

Shadaisy watched the two young women as they sat back against their chairs and laughed. What could make them so giddy and splendidly happy?

"Shadaisy?"

Shadaisy's gaze shifted back to her companion. "Umm. No, Upstate."

"Upstate? Really? That's unusual, isn't it? I didn't think foster care placed kids outside the city. How far upstate, dear?"

"I don't know. Hundred miles maybe."

"My heavens. That *is* strange. What county were you in?"

"Columbia, I think." Shadaisy watched the two young women gather their things and walk out the door, slender and elegant in their all-black outfits.

"My goodness. Columbia County. If I remember correctly, that's way up there. Near the Hudson River."

"Yeah, I guess."

"Why did they place you so far away?"

"They didn't. We just wanted to get out of the city."

"We?"

"Tristan and me."

"Tristan? You mean that boy who used to come by all the time when you were at home?"

"Yeah."

"So… you and Tristan wanted to get out of the city." Ms. Albright offered Shadaisy more tea, but she shook her head. "And foster care didn't place you there? In Columbia County."

"No, we just went."

Mrs. Albright poured herself more tea. "How did you do that?" she asked, keeping her eyes on her teacup.

Shadaisy looked at the top of the old woman's head with the neatly waved white hair. "Do what?"

"Get to Columbia County."

Shadaisy sat absolutely still.

"There's a train, Amtrack, that takes you right up the Hudson. Takes you upstate. Is that how you got to Columbia County, dear?"

Shadaisy remained silent.

Ms. Albright raised her head. "Do you remember that man, social worker he was, I think? Used to visit your mother at least twice a week."

"No."

"Sure, you do. He stopped coming by right after you left this last time.

Some neighbors say he was shot."

Shadaisy said nothing.

"With a shotgun, some say."

Shadaisy looked right into Mrs. Albright's watery blue eyes.

"Now why would someone shoot a man doing nothing but good? And with a shotgun, of all things."

"How would I know?"

"Of course you wouldn't know, dear. I'm just thinking out loud."

"Is he dead?"

"I can't say for sure. Some say yes. Some say no. Some say he's blinded for life."

CHAPTER TWENTY-EIGHT

Stupid, stupid, stupid," Shadaisy said to herself with each footfall as she made her way to the nearest subway station. She had told that woman everything. Even where she and Tristan lived. She pictured herself sitting in that silly tearoom with that silly teapot steaming away in front of her. Answering all those questions. Mrs. Albright was probably on the phone right now calling DSS. Or the police. Shadaisy didn't even have a phone to warn Tristan. She had to get back to Willow Bark to warn him as soon as possible.

Now that the initial shock was over, the image of her mother in prison with her rotten teeth, cracked lips, and sores had been overlaid by that of Tristan tenderly tending his glorious plants, totally unaware of the danger he was in. A runaway, a possible drug dealer, and a party to a felony. He could spend years in prison. Probably Sing Sing.

The subway wasn't very full, and Shadaisy made her way to the back. She found a seat where she could lean against the window of the car, settled her backpack on her lap, and began to ponder her fate. She couldn't exactly remember what she had told that nosy old bitch. She'd mentioned Columbia County and that right there was enough to bring the cops to their doorstep. She wondered if she should tell Josie everything. If she did, when the cops came to the door, Josie could say the "kids" had gone back to Ohio while they were in truth hiding out in the weeds. This was assuming either they or Josie saw the cruiser coming. If the cops questioned the bicycles in the shed, Josie could just say they left them behind. That and their flimsy, worthless clothes. They would have to hide the backpacks in a secure place as soon as she arrived home and leave them there. As far as Shadaisy could see, it was the only way they had a chance of evading the law. The thought of actually leaving the county and moving on never occurred to her.

Josie was so easygoing she probably wouldn't mind that Shadaisy had committed a felony. She'd mind if a bunch of detectives came around making a nuisance of themselves, but if she could convince them that she was there alone, she could stand one visit. Besides, she was so weird the police would probably think she was nuts and incapable of deception.

Shadaisy made up her mind to tell all as soon as she got home, and with that decision, her stomach stopped hurting and her muscles relaxed. There was nothing she could do until she got home. How she was going to get from Rhinecliff Station to Josie's she had no idea, but she couldn't worry about that now. Surely there was a pay phone she hadn't noticed before because she wasn't looking for one at the station. To distract herself, she looked around at her fellow passengers. The usual New York crowd at this time of day. Housewives rich and poor, high schoolers, bums, and artsy types. The car rocked gently. It would be a while before she had to change trains.

It was funny. She'd left her romantic infatuation with the city inside Rikers Island. She hadn't been there before. Her mother, as far as Shadaisy knew, had never been there until now. Why, she wondered, had she wanted to see her again so badly? She'd spent far more time in other people's homes. Yet she didn't care about or want to see any of them again. She wondered if she might still be in shock. Or was she a sociopath? The fact that she had probably blinded Mr. Lederer didn't bother her. Or not too much, anyway. She was glad she hadn't killed him. Even though alive he could bear witness against her. Over the past few weeks, when she thought about what she had done, her stomach hurt. So maybe she wasn't a sociopath. She tried to summon up remorse for blinding him by thinking about his family, if he had one. If he did, he probably abused them too. Especially a little girl. And then the image of him grunting away on top of her mother reasserted itself and her soul filled with murderous rage all over again. Of course, that old bat Ms. Albright might have her facts wrong. Maybe he got away with some buckshot in his fat gut and was fine now.

The train rocked and Shadaisy practiced in her head what she would say to Josie. The trip to Rikers Island. Her mother, the meth-head. The way she felt she had to get back to the city to see her mother. The murderous rage from the image of Lederer's naked fat ass pumping over her mother. No need to say she had blinded the man, just winged him, which was probably true. It was necessary to tell the pertinent facts so Josie would understand the need to lie to the police, but these facts weren't so terrible. She'd been protecting her mother from a monster.

Her mother stood in front of her. "You call that protecting me?" she shouted. "Forcing me onto the streets. Forcing me to become a whore? A thief?"

"You already were a whore. You just had one john instead of bunches and he paid you in oxy, so you didn't need to steal."

Shadaisy's mother hit her hard across the face and the girl startled awake, adrenaline making her entire body feel stuck with pins.

One didn't fall asleep on the New York subway. Shadaisy was instantly aware something was wrong, and of course that something was her missing backpack. She looked all around her, the seat, the floor, between her feet, under the seat, but she knew she wouldn't find it. Where was she? Shadaisy checked out the window. She'd have to change trains to get to Penn station. Standing up, she went through her pockets and came up with nineteen dollars and fifty-seven cents.

Out on the street, the girl looked up and down. It was late in the day. Shadaisy wasn't sure of the hour, and she didn't remember when the last commuter train to Rhinecliff ran. Anyway, nineteen dollars and fifty-seven cents weren't enough for the fare. I'm stranded, she thought. Instead of being filled with fear, a calm settled over her. This equanimity had happened to her before: When hearing heavy footsteps behind her on a dark night in a bad neighborhood, facing a bully who had a knife or a foster father after her with a belt, she'd had this same sensation. She had always felt a force, not a guardian angel exactly but perhaps an aura, a power settled on her by the universe that protected her when she needed it. A gift might be the best way to look at it. A gift that she could call on when in the most desperate situations. She didn't recognize it as the universal belief in her own immortality normal to teenagers.

Shadaisy looked at the tall buildings and their shadows lying across the street onto the sidewalk and thought about her situation. A blue sedan pulled beside her. "Hey, sweet thing, you want to party?" At first the girl didn't understand, thought she might know the person. Then it hit her. "Fuck off, shit face," she said and gave him the finger.

"Stupid cunt," the man said and peeled rubber into honking traffic.

Shadaisy put her hand on her hips. Think, she told herself. Jesus. She stared into the middle distance. Nothing came and nothing came. There was something though behind the curtain. A prickle or a nudge, a word. *Erik*. Hadn't he said something about a big deal show in Manhattan? Soho? The best part of Soho.

Another subway ride. Less money in her pocket. Nearly dark. Shadaisy walked the streets looking for art galleries with bright lights shining from their windows. She found a few, opened their doors, and looked inside. Some were art galleries, others just shops open late. None held Erik or any of his work. She kept walking. At the corner of an especially picturesque street stood a building bigger than the others. She opened the heavy door, went inside, let it sweep silently closed behind her and looked around. This was clearly where the beautiful people gathered in their skin-tight dresses, $1,000 haircuts, bare-shoulders, and $5,000 Italian suits. Shadaisy walked into the center of the room in her t-shirt and jeans and rumpled hair. She recognized some of the paintings. A waiter side-eyed her and gave her a wide berth. People stared openly.

And there was Erik also wearing a t-shirt and jeans, though his fit as though they were made just for him, which they were.

"Hi," Shadaisy said, as if showing up in his gallery was the most natural thing in the world. Even so, she didn't feel at ease or natural or anything like it. Her smile slipped, her grit failed, and her posture slackened, and there she stood, arms hanging at her sides, blue eyes round, not a dimple in sight.

Erik had spent enough time in New York to know his way around. "Shadaaaisy," he cried, "you came. I didn't dare think you would." He all but ran to her, plucking a flute of champagne from the snooty waiter and handing it to the girl while air kissing both her cheeks. "You must let me give you a tour, do you mind?" he said loudly enough for the room to hear and put his hand on the small of her back. "Now this big one, I know you always liked it," he said as he propelled her forward.

"It's always been my favorite," Shadaisy said.

"Alas, it is already sold, but what do you think of this one?"

Thus, they traveled around the room murmuring and exclaiming, pressed to each other's sides until Erik said again loudly enough for the whole room, "Do you really have to go? I'll have your pick wrapped and mailed to you, my dear. I can't say how glad I am you came." And smiling and whispering, he marshalled her out the door.

CHAPTER TWENTY-NINE

Erik half sat and half leaned on the pony wall outside of the gallery. He crossed his feet casually on the sidewalk and his arms loosely across his chest. "Go on," he said.

How different he looks here in the city, thought Shadaisy. In the country, his t-shirts were stretched, shapeless, and paint stained, his hair uncombed, and he had a three-day growth of scraggly beard. His movements were awkward, either from irritation or anxiety. Here, outside a gallery full of his paintings, he stood loose limbed, a man completely comfortable in his own skin. Too cool for school. Watching him at his ease, Shadaisy promptly fell in love with him. Fortunately, she had made a decision at thirteen to never, ever have a man in her life.

However, his looks compelled her and she told him everything, explaining how all of a sudden she wanted desperately to see her mother, to check on her because her mother was sort of a junkie and didn't take very good care of herself and how she had persuaded Josie to take her to Rhinecliff, and how she had left Tristan at the station and that upon arriving at the city of her birth she had made her way to her mother's place only to discover her mother was now a resident of Rikers Island. She told him about the neighbor who went with her to the prison and how her mother was more strung out than ever and looked exactly like what she was, a meth head. And how was that possible when you were locked up? Shadaisy told Erik that in her shock she had spilled everything to the neighbor, even that she and Tristan lived in Columbia County. That was really and truly a stupid thing to do because the old bat seemed to know that Shadaisy had shot the monster social worker who was raping her mother on a regular basis and well, possibly winged him. So Erik would understand that she had to get back to Tristan and Josie to warn them ASAP plus she had to get the hell out of Dodge, so to speak, but tragically she had fallen asleep on the subway and someone had stolen her backpack and she was practically penniless and then somehow divine intervention had brought her here to Erik's gallery.

When the words stopped tumbling out of her mouth, Shadaisy shrugged and looked at Erik with simple candor, instinctively knowing no amount of guile, whimsy, I'm-a-cherub-just-fallen-from-a cloud would do any good in this situation.

Erik stood, reached into a front pocket, and pulled out an electronic hotel room key, reached into the other front pocket, took out his wallet, retrieved two one-hundred-dollar bills and handed it all to Shadaisy. "Get a cab to the Omni hotel. It's not far. Get some rest. Stay the night. I won't be there tonight. Call Josie, tell her you're coming home so she can pick you up. Take the first train to Rhinecliff tomorrow morning." He turned to go back into the gallery, then looked over his shoulder at Shadaisy. "So, you're not from Ohio?"

Shadaisy shook her head.

"That explains a lot."

"I guess." Shadaisy did not want to know what it explained. She turned away, ran out into the street, and hailed the cab that, thank God, was right in front of the gallery.

CHAPTER THIRTY

When Shadaisy reached the hotel room, she pushed the sneakers off her feet, flopped on the bed face down, and promptly fell asleep. Sometime in the middle of the night, she woke and crawled under the covers.

Sun filled the room with gray light around six a.m,. which roused her. She reached for the hotel phone and began calling Josie. Shadaisy continued calling every fifteen minutes, to no avail. Then Erik arrived at seven from wherever he'd been. He took off his shoes and laid stretched out on the bed. After Shadaisy hung up the phone without saying anything, he asked, "No luck?"

"No. I've called over and over and she doesn't answer."

"No surprise. Just keep trying," and with that, he rolled onto his side and fell asleep.

Shadaisy was starving. She ordered room service: Rib eye steak well done, baked potato with butter and sour cream, Texas toast, Coke, and an ice cream sundae. Erik moaned a few times but never came fully awake until ten o'clock. In the meantime, Shadaisy had wandered down to the lobby and out into the street where she window gazed for as long as she could stand it. Back in the room, she found Erik sitting at the table in his boxer shorts with a pot of coffee. "There you are," he said. Shadaisy dropped onto the bed, picked up the remote and turned on the TV, stopping every fifteen minutes or so to call Josie. No answer. After his breakfast, Erik joined her, fluffing the pillows so he could sit upright to watch the TV along with her but dozed off and on until six in the evening when he woke with a snort and without saying a word, shoved off the bed and went into the bathroom.

By seven, he was dressed in an outfit very similar to the one he had worn the night before. "Last night tonight," he said, "then tomorrow we tear down, and I'll head home."

"I want to leave first thing in the morning."

"You haven't gotten a hold of Josie yet, have you?"

"No, but I'll call all night if I have to."

"Good luck. If I'm not here when you leave, that's okay. Just drop off the key. And help yourself to anything in the minibar. I can leave you some dope if you want, but it probably wouldn't be a good idea to smoke it here in the room. Don't you want to know how the show went?"

Shadaisy pulled her dazed glaze away from the TV. "How'd it go?"

"Great. Best one yet. Sold eleven smalls, five mediums, and one big."

"Congrats."

"Don't go overboard with the enthusiasm."

"Sorry."

"That's okay." Erik dropped a small baggie of weed on the bed. "Take the edge off. Just not in the room, okay?"

Shadaisy didn't feel like going back out into the city, so she drained a few bottles from the minibar into a can of Coke. She sipped her drink while staring mindlessly at the TV until she fell asleep.

Tristan thought the bed felt better. He pulled a pillow under his head, turned on his side, and curled around it. He finally fell into a deep sleep just before dawn when a loud wolf's howl startled him awake. Disoriented, he looked around the room before realizing the sound came from below him. He dove onto the floor, grabbed the phone, and stared at the screen. He didn't recognize the number, but then he didn't know anybody's number. The area code was familiar though. Manhattan. He fumbled for what seemed like forever trying to answer until accidentally he swiped the green circle in the right way, and he heard a voice. "Hello," he shouted at the screen. It was Shadaisy. She talked so fast he could barely understand her, but he gathered enough to go into Josie's room and wake her up. He handed her the phone. He could hear Shadaisy talking a mile a minute, something about her mother being in jail, Erik's show, something, something her backpack, and home right now.

Josie rubbed her eyes. "Yeah, what time?"

There was more babbling from Shadaisy that Tristan couldn't catch then Josie turned off the phone. "We're picking your friend up this morning at the train station."

As soon as Shadaisy stepped onto the Rhinecliff train platform, Tristan ran up to her and put his hands on her shoulders. She put hers on his and the two of them jumped around in circles while Josie felt her heart break apart.

Josie expected the kids to sit in the back so they could get reacquainted after being apart for forty-eight hours. Shadaisy, however, slid into the passenger seat. She buckled her seat belt and turned sideways to face Josie as much as the belt would let her.

"I want to tell you everything."

Josie glanced at her. "Okay."

Shadaisy talked all the way home. How her mother was her mother. You can't help worrying about your own mom. Shadaisy explained that her mom had been an addict for as long as she could remember. Sometimes she was able to function better than others and that was when social services would return her, Shadaisy, back home. But her mom always went downhill fast and back she went into foster care. She'd already told

Josie some of this, but now she made it more graphic. The girl explained what it was like to pull back a curtain and see a fat, flat, hairy ass humping over her mother. The creep was from social services, for God's sake, and came around every two weeks. She went into every detail about how she planned to kill him and with Tristan's help she managed to shoot him and, no, she didn't know if she'd actually killed him, they had booked out of there so fast there wasn't time to find out. But the neighbor who took her to Rikers to see her mom said she thought the social worker was only blinded, but what did she know, and blinding was bad enough, wasn't it? The old bat was sure to call the police or at least social services because Shadaisy had stupidly given her all the information needed to get them all hung. Most important, Josie mustn't think that Mouse was in any way guilty, he had merely been by her side like the great friend he was.

She sugar-coated nothing. Not her mother strung out on drugs in prison, her own horror and fear of getting caught, her need to warn Tristan and get back here, where maybe, just maybe they could be safe. Josie never interrupted, only nodded a few times, glancing at the girl. As Shadaisy talked, a strange sensation began to fill Josie. She couldn't say what this feeling was, but it seemed slightly familiar and the word for it hung at the back of her mind. The child had certainly led an awful existence so far, but other than showing the wear and tear of a night spent in the city, finding out her mother was in Rikers, and inadvertently spilling the beans to some nosy neighbor, then falling asleep on the subway and having her backpack stolen, leaving her without enough money to get back to Willow Bark, looking for Erik on the off chance he might actually be in the city and finding him, then scared to death, calling her over and over again, she looked normal. Anxious about the eyes maybe but not tragic. She told her story in a forthright, serious way without hysteria, and Josie was sure she told the truth. And she sympathized. She did not blame her for shooting that social worker. He deserved to die, or at least be stopped in some way from what he was doing and punished for it.

Tristan sat so his head was between the woman and girl. He nodded and said that's right, that's how it was, and smiled, commenting on how brave Shadaisy had been and how she had the plan all worked out ahead of time. He touched her on the shoulder and said, "Tell her how you got the shotgun," but Shadaisy told him no it wasn't relevant and to let her tell the story without interrupting. He had been a mess on the way to the station, staring out the window, sighing, asking how much longer, did Josie think Shadaisy made the train, asking again when the train would arrive, sighing again and saying maybe Josie could drive a little faster. Looking at him now, Josie was bemused by the smile he couldn't quite contain. He didn't sit back when Shadaisy finished her story but sat, grinning, with his chin on the back of the seat.

They turned onto Willow Bark's driveway, rounded the corner to the cottage, and there sat Sheriff Dobbs' cruiser. "This can't be good," Josie said in a low voice. Tristan burst into tears. He's getting too old for these tears, Josie thought. At the same time, she felt vexed and irritable herself, almost enough to shed her own angry tears. She parked behind the tan car with the word Sheriff printed on it in big letters.

Dobbs stepped out of the vehicle with his usually somber face. Deputy Bond unfolded himself from the passenger side. The two men waited, watching the folks in the SUV.

"Jesus Christ," Shadaisy said. "It's Superman."

"This really can't be good," Josie repeated.

Tristan dashed tears from his eyes.

Josie opened her door. Shadaisy and Tristan followed her lead and all three stood facing the law.

"To what do we owe this pleasure?" Josie leaned against her SUV.

"I would like to talk to all of you, but mainly the girl."

"Shadaisy. The girl has a name."

"Right. Shadaisy." Dobbs kept his eyes on Josie. "Where did you say these kids came from?"

"Ohio."

"Are you sure about that?"

"Yes, of course, I'm sure. We've had this discussion, you may recall. They originally came from Ohio. Then they moved to Hudson. Their mother is a friend of mine and asked if they could stay with me for the summer. To get them out of the city. Kids get in trouble in the summer in the city."

"I thought it was your aunt."

"What?"

"I thought you told me it was your aunt in Hudson."

"No, I didn't say that."

"You see, I've gotten this phone call. From a precinct in New York City. And they wanted to know..."

The sheriff was interrupted by a Lexus turning the corner of the driveway and parking behind Josie's SUV. The driver jumped out, slamming the door behind him.

"Will?" Josie said. She shrugged and flung out her hand palm up. "What are you doing here?"

Will put his hands in his pockets. He looked beautiful with the morning sun turning his hair golden and his perfectly proportioned body somehow relaxed and slightly aggressive at the same time. He shook his head. His ex-wife was barefoot, dressed in rags again and her hair bunched around her head. "What am I doing here? What am I doing here? Well, let's see. I come out of the bathroom, and you're gone. Just gone. No sign of you. So, I get dressed and go down to the lobby and look around. Not there, either. I think maybe you've gone out to get donuts or something. So, I sit in the lobby waiting, reading the newspaper. I wait twenty maybe thirty minutes, still no Josie. I'm hungry, so I go in the dining room and order breakfast. A large breakfast. Along with three cups of coffee. Still no Josie. I decide to talk to the guy at the counter in the lobby. He says the valet brought your car around some time ago. What the hell? I ask if you left a note. No note. Now I'm worried. But I'm also pissed. So, I head home to Syracuse. I can't stop thinking about what just happened, though. I mean, Josie, not even a note? I go back and forth between being furious and worried. I finally make up my mind to drive all the way back here to see what in the name of God is going on. I mean, we spend a lovely night together and you just walk away. That meal cost over three hundred bucks, by the way. Oh, and I called you about a hundred times, but no answer. What could have happened? I'm worried enough to drive back here in the hopes that you're at least alive. And to get an explanation as to why you walked out on me. I had to take a cab to get my car in Hollandtown, by the way. Here you are, but you're definitely not all right. No. You've decided to go back to being crazy. It's nearly noon. Why are you such a mess? I thought you turned the corner that night we were together."

"Turned the corner?"

Tristan glanced at Josie, whose voice had trembled.

Will turned his attention to Dobbs as though noticing him for the first time. "Something must be wrong to bring you out here. And with your deputy." The expression on Will's face was still a mixture of confusion, fury, and curiosity. He looked around at everyone. "Has anyone threatened to hurt someone… or themselves?"

Dobbs shifted his weight. "Nothing like that."

Will focused on Triston and Shadaisy. "These must be the mysterious teenagers."

Dobbs said, "Your timing is terrible, Will. This has nothing to do with you. Do you mind giving us a moment?"

"Take all the time you want."

"I meant could you…."

Wills' questioning gaze again roamed from face to face then to the scene in general. "Is that marijuana?"

"No," Josie said quickly.

Dobbs cleared his throat. "You should go, Will. This is none of your business."

Will stood as though rooted. Josie knew that stance. "He can stay. Nothing's wrong so he might as well stay while you say what you have to say. Though why he wants to, I can't imagine."

Dobbs looked uncomfortable. "Are you sure, Josie?"

"Sure. You don't mind, do you kids?"

They hesitated before shaking their heads.

Dobbs sighed a deep sigh. "As I was saying, I received this phone call from the city. About a girl Shadaisy O'Brian, who reportedly comes from New York, not Ohio, has lived there her whole life until a month or so ago when she disappeared from foster care."

Josie straightened away from the car. "This isn't that girl. This girl is from Hudson. Hudson, New York by way of Ohio, and I can prove it." She couldn't, of course, but hopefully it wouldn't come to that. Even after what had happened, she was well thought of in town. Her word should be good for something.

"This phone call from the city…" Dobbs was interrupted again by a large white van pulling in behind Will's Lexus. This time it was Erik. He rolled down the window and stuck his head out. "Well, well," he said. "Look who's here. Haven't seen you in a very long time, Will. To what do we owe the pleasure?"

Will stared at him.

Sheriff Dobbs attempted to continue. "It's also my understanding that this girl named Shadaisy had been in the city yesterday."

Erik slid out of the van and went up to the deputy. "I don't believe I know your name. Have we met?" He had lost none of his city languor. He held out his hand to John Bond, who took it. "Erik, Erik Whitt, Josie's brother."

"John Bond."

"Nice to meet you, John Bond. Nice name, too. I bet you get razed about it a good bit."

"A bit."

Erik smiled and continued looking into John's eyes, waiting.

"I'm Sheriff Dobb's new deputy."

"Perfect. I kind of figured cause of the uniform but nice to know for sure." Erik then made his way to the rain barrel, which he leaned against, his hand on the rim, ready to see what would happen next.

Dobbs heaved another deep sigh. "As I was saying. We have a report of a Shadaisy from New York City whose mother is in Rikers and who had a chat with a Ms. Albright who called the police about a shooting. I don't imagine you want to discuss this in front of all these people. Why don't you come to my office?"

"I still think that looks like marijuana," Will said.

"It's hemp," Tristan said.

"Hemp?" John Bond raised his eyebrows.

"Yes."

"Why are you growing hemp?" John looked from Tristan to Josie then glanced at Shadaisy, who was staring at him.

"For rope," Josie said. "For cloth, for a hammock, for baskets, for belts and bags. What difference does it make?" Her voice was getting shrill.

"Actually, it's Oleander. You don't recognize it because it hasn't bloomed yet. Has these beautiful huge white flowers. Really spectacular. Poisonous though." Erik crossed one ankle over the other.

Dobbs' expression was sliding from exasperation to anger. "To get back to the phone call..."

Josie pulled Shadaisy up against her side, her arm around her shoulder. "This child has been here with me all the time. She hasn't gone anywhere, and she's from Ohio. Like I said."

"I don't believe you," Bond said.

"Oh, shut up!" Josie knew she was treading on thin ice but couldn't stop herself.

Dobbs held up his hand palm down and made a patting motion. "No need to get upset. We just need to verify a few things. We can best do that by going to my office, making some phone calls, checking things out. I need you to come along, Josie."

Before Josie could respond, another car pulled into the driveway. Steve Getz fairly leapt out of his Cadillac as soon as it stopped. "I saw Will was back in town, so I drove out here to say hi." He lifted his arms, hands out wide. "My heavens. What's going on here? A reunion? Look at all of you.

Why, Erik is even here. And of course, Will. Why are you back so soon?" Getz swiveled his head, looking at everyone. "It's just like old times. The only one missing is Jess."

Silence fell with a thud.

No one moved except Josie, who dropped her head and looked at the ground. Shadaisy glanced at John, catching him staring at her. Everyone else carefully avoided each other's eyes until Tristan flung himself at Josie, wrapping his arms around her waist. He laid his head against her bony chest. "Don't cry," he whispered into her sternum. "Don't let them see you cry."

Josie raised her head, disentangled the boy's arms and moved him to her other side, leaving her arm around his shoulders. "Do you have a warrant, Sheriff Dobbs?"

"No, do I need one?"

"If you plan to harass Shadaisy again, you do. And don't think she's going to answer any of your questions."

"Are you saying she wants a lawyer present?"

"No, I'm not. She doesn't need a lawyer. She's done nothing wrong."

Dobbs looked at the woman with an arm around Shadaisy on one side and Tristan on the other. Like a Rodin statue, he thought. "Okay. Okay. John and I will go back to the office and do further checking. But I doubt very much this is over, Josie." He turned away from her. "Now if you all would leave so I can back up, I'd appreciate it."

Will opened the Lexus door. "I still think that looks like marijuana," he said.

Dobbs put his hands on his hips. "Erik, I can't get around that van of yours. And you too, Steve. You need to go." When Getz passed him, the sheriff took his elbow and murmured, "You really are such an ass, you know that."

CHAPTER THIRTY-ONE

There are those people who find the universe so vast and abstract they never think about it. For them, things happen or they don't. Events come and go randomly. They believe in coincidence. Josie was not one of those people. While she did not believe in a personal God, she believed in forces. People and events were drawn together, even if the reasons were beyond the pale. Voids were filled. The universe blew in, making itself felt. She believed in synchronicity. Therefore, when just two days after the "reunion" she heard a knock on the kitchen door and looking up saw Jess on the other side of the screen, she was not surprised. She went to him and let him in. He hesitated as though inertia held him in place. Like her, his eyelids were stuck at half-mast and the muscles in his face were slack. He said, "Hi, Josie," then leaned into her, his arms wrapped around her back, his head on her shoulder in a way that made it hard for her to stay upright. Disengaging herself, she led him to a chair at the kitchen table. Sitting next to him, she said, "Jessie, I am so glad to see you."

He squeezed her hand and looked straight into her face. He did not ask her how she was. He knew how she was. What he had to tell her would change things, but he didn't know if for better or worse. It didn't matter, he had to tell her. Without any pretense at niceties or preamble at all, he reached into his back jean pocket and produced a cell phone. Josie assumed it was his until he turned it on and held the screen in front of her face. "It's Jaylene's," he said. "I found it yesterday in a box of her things I was going through. The charger was with it. I don't remember packing them but there they were. The phone was dead, of course, so I charged it overnight. The phone still works. I checked it at three-thirty this morning and it works just like it was new." Jess removed the phone from Josie's gaze and poked at an app. A message came up. "Shall I read it to you, or do you want to read it yourself?"

"Jess?" Josie's throat felt like it was closing.

"This is Jaylene's phone."

"Yes. I know. You told me that."

"There's a message on it. From the day she died. It's from Will."

Josie dropped both hands in her lap.

"Okay," said Jess. "I don't mind reading it to you. I've read it to myself a hundred times. It'll be good to say it out loud." He drew in a deep breath and let it out. He leaned an elbow on the table, held the phone up to his face as if he were near-sighted though he wasn't.

"*Dear sexy, beautiful my own sweet 'Jaysie', you don't need to be so shy about your changing body. I swear your round belly is the sexiest thing I've ever come across. No pun intended. Well, yes intended. And then there's your breasts. My god. They were always beautiful but now, bigger, almost hard they are so firm standing up and out from your body, your hard nipples. I'm getting hard just writing this. Today was so damn hot. You were so slippery so full and plump, wet and tight and giving. I'll go mad if I keep thinking about it.*

I love that we'll be together tonight. Call me hateful, but I love it when the four of us are together and only you and I know what's going on. I love knowing that sexy bump under your clothes is mine. Or at least we think it is. You asked about the future. I don't mind knowing my child will be raised by you and Jess. Living so close I'll see him/her every day and you'll be a great mom. OOPS. I just had this sensation of your sweat-slicked skin under my hands, your nipple in my mouth. I'd better stop now before I'm a goner. See you tonight my love."

Jess put the phone on the table. Josie watched him, her eyes deep and smudged. She stared at the phone and said nothing.

"I have herpes. I can't remember if I was having an outbreak when the child was conceived. We used condoms when I did. But I never put the timing together."

Josie looked up from the phone to Jess's face.

"It took me time too, to let it sink in. Jaylene must have been keeping track. Of the days when we used condoms. I guess. Why else would she think the child was Will's? I couldn't make sense of it at first. Like I said, I read it for the first time at three-thirty this morning." He put the phone in Josie's lap. She looked down at it then back to Jess. "I believe you," she said. "I don't need to read it."

Her brother-in-law crossed his legs, tapped the table with his fingers, looked over Josie's head at the room, at the cupboards, the stove, the refrigerator. He looked bemused that such prosaic things could still exist, but not surprised by the poverty.

Josie placed the phone on the table with great care, as though it might explode. Her dress that day was made from sheets. If Jess noticed, he gave no sign. He seemed to understand her run-down house, the deadness in her eyes. "I think I need to lie down," she said. She rose, then abruptly sat back down. She knew in that instant lying in bed most of the day would no longer do. Dressing like a phantom was no longer an option. She thought of the rain barrel right outside the kitchen door. Never again would she spend hours pondering it, measuring the water levels, washing her hair, her clothes, the sheets and pillowcases in its waters. It was just a rain barrel, soon to become an eyesore as, through lack of use, it turned to rust. "How long can you stay?"

"Do you need me to?"

"Not if you don't want to."

"I hate to leave you here alone."

"I'm not alone. I have, um, some people staying here. They're not here right now but will be here soon."

"Josie... I am so sorry. About all of it."

"I'm glad you told me."

"Not just that. You didn't deserve this. Any of it. Will doesn't deserve to wipe your feet."

"What about Jaylene? Did she? Deserve to wipe yours?"

Jess dropped his head.

Josie wanted to hug him, croon over him, saying, "There, there." She loved this man, had for years.

Jess lifted his head. "I have to get back to work anyway." After the accident and leaving Hollandtown, he repaired bikes at a store in Rochester, New York. He never had to deal with a customer. He stayed in the dusty back room, out of sight. He was incredibly slow, going over the bikes from wheel to wheel, his long delicate fingers touching, with melancholy sadness each joint, each connection, each part. His boss put up with this slowness because Jess could return any disabled bike to usefulness, make some as good if not better than before. Also, he never took a day off. Not even Sunday. He could have stayed with Josie a week if he wanted to, but he didn't. She offered him some food, which he accepted and ate mechanically. He was very thin. Always had been. But this was a different kind of thin. Every trace of that merry, quixotic, musical man was gone. Now he just looked wounded. He wiped his mouth delicately with his napkin. "I guess I'll hit the road."

Josie couldn't wait for him to leave. She needed desperately to be alone. "I'm glad you came," she said. "I'm glad to know the truth."

"Does it make it better?"

"No, just different."

"Yeah, I know." He looked around as though confused, then turned toward the door.

Josie stood up. "I don't want you to disappear. I want to know you're out there where I can reach you."

"I'll stay in touch."

Josie didn't believe him, but she told herself she did.

Jess opened the screen door then turned to look at her. "I love you,

Josie Whitt."

"I know you do."

After Jess's car turned from the driveway onto the road, Josie went into the bedroom and dropped her sheet dress on the floor. She rummaged in her dresser until she found a pair of jeans and a t-shirt. When she put on the jeans, they dropped to the floor. She found the cloth belt she'd torn from the dress she was making the night she went out with Will and used it to hold them up. The t-shirt swam around her shoulders. Still, she found the clothes abrasive and annoying.

Tristan apparently had stayed to pick all day. He did that sometimes when there was nothing to do in the gardens. He and Shadaisy returned home around seven. Josie was waiting for them on the kitchen stoop. She did not move when they laid down their bikes on the grass and came to stand in front of her.

"Shadaisy," Josie said, "where would I get a gun?"

Tristan looked away. Shadaisy didn't. She examined Josie's face. "Why do you want a gun?'

"To shoot rabbits, I suppose," Tristan said, still not looking at Josie.

"Not exactly."

Tristan flicked his eyes over her. "You've changed your clothes."

"Jess was here today. My twin's husband. He brought some news." Josie's tone was formal. "You've used a gun, Shadaisy. I haven't. I've never even thought about them. That's why I'm asking you."

"I stole mine. From one of my foster parents. Did I tell you that? The dopes only had a shotgun. A Glock would've been much better. But I had to make do. You don't, though. You can buy a gun. Perfectly legal. You might have to apply for a permit. I'm not sure. But you'd have no trouble getting one."

"What kind do you recommend?"

"That depends on what you want it for.'

"Protection."

"Yes, of course. Protection."

"Oh, Christ," Tristan said.

"You should ask the seller. He can recommend something for you. I'll go with you if you want."

"That would be very nice."

Tristan put his hands up and took two steps back. "Hey," he said, "I don't want any part of this. Whatever it is. No ma'am. No sir. I don't want to hear another word." He turned and walked briskly to his marijuana garden behind the cottage and made his way to the very middle to sit on the tilled dirt among the rows.

CHAPTER THIRTY-TWO

Sheriff Dobbs liked to arrive at work before John Bond. It wasn't that he didn't like his deputy, he actually found him agreeable and for the most part easy to talk to. But he enjoyed starting the day on his own. He would get a regular coffee with cream from the café across the street, which opened at six. Opening at six seemed unnecessarily eager to the sheriff since this was a sleepy village with only the occasional commuter at that hour. Even so, Dobbs always thought as he stepped out of his car and locked it, good for you, Sherman, for being available to those few people.

The sun rose behind the strip mall and the office was dark when Dobbs opened the door. Normally, he flicked on the light and glanced around the room, put his coffee on his desk, rolled back the seat, and put his feet up. He sipped from the paper cup and looked out the window. He watched the sun turn the café's shingled roof from black to bronze then travel downward, bringing the golden bricks to life. Without thinking about anything, he'd watch the maple trees change slowly from silhouettes to distinct forms of varying color, depending on the season. When other merchants began to arrive, putting their keys into the locks of their shop doors and a car or two passed by, he'd take a last gulp of his coffee, throw the cup into the round metal waste can next to his desk, put his feet down, open his top drawer with a key, take out a day timer and begin the work for the day.

Today, however, John Bond's car was parked behind the cruiser in front of their building. The door to the office was unlocked. Inside, Shadaisy sat next to Bond's desk, her elbow resting on the top and her legs crossed. Dobbs checked her out for handcuffs. None. Instead of going to his own desk, he stood over Bond, who looked up at him.

"I'd like a word with you," Dobbs said.

John looked around the room. Having a word with someone generally meant going into a nearby empty office or some other private place. This was a single room concern with no place for privacy, not even a hall to the bathroom. John wondered if he was meant to go in there for a private chat.

Dobbs sighed and went to his desk, sat, and pulled his chair close. "What's she doing here?"

"I went out to Willow Bark and picked her up this morning?"

"He got there just at sunrise." Shadaisy smiled, producing her dimples. "Woke me up. Me and Tristan. We sleep in the shed."

The shed? Dobbs hid his surprise at this information. "And why did you do that, John?"

"I've heard from New York. The guy that got shot, the social worker, he thinks he remembers who shot him. He got a quick look at her before he was hit. The description matches Shadaisy. In fact, he knows her."

"So, you brought her here to interrogate her?"

"To question her, yes."

"What were they all doing when you got to Willow Bark?"

"Nothing. They were asleep. The kids in the shed, like she said. They like to hear the night sounds. Josie was asleep in the house."

"And you woke them up. Whom did you wake up first?"

"Ah, Josie."

"And she told you where the kids were."

"Yes."

"So, you gathered up Shadaisy to bring her here for questioning. Did you need force? Did you put her in handcuffs?"

"That wasn't necessary," John said, an edge to his voice.

"But it would have been protocol. That is, if she is a suspect. Is she a suspect?"

John said nothing.

"And were you successful? Did she confess?" Dobbs didn't know why he was so annoyed by his deputy's behavior, but he was getting more so by the minute.

Shadaisy uncrossed her legs, removed her elbow from the top of John's desk, and turned toward the sheriff. "I'm innocent. I didn't shoot anyone. That damn social worker knew me from coming to my house so many times. He probably thought I was an easy target to accuse being as my mother is in jail and I'm in foster care. But I'm a good person, not a cold-blooded killer. I want to stay with Josie, go to school. I'm only seventeen. After that I might even go to college."

Dobbs managed to hide a smile. "Shadaisy, why don't you step outside for a bit. Go next door and get a Coke or a cup of coffee?" He reached into his pants back pocket and pulled out a wallet. He held out a five then turned to John. "You didn't leave your keys in the cruiser, did you? Wouldn't want our suspect using it to flee."

"No, sir, I did not."

Shadaisy took the five and left.

Dobbs folded his hands and placed them on his desk. "I'm sorry. I shouldn't talk to you like that."

"No, sir."

"So, tell me what the NYPD had to say. All of it."

John's shoulders relaxed. "Apparently, this guy walks into the department and claims he had temporary amnesia from being shot. Now he remembers Shadaisy lifting the shotgun and shooting him. He describes her right down to the dimples."

"He's seen her before. Plenty of times."

"But why accuse her?"

"Why not? Like she said, she's an easy mark."

"That's what I thought."

Dobbs raised his eyebrows. "Did he say anything about Tristan?"

"No."

"Hmmm. Okay, so he's only focused on the girl with the gun. That's natural. Any other evidence?"

"Not so far."

"So, it's a blind man's memory and a faulty one at that. A lawyer could shred his testimony to bits. Does the prosecutor seem aware of that?"

John pushed his seat back. "Yes, Sheriff, I think he is."

"Why?"

"I sensed a certain reluctance from the guy I spoke with to follow through on this."

"You sensed. I see. Did he call you or did you call him?"

"Actually, he called me. But it sounded more like a courtesy call. Little more."

"And you followed through, which is the proper thing to do." Dobbs relaxed into his chair. "What are your plans?"

"I thought I would drive Shadaisy home."

"And then we can close this case."

John blushed and looked away.

"She's young but not as young as she looks. She's lived a lot in her seventeen years. Probably more jaded than most. And that baby face could get her out of a fair-few-scrapes. I can see why someone might find her suspicious. And attractive. There's always that. Okay. Take her home. Who knows what really happened? She seems good for Josie, though, and that's fine by me. I like knowing she and that boy are out there with her. Growing their Oleander plants."

CHAPTER THIRTY-THREE

As it turned out, it was not easy to buy a gun in New York state. First, you had to get a permit either from the County Clerk's office or the Sheriff's. Going to Sheriff Dobbs was obviously not an option so Shadaisy drove Josie to Hudson and city hall. The building, dating from the sixteen hundreds, was beautiful on the outside. Inside, the ground floor kept its original structure and charm. To make space for more offices, the upstairs, however, had been renovated with no consideration given to aesthetics. The room they were directed to was small and plain. The most noteworthy thing about it was the people who lined down the middle then curved and continued along the length of the left wall then circled back to continue down the right wall. There was just enough space for Josie and Shadaisy at the end. The focal point for this line was a tall, thick woman with short, gray hair and large breasts standing behind a counter looking as though she wouldn't mind taking out her own gun and mowing down everyone in the room.

When they finally reached her and asked for the requisite paperwork, Mrs. Dorchester, (according to the wooden rectangle placed in front of her) looked at Josie, her expression saying she thought Josie was planning to murder her mother. Mrs. Dorchester reached under the counter and pulled out an intimidating pile of papers and dropped them in front of her without saying a word.

Josie searched through her purse. "Um," she finally said, "I'm sorry, do you have a pen?"

"You can't fill those out here."

"It said on Google I could."

"Google? Google doesn't tell you about *these* lines now, does it. Look behind you. I can't have you standing here filling out forms with all those people waiting behind you. Go next door and someone in there will take your picture." She looked around Josie's shoulder. "Next!"

After waiting in line to have her picture taken, Josie was sent to a third line to be fingerprinted. This took the longest time of all, since apparently you couldn't simply place your fingers on an inky sheet. You had to roll them in a very precise way to get a clear enough set of swirly lines. This proved difficult for just about everyone, including Josie who had to wipe her sweaty hands on a gooey substance called Gojo and wipe that off three times before producing an acceptable row of her own delicate swirls.

Once they were back at Willow Bark, Shadaisy helped Josie fill out the forms, muttering that they should have done this online, and Josie really should think about getting a computer. Smart phones were all right for some things, but they didn't replace a computer. Or a printer. And thank God Josie had no history of criminality or… well, mental illness. Being sad didn't mean you were insane.

Shadaisy didn't know who Josie wanted to kill or why, but she'd been around the woman long enough to know she must have been through something terrible. A person didn't dress like a ghost and hover over a rain barrel when she wasn't in bed with her dog unless someone had hurt her and hurt her bad.

After Josie and Shadaisy had gone back to Hudson and once again waited in line to turn in the papers, they waited days while the forms, the picture, and the fingerprints were processed. After that, it took days for the official permit to arrive in the mail. When it did, Shadaisy said, "Now this is the fun part. Let's go get us a gun."

The gun shop, located on a picturesque side street in Hudson, looked like something out of a Norman Rockwell painting. The square, one story building was made of worn red brick with the words "Weber's Gun Shop" painted in an old English font on the glass door, centered between two large windows. The frames around these windows were wooden and nicely molded. Josie imagined them draped in Christmas evergreens straight out of Dickens. When she opened the door, sleigh bells jangled from a leather strap hung on the inside handle. Shadaisy lifted it and shook it.

"I put those there so I can hear when a customer arrives. I spend a lot of time in the back room going over inventory and doing paperwork." The man who said this was tall and slender with dark hair and light skin. He watched Josie so attentively as she approached him that she stopped just shy of the counter. He had unnerving yellow eyes with dark streaks, yet his smile was friendly.

Josie looked around briefly. There were guns displayed on three walls. They looked old and useless and gave the place a homey feel, like a room in a collector's house. "I've come for a gun."

"I sell guns."

When Josie didn't laugh, Mr. Weber continued, still smiling. "What sort of gun are you looking for?"

"Something for protection."

Mr. Weber's smile deepened. "Well, you've come to the right place. Did you have a particular gun in mind? I recommend a nine-millimeter."

Shadaisy had told Josie she should get a Glock, but Josie didn't like the sound of it. As an adult, she never thought about guns. As a teenager, many of her male friends hunted and when they offered to share some venison bologna with her, the manner in which the deer had been brought down never crossed her mind. However, from the ages of four to ten she'd been in love with westerns and the "peace maker" had played an important role in her games and fantasies. She especially liked The Lone

Ranger galloping his beautiful white horse into a scene, the reins loose on the horse's neck, both six-shooters blazing, killing off the bad guys and saving the damsel from a fate worse than death. The peace maker meant the wild west, where folks lived by a moral code of their own. Out there, if a woman shot a man, it meant he deserved to be shot and the law would know he deserved it and the woman shooter would go unpunished. Even more important, she wouldn't feel guilty. The code of the wild west would have been fulfilled. No judge, no jury needed. Justice done.

She told Mr. Weber she wanted a six-shooter. A peace maker, to be precise.

Mr. Weber stared even more directly into Josie's eyes; his smile gone. To his way of thinking, there were only two reasons to buy a revolver. Either you were a collector, or you didn't want to leave casings around for the police to find and use to track you down. This woman didn't look anything like a gun collector. She didn't look like a killer either, but you could never tell, especially with women. He looked down at the permit. "Josie Whitt," he said.

"Yes, that's me."

"Collect guns, do you?"

"No."

Shadaisy kicked Josie on the ankle.

"I don't recommend the um… peace maker. It's heavy, inefficient after six shots due to the need to reload. Awkward for a woman to hold."

"That's okay."

"The nine-millimeter is a much better choice. Let me show you one."

"That's okay. I want a six-shooter."

Mr. Weber looked over the paperwork page by page. He then went into the back room and returned with a box. "Do you want a case for this?"

"How about a holster?" Josie said.

"Think this is the wild west, do you?"

"As a matter of fact, I do."

Shadaisy gave Josie another kick.

Back in the SUV, the girl nearly vibrated with glee. "Holy shit, this is so cool. You are so cool. Look at you. Owning a Colt 45. I still think a Glock would have been better, but you're a regular Annie Oakley. Have you ever shot a gun before?"

"No."

"Well. We'll start practicing as soon as we get home."

It's a peace maker. Not a Colt 45."

"Same diff."

When Shadaisy told Mr. Raymond she wanted to take a few days off, he said, "You may be good, but you're not that good. I need someone reliable. Plenty of people who'd take this job and show up every day like clockwork. I need to get this fruit picked at just the right time, and I need to know I'll have enough people to get the job done." He put his hand on the nearest tree and leaned into it. "This is the second time, young lady, that you've called off."

"I know. I'm sorry, but this is really important. And Tristan will work extra hours."

Tristan stared at her. Raymond looked at Tristan. He was the worst worker of the season. It barely paid to keep him on. But he had lied about people waiting for their jobs. This late in the season, all the reliable workers had steady jobs they wouldn't leave. Raymond sighed. "Okay. But get back here as soon as you can. And remember, I don't like it. I don't like it one bit."

Shadaisy arranged a six pack of empty Coke cans in a row on a sawhorse she found in the shed. "Now don't go getting discouraged. This takes practice. We're not on a schedule, are we? No. We've got plenty of time and plenty of bullets. Just keep at it. You'll probably miss the first six and maybe the next six, but you'll get it. Just practice, practice, practice."

As luck would have it, Josie was an astonishingly good shot. Weber had been right. The gun was heavy and made her forearms hurt. She held it with two hands and hit four out of the first six cans. Tristan ran back in the house to get another six pack, this one full. Josie hit them all, leaving a wet, sticky, fly-magnet mess on the sawhorse. Though he would not talk about Josie's "project," Tristan found he could not stay away. He tried to go picking, but he was so preoccupied by what he thought might be going on at home, he fell out of a tree again. Mr. Raymond just shook his head, didn't even ask if he was all right. By the end of the day, the boy had picked less than half of what the other workers had. When he told Raymond he wouldn't be coming back for a while, the farmer said, "Make it forever."

It seemed Tristan's job now was drinking cans of Coke and lining up the empties for Josie to pick off. If he never saw a Coke again, it would be fine with him. When he tended to his marijuana, he had to leave his plants and piss in the weeds every five minutes. After two days of practice, the woman never missed.

When she wasn't shooting, Josie helped Tristan in his gardens. She examined the leaves and the stems with the same tenderness the boy did. She fertilized and misted with the same loving care, going along each row slowly, bending to pick away a yellowed leaf here, a twisted stem there, digging ever so gently with a tined fork to loosen the soil. Rambles stayed close enough that her fur brushed Josie's leg. The dog didn't like all this shooting one bit.

Once, when Tristan came back from a pee break, Josie said, "You know you don't need to drink all that stuff. You can pour it out in the driveway."

She went to bed bone tired but unable to sleep. Her shoulders and hands ached. As she stared at the ceiling and rubbed her fingers, a single question circled in her mind until, sometime in the hours before dawn, she dozed off, exhausted. The question she could not find an answer to was whether she should kill both Will and Lisa Wong or just Will.

CHAPTER THIRTY-FOUR

Josie had one more thing she wanted to do before she killed Will. She wanted to see Jess. With Shadaisy's help, she located exactly where he worked in Rochester. She could have called him, but she didn't want to let him know she was coming for fear he would tell her no. When Josie brought the kids into the kitchen to tell them she was leaving early the next morning, Shadaisy put her hands on her hips. "You hate driving. Why aren't I going with you?"

Tristan put his fist to his mouth, and Shadaisy put her hand on his shoulder to keep him from crying. Everything upset him since Josie had started shooting her gun.

"Because I want to go alone. I won't be gone long, anyway. Just the day." Josie regretted taking Shadaisy with her to buy the gun and even to the county clerk's office for the permit. The girl had troubles enough with the law. Josie didn't know what had transpired at the sheriff's office when John Bond hauled her in there because the girl blew her off when asked and said everything was settled. They could forget the whole thing.

And then there was Tristan. Growing his marijuana as fast as he could. Soon enough it would be ready to harvest, and she had already overheard him talking to Erik about buyers.

To her surprise, Josie didn't mind driving out of town by herself. She took the highway to Rochester instead of the back roads, which would have been pretty this time of year. This was not a pleasure trip. The idea was to get there as fast as possible and say what she needed to say. Jessie deserved so much more than what life had dealt him. It was as though someone, something, had noticed this bright, joyful being singing his song and said, "Well, we'll just see about that."

As she approached the city, Josie did not experience the anxiety she had expected but an intense urgency, almost an eagerness instead. She imagined it was the way a mother might feel rushing to comfort an unhappy child. Jess was not a child and was more sophisticated than Josie. Nonetheless she felt, in that moment, the stronger of the two. Maybe it was because she knew this tragedy would soon reach a finality of sorts and Jess did not. At any rate, her momentum continued through the process of finding the bike store and pulling into a parking spot two doors down. The store front was small but painted a cheerful yellow with red letters reading Cycles and Things. Inside was busier than Josie expected for a weekday morning. Two clerks were showing three people bikes and four customers waited in line while a man and a woman stood behind a counter helping them. Josie went to the counter and managed to catch the woman's eye. "I just want to see Jess Hart. Is he here?"

"Oh, yes. He's in there, through the door. Go on. He won't mind." The woman smiled and pointed toward a door at the back of the store.

The back room was filled with bikes in various stages of repair hanging from ceiling hooks. A long, six-foot-high row of boxes filled the center aisle. These boxes were attached at the sides and their openings faced outward. There must have been at least twenty of them and each was filled with bicycle parts. The room was narrow and dimly lit except for a space in the very back where Jess stood working at a table made brilliant by overhead LED lights. He looked up when the door closed and the lighting cast dark shadows under his eyes and from his nose to around the corners of his mouth. My God, thought Josie. She waved at him. He didn't seem surprised to see her. She made her way around the boxes to him and put her fingers on his forearm. "I'm sorry to just show up like this, but I thought you might not see me if I called. Will you see me? Will you talk to me? Can we talk now? Just for a while? I'll take you for an early lunch."

"I brought my lunch." Jess picked up a rag with a strong-smelling liquid on it and began wiping his fingers. "But I can talk to you now. Why would you think I wouldn't want to talk to you?"

Josie shrugged.

"Let me just tell my boss I'm taking a break, and we can go outside and sit on the bench out front."

Josie had noticed a nice wrought iron park bench in front of the store. "Okay, that's fine. It's a lovely day, anyway."

They sat on the bench, and the anxiety hit her. She sighed. They weren't looking at each other but at the street in front of them and the stores on the other side. "Um, I came here to tell you that I understand what you're feeling. I'm probably the only person who does, and I wanted you to know that wherever you are or whatever you're doing, someone knows what you're going through. And always will. I just wanted you to know that." New York State no longer had the death penalty. Josie didn't think she would be killed in prison. Unless maybe by a guard. She reckoned the inmates would be sympathetic. A man who cheats on his wife with her own twin deserves to die. She might live a long time, and though she wasn't a praying kind of woman, she would pray for Jess every day.

Jess said, "You could have called me."

"This is something I wanted to say in person."

"That's really nice of you. I think I knew that already, but I'm glad you came here to say it anyway." He paused for a long moment. "I still miss her every minute of every day. Even knowing that baby might have been Will's, I can't help missing her. I hate him, though. It's a good thing we're not in the same town." He took Josie's hand, but he didn't turn to look at her. "I don't want you to think I blame you for the accident. I know we've talked about this before, but I'm glad you came today so I can tell you again. In a way that will convince you. I don't want you to go on thinking it was your fault. You tell me you want me to know someone out there understands what I'm feeling. But what about you? It's got to be so much worse for you. The guilt and now knowing they both betrayed you. Will was your husband. Jaylene your twin. Think about that. Just think about that. Maybe what happened—"

"Don't say it."

"Well, doesn't it make—"

"Don't say it. Don't say anything. Nothing makes it better."

"I wasn't going to say that. Or maybe I was. Just that Jaylene owns some guilt too. And her death was an accident. You didn't mean to hurt anyone."

"I miss her, too. Every day. I miss her more than I miss Will. He was the love of my life, but Jaylene was with me from the very beginning. I thought we'd die on the same day." Josie laughed. "I really believed that. I couldn't imagine it any other way."

"Was he? The love of your life?"

"Yes, after a while. I never would have married him if you hadn't come along and swept Jaylene away. She was all I needed. There might have been boys or men but nothing serious. A day never went by, or something happen that I didn't think, oh, I can't wait to tell Jaylene or what would she think about this. At the end of the day, I would look into those eyes, into that face and feel completely safe."

Jess sighed and the muscles in his face slackened even more.

"But after Will and I married I became, I guess you could say, enthralled. He was so good physically. It never grew old. The way he moved in general enthralled me, the way he moved through space." Josie heaved a deep sigh. "I guess it's wrong. To find someone so beautiful. An aberration, really. Or rather to be so drawn to it. Others were too, though.

I remember an afternoon when we were fixing up our old farmhouse. Jaylene was over and the three of us were upstairs in one of the bedrooms. Jaylene and I sat on the floor watching Will take out an old window and replace it with a new one. We were all talking as he worked. The window frame wasn't level and Will had to shim it with a very thin piece of wood. And then he had to cover it with some sort of goop so that when it was painted you wouldn't see the repair. It was perfect. You couldn't tell it had been rigged at all. Jaylene talked about that later. She said, 'Did you see how effortlessly Will fixed that window? He kept right on talking and working and everything looked so easy for him. Amazing.'"

Jess stared at Josie then turned away.

"Damn. I'm sorry. That was a stupid thing to say."

Jess squeezed Josie's hand. "That's okay. The cat's already out of the bag, so to speak."

"Jaylene was crazy about you. She would never have left Will and me to go and hang with you if she weren't. You were the new guy in town. In a town that didn't have many new guys, believe me. And you were so exotic, playing in a band, having actual gigs. You swept her off her feet. You weren't like anyone around Hollandtown. You still aren't. Will was just a passing thing. I'm sure."

"Not with the baby, he wasn't." Jess turned back to Josie. "Do you hate her now? Maybe just a little?"

"Jaylene? Oh, no. Maybe I should, but I can't. I hate Will, though." Josie laughed again, a bitter laugh. "All along I felt sorry for him. Sorry I messed up his life so much he had to divorce me, find another woman, and move away. He loved it here… I mean Hollandtown. But why don't you hate Jaylene?"

"I didn't say I didn't hate her. I said I missed her."

"Jessie, come back to Hollandtown. I miss *you*. It would be so nice to see you around. You could open your own bike store again."

"No, Josie, I couldn't. It's not just the memories. It's not the place for me."

And Rochester is? Josie thought.

They sat in silence then, still holding hands, watching the ordinary people walking down the ordinary street in this ordinary city. Finally, Jess said, "So, do you believe me? That I don't blame you?"

"I think so."

"Do you blame yourself?"

"Always."

"Oh, Josie."

"It's going to be okay. You'll see. Things are going to work themselves out." She kissed him on the cheek then he hugged her with an extra squeeze at the end. Josie rose and smiled down at him. "You know where I live. My door is always open."

Driving home, Josie felt the tension ease. She liked the idea that Jess would know someone out there knew and understood. She hoped it would ease his days. She hoped that when he woke in the middle of the night, he'd remember he wasn't alone. She thought of the universe and imagined their two souls floating like mist, aimlessly whirling and twirling and then somehow coming together into a vortex, the droplets all mixed into one and then she thought, what utter crap. Still. She was glad and relieved she had talked to him.

She took the scenic road home. It was still early enough in the season and there had been enough rain that everything was lush. The sky so blue, the leaves so green and turgid, the wild daisies so plentiful, the brush so thick and emerald it was almost painful to look at. No one should be able to drive through such beauty without paying a toll of some sort.

CHAPTER THIRTY-FIVE

Tristan stood at the stove making spaghetti. He made it at least once a month, sometimes twice, and so far, no one had complained about getting tired of it. Lately, he had taken to adding zucchini from the garden. Being babies, they were tiny and almost tasteless and made little difference in the flavor of the Bolognese. Tristan added them anyway. He liked chopping the firm, small vegetables into tiny discs and watching them disappear into the dark red liquid. He enjoyed cooking for the others. Shadaisy came home from picking hungry and tired and appreciated the nights when he prepared a meal. Josie didn't seem to notice what she was eating and ate only a little, but Tristan thought it was probably the only food she got at all, so he was happy to put a meal in front of her. He looked over his shoulder and smiled when Josie and Shadaisy came into the kitchen. Josie had been sitting on the back stoop waiting for the girl to come home. It was seven o'clock, time for dinner, and the sauce was ready. Tristan picked the noodles out of the pan of boiling water with tongs and dropped them into the sauce, lifting and turning the pasta making sure every noodle was covered. The others were still standing just inside the doorway. Normally they washed their hands when they came in, then Shadaisy would peer into the pots on the stove and make appreciative comments while Josie set the table. Today his friend stood by the door, looking uncharacteristically perplexed, and Josie's body had a determined straightness Tristan hadn't seen before. He set the table himself and lifted the heavy pot of spaghetti and put it there.

"Sit." He waved his hand like a maître d'. "Dinner is served." The women moved from in front of the door and sat in their customary places: Josie at the head of the table, Shadaisy to her right. Tristan took his seat on the left nearest the stove so he could get up if they needed anything. "I forgot the water."

He started to rise but Josie put out her hand palm down. "Wait. I have something to tell you."

Tristan sat down and began filling plates with the pasta. He avoided looking at Josie. When all three plates were filled and in their proper places, he picked up his fork.

"What?" Shadaisy asked.

Tristan glanced at her with his fork in mid-air.

"What do you have to tell us?"

Josie put her paper towel napkin in her lap and smoothed it. She looked up. "I'm leaving again. First thing tomorrow morning. This time I'm not sure when I'll be back."

"Oh, my God." Tristan's ears were already turning pink. He dropped his fork onto his plate of food.

"Go on," Shadaisy said.

"I've been to a lawyer and made arrangements. If something should happen to me, this property will be held in trust for you two."

"A lawyer?" Tristan nearly shouted.

"Yes. I don't like it either." Josie's voice was very formal. "It shouldn't be anybody's business but mine what I do with my things. But to be on the safe side, I had my will drawn up and notarized. It's a legal document that no one can contest. There's a copy of it at the lawyers, Mortensen and Son, and I put another copy in a lock box and planted it under the third tomato plant from the front. The key is in my room, in a chest of drawers in a small, dark, handmade box in the bottom drawer. The house, the land all goes to both of you. There is no mortgage, so it's free and clear. The only thing I ask is that you let Jess Hart stay here if he ever wants to, which I don't think he ever will, but you never know. I believe you've met him... maybe not. I can't remember."

"But..."

"Let me finish. There is also a letter to Erik in the box. I have savings and that is going to him. He doesn't need money, doesn't really like it. As long as he has enough for whatever he wants, mostly paints, he doesn't want to be bothered thinking about it. He certainly wouldn't want this place to worry about. Even selling it would be a hassle for him. So go to the lawyer's office. You'll need some sort of ID, I guess. I'm sorry about that Shadaisy, but you said that business in the city was all taken care of, and you will be eighteen soon and out of foster care. You can contact the authorities to get a birth certificate. Tristan, do you have an ID?"

"Of course, I don't have an ID. You've gone full-blown crazy now. I thought you were getting better, but you're getting worse."

"What the hell is going on?" Shadaisy demanded.

"I want you kids to always have a home. Free and clear. You can sell it if you want to, but it's yours."

"You're going to kill someone, aren't you?" Shadaisy said.

"I'm not—"

"That's why the gun and all that target practice."

"I'm not—"

"What the hell did you think she was getting that gun for, anyway?" Tristan's voice rose to a squeak. "She's gone crazy."

"No, she hasn't. She's completely sane. She's been planning this and now she's going to do it. She's going to kill someone. Who, Josie? Who do you plan to kill?"

"I never said I was going to kill anyone. You have no idea what I'm planning to do."

"Then tell us where you're going." Tristan's ears were bright red. Redder than Shadaisy had ever seen them.

"I don't want you two involved in this."

"I'm going with you," Tristan said.

Josie shook her head.

Tristan threw his paper towel napkin at her. It landed in her spaghetti. "You think I want this place? Why the hell would I want to live out here in the middle of bum-fuck nowhere?"

"Your plants. You love your plants. And there's so much more land you could cultivate. Recreational marijuana will be legal soon. You could have quite the business. You have a gift for growing things."

"Without you? That's just wonderful." He flipped his fork, jettisoning saucy noodles all around the table and himself.

Josie stared at him in disbelief, not because of the mess, but because of the words. "Tristan," she said, "I don't matter."

"Oh, shit. You are so unbelievably stupid." Now the boy's eyes were turning pink.

Shadaisy's face under her picker's tan had turned the almond color of a heavy-on-the-milk latte. Her muscles were Botox stiff. The girl who could sparkle at the drop of a hat had disappeared. "You are not going to do this," she said.

"You haven't a clue what I'm going to do and besides, you can't possibly stop me. And I'm not saying positively I won't be back. I'm just making arrangements because I want you to have a home. Now I don't want to talk about it anymore. Let's eat our dinner." She carefully picked the soaked paper towel out of the spaghetti, set it next to her plate, twirled a fork full of noodles and put them in her mouth, chewed and swallowed. "This is really delicious, Tristan. Your cooking gets better and better."

Tristan picked up his plate, walked it to the sink and threw it in, food and all. Then he slammed out the door.

"When did you say you were leaving? Tomorrow morning?"

"Early, so I'll say goodbye tonight. Please tell Tristan goodbye for me."

"I thought I liked you. But what you're doing to Mouse… I'm not so sure now."

"I don't want—"

"He loves you. Like a mom."

"Oh, that's—"

"Ridiculous?" Shadaisy raised her eyebrows.

"Not possible is what I was going to say."

"You're not really that stupid, so don't even go there."

"Why do you think I got that gun, Shadaisy? To shoot skeet?"

Shadaisy continued studying Josie. Finally, she said, "You know, you're right. It is possible to be that stupid."

Tristan and Shadaisy sat cross legged, facing each other in the loft.

"This is your fault," Tristan said.

"I didn't know it would go this far."

"If you hadn't helped her with that gun, things *wouldn't* have gone this far."

Shadaisy put a stalk of hay in her mouth and chewed, making it bob up and down. "I guess I wasn't thinking," she finally said.

"I guess you weren't."

"Do you really love her that much?"

"I don't love her."

"Yes, you do. You might as well admit it."

"She's been good to us, that's all."

Shadaisy thought for a while. "Yeah, I guess."

"You guess!"

"Imagine leaving us this place. That's incredible."

"You're a mercenary little bitch. Is that all you care about? A place to stay? A meal ticket?"

"No, I care about her. A lot. Funny. She was hardly even there in the beginning. Just a ghost. And now she's going to go out and shoot someone. Probably that ex-husband of hers. That's quite the leap, if ever there was one."

"Ghosts kill people all the time." Tristan snatched the hay out of Shadaisy's mouth. "You can't let her do this. She's not a ghost. She can't just vaporize. She'll go to prison."

"Can you believe she went to a lawyer? On her own? Amazing."

Tristan stared at her, his face a cloud of fury.

They sat in silence.

Shadaisy picked another stalk of hay and put it in her mouth. Around it, she said, "You know, I wish I never shot Lederer."

"*You do?*" The cloud lifted a little.

"Yes, I do. I'm really glad I didn't kill him. I'll tell you something, Mouse. If he died it would have been like—what do they call it—that thing that peasants used to carry across their shoulders so they could haul things."

"A yoke."

"Yeah, that. It would have been there all the time. It would have changed my DNA. I would have become a different person. Yoked to the ground. Less… less—free. It's bad enough I blinded him. I hate the idea of that now."

"Huh."

"If I had just minded my own business, Mom wouldn't be in Rikers. Lederer would still be coming around and doing her, which still makes me sick by the way, but she wouldn't be in prison. God knows what's happening to her there."

"But it's all women there, isn't it?"

"Oh, Jesus, Mouse, you can be so naïve sometimes."

Tristan didn't know what to say. Or even think.

"We could have still run off. We should have just made a plan to get out of the city and strike out on our own." Shadaisy had forgotten they had planned to stay away only until things settled down and then go back to the city before Christmas. "I wouldn't have had to watch what Mom was into and you, we, could have stopped being passed from foster home to foster home. No one would have spent much time trying to find us.

Not even Mom." Tears sprang to Shadaisy's eyes, threatened to run down her cheeks, but stopped, suspended on her lower lids.

The cloud lifted from Tristan's face, leaving it open, wide-eyed and astonished.

"Don't get me wrong. I like guns. And Josie's Colt 45 is cool as shit, but you don't ever want to shoot a person, Mouse, believe me."

Tristan closed his eyes, squeezed them shut for a few moments then stared at Shadaisy. "Shadrack, you have got to stop her. You have to."

"How?"

"I don't know."

"We could tackle her and tie her up," Shadaisy said.

"Okay."

Shadaisy threw away the stalk of hay in her mouth. "I was kidding. We'd have to let her go sometime. If she doesn't leave tomorrow, she'll just wait until she has a chance. She's a very determined woman, you know."

CHAPTER THIRTY-SIX

Josie knew the only way she was going to be able to pull this off was to create a box in her head and put a lid on it. Only the digital, practical, concrete brain cells could be allowed into her consciousness. It would take three hours to get from Hollandtown to Syracuse, not counting stopping for tolls and the fact of hitting rush hour traffic. She had found out, this time without Shadaisy's help, exactly where Will lived and the location of his Lexus dealership. She also knew that Lisa Wong worked the seven to three shift at the hospital. Josie wanted Will to be alone in the house when she arrived. If she was going to catch her ex-husband at home, it was also important that she know his habits. It was helpful that Will Elliott had a very set routine when he performed his morning ablutions.

He rose at seven, went into the kitchen and made coffee which he drank while watching the news for half an hour. Next, he fixed his breakfast: cheese eggs, two pieces of buttered toast and bacon, a water glass tumbler of milk and one of orange juice. He sat at the dining room table while he ate. He was a very deliberate, even fastidious eater, taking every bite seriously and enjoying it a great deal.

After breakfast, he enjoyed a fifteen-minute shower, stepped out and wrapped a towel around his waist and proceeded to shave, moving his mouth from one side to the other, his razor strokes slow and considered. When satisfied, he washed off any remaining lather with a washcloth while examining his face closely in the mirror. He patted his cheeks with astringent, holding his mouth in the shape of an O. He tilted his head back and examined the insides of his nostrils. If there were any stray hairs there, he plucked them with tweezers. Next, he examined his ears in the same careful manner. He finished his duty to his face by using the washcloth to clean out the insides of those beautifully shaped orbs.

If it was a work week, Will wore a white or blue good quality, Egyptian cotton, custom-tailored, button-down shirt. His slacks, either light or charcoal gray, would be a fine quality wool or gabardine depending on the weather. His shoes, made from Italian leather, were always cordovan oxfords. It took him three to five minutes to arrange their laces to the correct tension across his feet and tie them in perfect bows. The last item to don, his tie, never cost less than eighty dollars.

By the time his ablutions were finished, it typically was between eight-thirty and eight-forty-five. That was when Josie wanted to arrive at his house, ideally just as he came down the stairs. This meant she needed to leave Willow Bark at the latest by four, to allow for getting lost and the heavy morning traffic.

There had been no need to set an alarm. Her biological clock woke her. All she needed was to say to herself, "get up at three," and she did. She needed only half an hour to dress and load the car. Loading the car entailed putting in an overnight bag and the bullets to the six-shooter. New York State gun laws were so poorly written and contradictory, Josie wasn't sure what they actually meant when it came to carrying a gun in your car. On the one hand, it read you could not have a gun in the car at all. However, the rules stated that if you were just traveling through, you might be able to have a gun in your vehicle, but it had to be empty and the bullets stored in a tag-a-long trailer, or, at least, in the trunk. Josie had no intention of standing in back of the SUV on a residential street in Syracuse and loading her Colt 45 in plain view of all the neighbors.

She decided to wrap the box of bullets in a towel and put them in the backseat. A thin disguise she knew, but she couldn't think of a better one.

The other gun law, which was very clear, stated open carry was a huge no-no. Concealed weapons, on the other hand, were legal if you had a permit. To Josie this was pure madness. In other words, you could walk into a bank with a gun hidden in your pocket but not in plain view for all the witnesses to see. How did that make sense?

Nonetheless, she chose her outfit accordingly. First her jeans and sneakers. Then she buckled the holster around her waist. The firm leather pouch for the gun settled against her thigh as though it belonged there. The gun slid into the holster as if going home. A baggy t-shirt covered everything.

Toothbrush, toothpaste, fresh panties, bra, and a clean t-shirt and nighty went in a nylon zippered tote. She looked at the clock on the stove. Three-thirty. Plenty of time. She wrapped the box of bullets in the kitchen towel, opened and shut the kitchen door quietly even though there was no need since the kids were asleep in the shed. Rambles waited for her next to the SUV.

"You can't go with me, old girl, not this time." The dog stayed where she was but followed her owner's movements with her eyes. Josie opened the car's back door and threw the overnight bag and bullets on the backseat, climbed in the driver's side, and started the engine. She rolled down her window and called to Rambles. The dog put her feet on the sill. Josie patted her head and said, "Goodbye, old friend." Straight out of Hollywood, she thought, embarrassed. She carefully pushed the dog away and rolled up the window before memories could slip out from under the lid on the box.

The SUV's GPS held Will's home address. Josie brought it up, and at the end of the driveway a soothing voice said, "turn right." Josie elected to take Route I-60 instead of the back roads for fear of getting lost. The highway had tolls to worry about and the state boys cruising along could be a problem, but Josie had an E-Z pass so some nosy toll booth attendant wouldn't be looking into her car, and she hadn't gotten a ticket since she was nineteen. At twenty-six, blonde, and driving a high-end SUV without a hint of tint, she figured she was as low risk as they came. The stars surrounded her in a black, cloudless sky. Even on the back roads before I-60, Josie followed every rule of the road. Once on the highway, she stayed in the right lane going with the flow of traffic which was minimal until six-thirty when the air turned gray as the sun climbed to the horizon. Within ten minutes, there was a steady stream of cars and Josie's heart rate increased a few beats. She touched the peace maker on her hip. New York State was a real pain in the ass when it came to gun laws. Josie couldn't see any reason why a hitherto law-abiding citizen couldn't carry a gun while driving. You'd have to be an awfully good shot to hit someone while moving. Unless you were using an AK-47 or some other assault weapon. But an ordinary gun? In West Virginia, a rifle hung proudly in the back window of every truck. And what about Texas? Everybody packed in Texas. Josie remembered going with her parents to visit a cousin near Austin. Supermarkets, stores of any kind, were few and far and usually an hour outside the city. HEBs, a market the size of Hollandtown, serviced ninety percent of the rural population. Josie would never forget pulling into the huge parking lot. A row of at least a dozen gas pumps stood in front of the store. Even so, pick-ups waited in line to get fueled. Josie's eyes had popped when the doors opened and long, lean men, wearing jeans and cowboy hats glided out. Every one of them had a revolver on his hip. Maybe I'll move to Texas, she thought. A surprising flush of affinity for that gun group with so much power ran through her. Nothing was as American as the right to bear arms. The forefathers said so.

A blood orange sun rose over the horizon. Cumulous clouds, high, white and still as death, floated above her. It would be a lovely day. "There is nothing more rare than a day in June," her mother used to say. Of course, it could be cold and wet or miserably hot and humid as well, but when June got it right, her mother was correct. There was nothing like it. Josie sighed. The scenery along the highway was boring as hell. The back roads around Hollandtown would be glorious though: the tree branches swaying and the sunlight glinting off their leaves. The lid on the box creaked open and Josie slammed it shut. She checked her speedometer. Perfect. She glanced at the clock on the dash. At this rate she would arrive at her destination in plenty of time, maybe even too early. She'd have to drive around Syracuse for a while. A strange car sitting on a residential street for any length of time might be noticed. She sighed again. Then she heard it. A siren. A siren blaring on her left. She looked in her side view mirror. Yup. A state police car barreled toward her, came along side, stayed steady for a few moments then zoomed past. Terror and relief sent pinpricks of electricity through her. She glanced in the rearview mirror to see if a back-up cruiser followed and there was Shadaisy's angelic face smiling back at her.

Jesus Christ." Josie jerked the wheel left then right.

"Easy does it," Shadaisy said calmly.

Josie got her arms under control. Even through her tunnel vision and difficulty in breathing, she managed to get the SUV on the same trajectory as the car in front of her. "What the… I mean how… how did you get in my car?"

"You don't lock your doors, Josie."

"But I didn't see you."

"It was dark, remember? When you left Willow Bark."

"But…"

"I got in the car in the middle of the night. After Mouse had finally fallen asleep. He was terribly upset. You shouldn't have done that to him, Josie. Just dropping a bomb like that on him. It was cruel. Me, I can handle that kind of stuff. Not Mouse. Anyway, once he was sound asleep, I snuck out of the shed and got in the car. I lay down on the seat and fell asleep. I figured I'd hear you moving around in the house, or a light would come on and I'd wake up. And I did. When you turned on the bedroom light. I got down on the floor and lay there. It's damn uncomfortable, by the way. And, of course, I had to stay there until you'd gone too far to turn around and now I'm stiff as a board." Shadaisy rolled her shoulders.

"But I opened the back door to put some things back there."

"And I nearly pissed my pants when you did, I don't mind telling you." Shadaisy shook the towel and box of bullets. "What do you plan to do with these exactly?"

"You can't be here. You've really made a mess of things by sneaking along with me."

"What are you going to do? Dump me on the side of the road? And why can't I be with you? What are you planning to do?"

Josie glanced at the GPS. "There's an exit in two miles. I'll drop you somewhere, and I'll give you my cell phone. You can call someone to come and get you."

"Like who?"

"Um…Erik."

"Erik turns his phone off as soon as he starts to work."

"He's not working yet."

"He turns it off as soon as he wakes up, and he's up around six." Shadaisy had no idea if this were true, but it could be.

Josie thought for a moment.

"I guess I could call Sheriff Dobbs. Or John Bond." Shadaisy's eyes beamed innocence. She sat on the edge of her seat, rested her arms on the back of the passenger seat and watched Josie. After a short while, she sat up straight and pointed. "Did you see that sign? There's a Denny's. I'm starving. Haven't eaten anything since lunch yesterday, you might remember."

"We are not stopping for breakfast. This isn't a joy ride. I can't believe you snuck into my car." Josie stared out the front window, thinking. She couldn't leave her cell phone with the girl. If she called Dobbs or Bond, they would call the police in Syracuse, and everything would be ruined. Maybe. Having a gun and bullets in her vehicle might be enough to interest the cops but probably not. No other crime had been committed. Actually, she doubted if the police would bother themselves about a woman without a rap sheet of any kind heading their way to maybe or maybe not shoot someone. It was Shadaisy who should be worried if they did. It could open up that whole can of worms concerning the shooting of a social worker. And there soon *would* be a crime, a serious crime and Shadaisy right in the middle of it.

Shadaisy sat back. "I can tell by the bulge in your baggy shirt you've got that sweet Colt strapped to your hip. What's in the tote bag?"

"Nothing." Josie pulled onto the exit ramp, flicked her eyes to the clock. She was way ahead of schedule. Denny's waited for them two stop lights off the ramp on the right. She pulled into the lot, parked, turned off the ignition, jerked her door open and clambered out of the car. "Come on," she said without looking back.

Inside, the restaurant was nearly empty. A waitress showed them to a booth. "Coffee?" She held out the pot. Shadaisy said, "Yes, please. I already know what I want. I'll have the super breakfast. Fried eggs over easy, sausage, hash browns, and pancakes." Josie ordered tea and pancakes. The waitress poured the coffee and placed several paper cups of cream on the table. When she left, Josie said, "Shadaisy, this is serious. I'm about to do something that could get you right back into the foster care system, possibly the court system. The criminal court system. I am going to do this thing, and you could be seen as an accomplice."

"You're going to shoot someone. I already know that."

"Yes I am."

"Why?"

The waitress appeared with their food. When she had left, Josie began. "I'm not sure how much you know. Frankly, I can't remember what I've told you. There are large gaps in my memory since... um, never mind." Josie cleared her throat, leaned her forearms on the table and described to Shadaisy what it was like to have a twin sister. She explained the difference between that kind of love and any other; how they went through the world together, shared every experience. She frowned. "I can't remember a moment when Jaylene wasn't actually with me or in my thoughts." Then

Josie talked about Will coming along and fitting in just as easy as could be. She talked about the three of them being so close. How he would toss a pebble against their bedroom window and when they looked down at him, he would say, "Let's go swimming." When they swam, they held hands and jumped off Dales Bridge into the local river many feet below, something no one else dared to do. They rubbed suntan lotion all over each other, laid on a beach towel, their sides touching. If it was winter, they went to Abram's Pond to go ice skating. They held hands when they skated, ventured up the small streams that fed the pond and where lovers went to kiss. When they grew cold, they snuggled in front of the fire in the shed built by the Lion's Club for all the youngsters in the area. They did their homework together. Sometimes curled on the twin's bed. Hugs, kisses, heads on each other's shoulders, back rubs. They were inseparable. When Jess came along, they drifted apart, leaving a gap that Josie and Will didn't know what to do with. Then Jaylene married Jess and Josie married Will. They bought property next to each other, and when they weren't working, they were once again inseparable, only this time there were four of them. "We saw each other all the time. They were coming over to our house for dinner one night, in the spring or maybe summer, I can't remember, and Jaylene apparently decided to walk over through the woods. She'd made a blueberry pie. She was carrying it when she came out of the woods. The trees grew right down to the road, you see. There were a lot of them, and you couldn't see into them. She was wearing headphones, so she didn't hear my car. She just stepped out of the woods onto the road, and I ran into her. She and the pie flew into the air and landed on the road. She was pregnant, and they both died. Her and the baby."

Shadaisy opened her mouth to say something, but the waitress arrived to ask if everything was all right and did Shadaisy want more coffee? She shook her head no.

"The thing is," Josie continued after the waitress had gone, "the baby could have been Will's. Probably was Will's, since Jess was having a herpes outbreak when the baby would have been conceived and he and Jaylene weren't having sex without a condom. Or at least that's what Jess figures"

"How do…?"

"How do I know? I know because Will left Jaylene a text on her phone saying so. The afternoon she died. A very sexy text. Jess found it when he went through some boxes of her things. That's why he came here… I mean to Willow Bark. To show it to me. He wanted to free me of my guilt."

Shadaisy, who had been eating her food while Josie talked, looked up. "I already knew what happened to Jaylene," she said quietly. "Erik told me. I know that's why you act different than other people. Why some people think you're crazy, but you're not. If anything happened to Mouse, I don't know what I'd do. And he's not even my twin." She frowned. "I didn't know the baby was Will's though. No wonder you want to kill someone."

Josie leaned back against the booth. The lid had come off the box, synapses ran free, and she was having trouble holding still. She felt sick.

Shadaisy nodded at her companion's untouched food. "Aren't you going to eat?"

"I'm not hungry. You go ahead."

"You sure?"

"Yes." Josie watched the girl as she finished the platter of eggs, potatoes, and sausage; she watched how when everything was gone except Josie's pancakes, she poured the fake maple syrup over them. The sticky liquid slid over the stack and coagulated on the plate. Josie signaled to the waitress for the check, pushed her way out of the booth and went to the counter. She sensed the girl standing next to her as she put her change in her wallet.

CHAPTER THIRTY-SEVEN

The soothing voice guided them back to I-60 then on into Syracuse, through the city center and into a nearby residential area where it said, "Arriving at your destination."

It was a nice neighborhood. The houses were semi-grand with large, old trees in front of them. Josie drove around the block and parked three houses away from Will's. She didn't want the neighbors to see her vehicle in front of his house. It really didn't matter since she wasn't planning on a get-away, but she followed her instincts anyway. Once parked, she reached into the back seat for the bullets. Shadaisy sat beside her in the front. They hadn't said much since leaving Denny's and none of the conversation referenced the purpose of this trip.

Josie unwrapped the box of bullets from the towel, lay the box on her lap, and pulled the Colt 45 from its holster. She opened the box, rolled the revolver chamber open and proceeded to slide six bullets into place.

"Hey." Shadaisy lunged at her and tried to grab the gun. "When I said I understood, I didn't mean you should go through with it. Hey, quit it."

Josie had elbowed Shadaisy in the ribs, pushing her back in her seat. She fixed the girl with a blazing glare, holding her in place. "Don't touch me or try to stop me in any way. If the police come, tell them you're a hitchhiker I picked up and don't give them your real name. Or you could start walking right now." Josie reached for her wallet on the console with her right hand and with her left, nestled the bullets and gun in her lap between her thighs. She took a fifty out of her wallet. "Here, use this if you need to. No, wait." Josie took out another fifty, handed them both to Shadaisy. "Whatever you do, don't connect yourself to me in any way. Get back to Willow Bark as fast as you can. Hitchhike if you need to or find a taxi to get to the bus station. Call Erik from a pay phone. If the police come to Willow Bark, act as though you've been there all the time. You had no idea where I was or what I was doing."

"You're going to regret this."

"I really didn't want to get you involved."

"I don't mean that. I mean shooting someone. Anyone. Don't do it. Just don't do it."

"Please, just get back home and if the police come around for any reason act like you don't know anything." Josie stepped out of the car and carefully closed the door. The lid on the box in her head firmly in place, she began walking along the sidewalk starting at house two hundred and two. She kept her pace even and unhurried, a typical suburbanite out on a walk.

All the mailboxes had the house numbers painted in black letters on a white background. It was an exceptionally nice neighborhood: the houses in excellent repair, the turf lawns manicured in a way that had to have come from a professional landscaper. Some had flower beds. All had mailboxes painted in sparkling white. Perennials surrounded some of their bases.

Two hundred and four. Step, step. Josie did not hurry or linger. Two hundred and six. Just an ordinary person strolling along. She could not imagine Will living in a place like this. A high-rise condo in the middle of downtown, maybe. Or an artist's loft in a renovated factory building. But this: both parents, two and a half kids, a dog, corporate America. It didn't suit him. It must be Wong's doing.

Two hundred and eight. The house was two story, white with black shutters and a pristine lawn. No flowers though. Josie did not change the rhythm of her footsteps. She walked up the driveway, up the front porch steps and rang the bell. It rang loud and clear. Josie listened intently but did not hear anyone moving inside. When the door opened and Will stood right in front of her, she nearly jumped out of her skin. Recovering quickly, she stepped around him and over the threshold.

He turned as she passed him. "Josie… what on earth?"

"We need to talk." In a glance, Josie took in the layout of the house: central hall with a staircase leading upstairs, dining room on the left, living room on the right. The place was as well-appointed on the inside as it was on the outside. She made her way quickly to the couch, a striped rose and yellow satin Victorian piece, and plunked herself down.

Will followed her more slowly. He sat in a winged chair, facing her. "This is a surprise. What's happened? Why didn't you call? It's good to see you out and about though." He smiled.

Josie briefly looked around. This house was not like anything Will would choose. It definitely must be the Wong woman's doing. How had she managed to talk him into it? Josie turned back to him.

"Jess came by a few weeks ago."

Will waited.

"He brought Jaylene's phone. To show me. It had a text message on it. From you. Sent the day Jaylene died." When Josie had sat down, she sat on the back of her t-shirt. Now, she lifted her bottom an inch off the sofa and pulled her t-shirt up and away, revealing the peace maker.

Will had this thing he did when knocked off guard. In only a heartbeat the surprised look on his face was gone. He settled into a relaxed, loose-limbed ease that showed no evidence of alarm, only a calm interest in what might happen next. Josie had never seen anyone else capable of such control. Now, he stretched his shoulders easily along the back of the chair, his arms resting on its arms. His legs, slightly parted, stretched before him. This thing that he did wasn't like a big cat ready to spring on its prey, though knowing him she knew it held the same tension. She'd seen

Rambles do it a few times: head resting on her forelegs, lids half closed, dreaming, it appeared, in the soft afternoon. Then before you could see her, she jumped onto a nearby, hapless rabbit.

Will could move that quickly.

"I'm going to tell you what's in that text," Josie said. She rested a shaking hand on the butt of the gun. The lid on the box had flown off completely, letting all her brain synapses loose. "It's a sex text. In graphic detail. Apparently…" Josie stopped. Feet daintily pitterpatted down the stairs. Lisa Wong called out, "Who was at the door?" She stepped off the bottom step and came into the living room, her face bright and questioning. She froze. "Josie… what are you doing here? What…oh, my God, she's got a gun. Will?" She looked to her fiancé. "What's happening?"

"Josie just came for a short visit."

"But she's got a gun!"

Will turned his head to look at her. "I can see that."

"I'm calling 911." Lisa Wong put her hand in her jean's back pocket.

Josie kept her trembling grip on the handle of the Colt. "It's perfectly legal to carry a gun if you have a permit," she said, silently cursing the quiver in her voice. "What are you doing here anyway? You should be at work."

"I changed shifts. And how do you know when I go to work?"

"You can find anything on the internet," Will said.

Lisa Wong pulled the cell from her pocket.

"Put that away." Will's voice was quiet.

Josie's eyes went from one to the other, then she focused on Ms. Wong who opened her mouth to say something then shut it. Her delicate Asian skin stiffened. She put the phone back in her pocket. Josie said, "Will got my twin sister pregnant. Did you know that?" The look on Lisa Wong's face made it clear she didn't. She reached out and put her hand on the empty chair matching the one Will sat on. Josie wondered why she'd been so obedient, putting the phone away like she did without any protest. Had she already become suspicious, shrewish, asking too many questions?

Will would hate that. The way he would hate this house. And he would let her know it. Perhaps she was afraid to lose him.

She looked back at her ex-husband. He really was beautiful. So were other men though, a few even more so, but they didn't make you want to touch them, didn't mesmerize you, throw a net over you and make you crazy. He had left broken hearts all over Hollandtown. *Of course* he had made love to Jaylene. How could she have been so stupid not to know that?

After the accident, Josie had felt as black and empty as an unused operating room. Sterile of history, of knowledge, of awareness. Now a switch turned on and brilliant light filled the space, bounced off the stainless-steel tables, emphasized the sharp edges, did away with any shadows or places to hide leaving only an illuminated space, agonizing in its clarity.

There was no point in shooting Will. It would be like shooting a stud horse for jumping the fence and breeding all the mares in the next pasture. Josie's heart slammed against her ribs at what she might have done. She catapulted off the couch, walked as fast as she could through the living room, through the hall, and out the front door, nearly falling over Shadaisy who sat, leaning against it. The girl grabbed Josie's wrist to steady her.

Josie took hold of the porch railing. "I'm not even going to ask what you are doing here."

"I couldn't let you go in there alone."

They rushed down the steps and onto the sidewalk. "I didn't hear any shooting, so I guess everyone is alive and well?"

Josie felt shot through with Novocain, the relief almost making her topple over. She put a limp hand on Shadaisy's shoulder, who had the sense to say nothing.

When they got to the car, she emptied the revolver and threw the bullets in the hatch. "Go get the rest of them," she told Shadaisy. The girl went to the front seat, retrieved the box, and returned it to Josie who took it and dropped it into the wheel well. "You know," she said, "I should never have been allowed to buy a gun."

"But it's our right."

"Doesn't matter."

As soon as both were in the car, Josie hit the electronic button just below the window, the one that locked all four doors and the hatch. Her hands continued to shake. Shadaisy turned sideways to inspect her. "What happened in there? Tell me everything."

"Shhh. I have to listen to the GPS to get us out of here."

Shadaisy looked out her side window, watching to see if Josie's ex was walking toward the SUV. The sidewalk was empty. When they passed Will's house, he wasn't standing outside. "I didn't hear any shots so I'm guessing no one was hurt, right? You'd think Will would come out to take down your license plate numbers for the police."

"That's not his style. Besides, he knows where I live. And nothing happened. I told you that. Now can you be quiet? I have to concentrate on getting us out of this place."

When they reached I-60 and the familiar voice told them to stay on this road for hundreds of miles, Shadaisy felt safe to talk again. "So, you realized I was right? Shooting him wasn't worth it?"

"Mostly I realized what a fool I am. People don't change." Josie's voice was tight. "Will always had a lot of women. He was a magnet. Everyone knew that, including me. Until we got married. I actually thought he'd stopped running around and I was the only one. I was so stupid. I thought we were happy. All of us. We *were* happy. It's just that Jaylene and Will had something extra to be happy about."

"So, you're saying the reason you didn't shoot him is because he'd always been a player? I don't get it."

"Will is who he is. I should have known when we got married, he wasn't going to change. There would always be someone else."

"I still don't get it."

"Will is just Will. Why shoot someone for being who they are?"

Shadaisy, who'd been watching Josie, turned and stared out the front window. "He's a hound dog is what he is. I'm never getting married. I'm never falling in love." She paused then went on, "So you're saying you forgive him cause he's too hot to be shot? That's a new one."

Josie stared at her then turned back to the road. "I should never have married him." She took a deep breath and exhaled slowly.

"You okay? You want me to drive?"

"Yeah, but not until we're on the back roads. I can't chance a trooper pulling us over because you look so young."

"What about Jaylene? Was she just being Jaylene?"

There was a long silence. Finally, Josie said, "The three of us had always been so close. I mean really close. Then Jess came along. He was so beautiful and daring and cool. It was no wonder she went with him and left us. I guess it was just unfinished business between her and Will."

Shadaisy made a disgusted sound with her tongue against her teeth. "She betrayed you."

Josie sighed again. "That's what Jess said… more or less."

"Don't you hate her? Just a little?"

"I could never hate her."

Shadaisy shook her head. "I still don't get it."

"You know it might have never happened if they weren't fucking each other. Jaylene was so besotted and stupid in love she walked right into my car." Josie's thin face looked like blades. She smiled. "You should have seen Lisa Wong in there. I told her about Will and Jaylene. She almost flipped out when she saw the gun, but I thought she would faint when I told her what her fiancé had done. That marriage will never last. If they ever get married."

Shadaisy leaned against the back seat. "Well, at least he'll die a lonely old man."

"You think?"

"Sure. Everyone gets old. He might be a hunk now, but he won't always be. He'll be old and wrinkly and hunched over and no woman will have him. Unless he makes buckets of money. He can buy himself a trophy wife then, but he'll always know she's just in it for the money."

Josie pictured an old man hunched and teetering down the street, a Barbie on his arm.

Jaylene would never grow old.

"Did you threaten him with the gun? Shame to waste that Colt." Shadaisy laughed and glanced over at Josie, who, feeling a little giddy, laughed too.

"No, I didn't. I didn't do anything illegal. Except carry this gun around in my car." She laughed again.

"So, you didn't have a lightbulb moment about the sin of taking a life?"

Josie looked at the girl, recognizing for the first time a maturity in her. "I don't know. Maybe I did. I don't understand it. Don't try and make me. Stop asking so many questions. All I can say is I scared the hell out of myself."

"I'm glad you didn't shoot him." Shadaisy leaned her head against the car door. "I don't know about you, but I'm tired as hell. All this excitement has worn me out." She wiggled around finding a comfortable position. Soon she was breathing slowly, her mouth slightly open.

Josie looked over at the sleeping girl then back at the road. I almost murdered a man, she thought. The wobbly-kneed relief she had felt walking to the SUV was slowly being replaced by a sickening new guilt. In her heart of hearts, Josie knew Jaylene's death was technically an accident. But she'd been driving too fast, had slammed on the gas instead of the brakes and then in a mad effort to undo the unthinkable had reversed the car. Her chest felt tight. Josie knew she would have died rather than hurt her twin intentionally. Yet, today, she had, with malice aforethought, come within a wink of killing someone in cold blood.

You're a peach, she told herself. A real swell.

CHAPTER THIRTY-EIGHT

It was not coincidence. It was synchronicity that brought Sheriff Dobbs to Willow Bark the morning after Josie and Shadaisy went to Syracuse. Josie was dipping water out of the rain barrel with a large saucepan when he stopped in front of the cottage. Technically, it was his day off, but he was on call twenty-four seven, so he always drove one of the cruisers. He stepped out and came over to Josie and stood with his hands in his pockets. He smiled. She looked different. Her slack face had turned ascetic and focused.

She smiled back. Seeing the sheriff, unaware of her felonious heart, standing there looking at her with such friendly interest, she wanted to tell him that she had, with malice aforethought, bought a gun and driven that gun to Syracuse with the intention of killing Will. That she had walked up his front porch steps and into his house, on into his living room where she sat on his couch facing him with her hand on the butt of the gun. That she had come within a few breaths of shooting him in the chest. Possibly of shooting Lisa Wong as well. Instead, she said hello to him as though nothing could be more natural than this early morning call. Dobbs said hello back and after a few quiet seconds asked her what she was doing.

"I want to empty this barrel so I can roll it over there in the woods.

Out of the way." The water's surface was covered in algae and thick moss whose neon tendrils, lit by the slanting sunlight, hung below it. The saucepan Josie used was covered in algae and green slime, some of which had slipped down her arms and into her elbows and over the front of her shirt. The water came to two feet from the top of the barrel.

Dobbs peered into it. "It's going to take you a while."

"I don't have a deadline."

They stood silently as Josie dipped the pan and lifted it out, filled with brown water and wild growth. She tossed the contents into the driveway. It was around nine o'clock, but the morning was already warm, and she didn't mind being wet.

Eventually Dobbs said, "Where are the kids?"

"Not sure. They went off on their bikes. I think Tristan's been fired. Shadaisy still has a job though."

"Huh."

"So, what brings you out here?"

"Oh, nothing really. It's my day off, and I thought I'd take a drive that didn't have calamity waiting at the end of it for once. That's all."

Josie laughed. "And you ended up here?"

Dobbs smiled. He continued watching Josie's hands disappearing into the fecund liquid, the way she threw the mixture onto the gravel driveway and surrounding yard, letting it splash against her jeans. "I can help you with that," he said.

Josie looked up. "Really?"

"Do you have a hammer and nails?"

"Um, I might. I think I remember when I was cleaning out the second bedroom that I put some tools under the sink. You can go and look if you want."

Dobbs disappeared into the kitchen and returned holding a hammer and a small rectangular box of nails. Josie thought of the Peacemaker and the bullets hidden under her bed.

"Now if you don't mind, I can drain that barrel fairly quickly. It will make a mess all around it, but the ground is dry, it should soak it up shortly."

"No, go ahead. That's fine."

Dobbs knelt down and began hammering a nail an inch above the bottom of the barrel. It was a medium sized nail and he pulled it out once it had penetrated the metal. By pounding the hammer's claw against the hole, he made it bigger. Water immediately gushed onto the ground. Dobbs repeated this maneuver until he had circled the barrel. Water poured out all around, forming a circle that spread quickly, approaching Dobbs' and Josie's feet. They stepped back, then back again. They watched until the water slowed to a trickle then stopped. Dobbs walked on his toes through the mess and looked into the barrel. "The holes are blocked by a lot of algae and gunk." He still had the hammer. Bending over, he stretched his torso inside and, using the claw end of it, cleared the holes. It took a while but eventually water began trickling out again. He tiptoed back to Josie and shook his feet to get rid of the slop.

When the trickle stopped, Josie walked through the swampy water and peered into the barrel. "The water's gone, but there's a lot of greenery hanging around in there. I want to roll it into those trees over there out of sight."

"All right." This time Dobbs gave up on trying to keep his sneakers clean and sloshed over to her. He pushed the barrel onto its side and looked at Josie. "You want to help?"

"Sure."

"Let's roll then."

It turned out to be extremely difficult getting the heavy cylinder through the tall grass which seemed to want to hold on to it, kept wrapping itself around and into the metal barrel. They needed to stop several times and yank the weeds out of the ground and rip them free. Finally, they got down on their knees, pressed all their upper body weight against the barrel and shoved as hard as they could. There was a lot grunting and some swearing. At the edge of the tree line, the two of them stood up. Dobbs pulled out his t-shirt from his jeans, a nice one with a collar and alligator on it, and wiped his brow. Josie did the same with her well-worn shirt. They looked at each other and smiled. "I'll do the rest," said Dobbs. He bent over, put his arms around the barrel in a big bear hug, stood upright with a grunt, then duck walked it into the woods. After he was satisfied it could not be seen by anyone at Willow Bark, he rocked it firmly upright and walked over to Josie. She looked him up and down. "You're a prince, but my God, I've never seen anyone such a mess."

Dobbs looked down at himself. He was covered in slime, dirt, weeds, and rust. He shifted his gaze to Josie. Her small, triangle shaped breasts were visible through her wet t-shirt. He looked away. "You're a bit of a mess too."

They made their way silently back to the cottage. When they emerged from the tall grass, they stopped and turned to face each other. Without giving herself time to think, Josie reached into the bathtub, gathered up one end of the hose lying there, dragged it into the kitchen, screwed the nozzle onto the sink faucet and adjusted the water to warm. Next, she went into the bathroom and grabbed two towels and carried them outside and hung them on a tree branch. She put the plug in the tub's drain and opened the nozzle on the hose all the way then dropped it into the tub and straightened up. Avoiding Dobb's eyes, she pulled her t-shirt off in one easy motion.

"I can think of about fourteen dozen reasons why this isn't a good idea," he said.

Josie threw her shirt onto the ground. "You can't get in the cruiser as dirty as that." She tugged at his shirt, meaning he should take it off, meeting his eyes for the first time. Dobbs pulled it over his head. Josie undid the button on the waist band of his khakis then pushed her jeans down her hips and stepped out of them.

Hip bones of Christ, he thought.

She stepped into the water, facing front, and sat down. Dobbs unzipped his zipper, pulled off his pants, bent and removed his shoes and slid in behind her. Josie took a washcloth and soap from a metal dish hanging from the rim of the tub. She handed them over her shoulder to Dobbs. "Do you mind washing my back?" The water was up to their waist by now. Dobbs soaped up the washcloth and began making circles on Josie's back.

"Will was the love of my life, you know."

Dobbs rinsed the washcloth and spread it between her shoulders.

"I need you to know that. And I thought I was his. I wasn't, but that doesn't change the fact that other than Jaylene, he was the whole world to me. I've never even come close with anyone else. The fact that he wasn't faithful doesn't change anything." Josie closed the nozzle to the hose.

Dobbs dipped the washcloth in the water and soaped it again. He touched Josie's head to show she should bend it forward. She lifted her hair out of the way. Dobbs washed and rinsed her from her shoulders to her hair line then leaned forward and kissed the back of her neck.

Josie moaned, straightened, and let her hair drop. "I can't get that close to anyone ever again."

"I'm sorry. I shouldn't have done that." Dobbs put his hands on the side of the tub and stood up.

"Don't leave. I'll wash your hair. You look like the scarecrow of Oz with all that debris in it."

Dobbs turned around and eased himself into a sitting position again. Josie wiggled her body so that she faced his back and began to scrub him between his shoulders and down his torso as though she had been doing this all her life. She said in a conversational tone, "What about you? You never married after Sally."

Dobbs waited so long Josie started to wonder if he was going to answer. "I was crazy about that girl," he finally said. "When I wasn't with her, she was all I thought about. To be honest, I've never had as much fun as I did that year we dated. But the marriage was a train wreck. I was crazy about Sally, but Sally was just plain crazy. I've had other women friends since, good women, but every time I get close to asking one of them to marry me, I break it off. It wouldn't be fair making them a consolation prize."

Josie soaked Dobbs' hair with the washcloth, shampooed and rinsed it. She stepped out of the tub, unplugged the drain, and walked to the tree to get a towel which she wrapped around herself. Dobbs did the same.

They sat next to each other on the side of the bed. Josie held onto Dobbs' hand then dropped her towel to the floor. She rolled onto her back and stretched out. Dobbs followed her and the two laid naked, side by side.

"The baby Jaylene was carrying when she died. It was Will's."

"Oh, Josie."

"Jess came by the other day. He found a text from Will on Jaylene's phone… a sex text. It was graphic."

"God." Dobbs leaned over and smoothed the hair away from her face. "I am so sorry." He felt himself reacting to her nakedness, and ashamed, started to move away but she pushed him onto his back again. She sat up and turned toward him, then placed her left knee next to his right hip, her right knee on the other side, and lowered herself. The pleasure that is like no other burst and took hold, synapsis firing lightning all over her body then zinging between her hips, overtaking that bowl of conception, astonishing her with its force. Surfer's waves rolling and rolling, controlled by the moon, subsiding then startling with aftershocks over and over again.

She put her hands on his shoulders and he put his hands around her waist and held on and on until they both cried out, and Josie slid off and nestled along his sweaty side, her head on his shoulder. She began to sob. He put his arms around her and held her close until finally she was still.

He kissed her forehead. "I think you needed that."

"*I* think I needed that."

Both were wise enough not to linger in the moment, turning it maudlin. Josie sat up and left the bed. She rummaged around in her dresser for a t-shirt and shorts.

Outside, she arranged a clean towel around the cruiser's seat to protect it. Dobbs put on his filthy clothes. "At least my hair is clean," he said as he opened the car door and gingerly arranged himself on the carefully covered leather. He smiled up into her face.

Back in the kitchen, Josie pulled out a chair and sat at the table. She folded her arms and settled her head on them. This time the tears were silent as they ran across her mouth, over her arms, onto the wood. More than anyone else, the sheriff had followed the pathways of her sadness.

When Dobbs returned that night, Josie was sitting on the kitchen stoop. She had just finished mowing the yard with the garden tractor. The once knee-high grass now lay in rows and clumps all over the place. Dobbs sat beside her, leaned over, and picked up a fragrant blade and placed it across her thin wrist. "I don't want this to be just another booty call," he said. "This isn't about sex."

Josie put her hand on the back of his neck and looked him in the face. "Be careful," she said.

CHAPTER THIRTY-NINE

After the morning Dobbs and Josie made love, he became part of life at Willow Bark. When work permitted, he was there two or three evenings a week. Sometimes he spent the night, and sometimes he didn't.

Erik became a frequent visitor as well. He and Tristan would walk through the rows of crop, stopping to inspect this or that plant. Occasionally, Erik took Tristan to his place after dinner and brought him back as it turned dark. Josie assumed he was giving the boy lessons on harvesting.

A year later, on an evening toward the end of June, Josie, Erik, Shadaisy, and Tristan were gathered outside of the kitchen. Josie and Shadaisy sat on the top of the stoop with Erik just below them on the second step. Dobbs had just arrived and leaned against his cruiser, arms crossed and his weight on one leg. Tristan laid on his back in the grass next to the stairs, knees up, one crossed over the other, bobbing the free foot and looking at the sky turning from lavender to rose. "Pink at night, sailor's delight," he said. "No rain tomorrow. We need rain and we need it bad."

Dobbs smiled at Josie, and she smiled back. "The vineyards are loving this dry weather," he said. "I don't like New York wine, but it should be a good year."

Erik looked up at Josie. "You've got a good well, don't you, Josie?"

"I guess."

"You could always use the hose to spray the fields if you need to, Tristan." Erik stretched a leg and poked him with the toe of his sneaker.

"It's not the same."

Dobbs shifted his weight to his other leg. "No way the corn will be knee high by the fourth of July, if we don't get rain. And the apple crop will be small. It'll be hard on the moonshiners as well as the growers of… Oleander."

Tristan stopped bobbing his foot. Erik laughed.

"Guess what," Shadaisy said. "Today, one of the pickers, Carlos, was acting real edgy. He kept moving closer and closer to the road. He even told me to get out of a tree so he could pick it. No one ever does that. I went ahead and let him anyway. It's shadier inside the orchard. So, he's up in this tree and he's got three or four full bushels underneath on the ground and along comes this bashed up blue sedan and stops right next to him. Carlos leaps out of the tree, the four car doors fly open, and out jumps four guys about the same age as him. They grab up the bushels of cherries, throw them in the trunk and back seat and drive off with Carlos. Mr. Raymond was spitting mad. Those late season Bing cherries are real expensive."

Erik laughed. "They'd make some fine cherry wine."

Josie looked over at him. She liked having him around. She liked having all of them here. She straightened her back and slapped her hands on her thighs. "You know what? I'm going to put a screened-in porch right here off the kitchen. No point sitting on this uncomfortable stoop that only holds a few anyway. Rob, who should I get to do it?"

"Me. I love doing that sort of thing. And there's no room nor need to do any carpentry at my place. Or to pay someone to do it here."

"I'll help," said Erik.

It occurred to Josie that her brother might have missed her when she was a ghost spooking around Willow Bark. In fact, she thought with a sinking feeling, he may have missed his twin sisters all along. They had rarely included him in their games when they were little and never in their activities when they were older. Had he been lonely? Had he resented them? She never asked herself before now.

Something else happened after Josie and Dobbs became lovers. The following morning, she threw off the sheet, leapt from bed, and began thrashing around in her closet, fighting the dresses and shirts on hangers to get to the back corner where she had stashed her easel. She managed to drag it through the clothes, knocking several garments onto the floor. She set it up in the kitchen where the light was best. Next, she crawled under the bed to retrieve her box of paints, pencils, linseed oil, pallet knives, and other painting paraphernalia. When she sat in front of the easel and began mixing paints, the colors seemed to pick themselves. When she put paint to canvas, the brush took control. This happened every time she sat down to paint, and she sat down to paint every morning for a year. Her work was somewhere between abstract and impressionistic: greenish blues, gray blues, deep blues with flashes of white, hints of a figure here and there. Moody, mysterious, subject to interpretation.

Erik looked over what she had done and liked the paintings well enough to take them to his agent, who arranged a two-woman show with a well-established artist. Josie's paintings sold out, and those patrons who weren't quick enough commissioned pieces two years in advance. Josie's second show was a one-woman show and that too sold out. New York City had taken her up. The same thing had happened to Erik when he started, and both he and Josie knew better than to see it as anything more than a passing wave. The city would drop her as easily as it had picked her up, moving on to the new, new thing. If she were lucky like Erik, Josie would end up with a moderately sized group of loyal followers.

The year that Josie spent painting was like living in a fever dream. As she stirred paint and followed the brush around the canvas, her memory cells went underground. Gone the memory of Jaylene stealing Josie's bike and hiding it in the woods causing the one and only fight they ever had; gone the memory of holding hands and squealing, thrilled by seeing Sanford Gifford's work in a special showing at the Metropolitan Museum of Modern Art in New York. He was an ancestor and their parents owned several of his paintings.

Gone as well was the memory of the two of them and Will going to the prom as a threesome wearing rented tuxedoes and being refused admittance. The memory banks were shut down until, after five or six hours of intense concentration, Josie wilted to a stop, dazed and vulnerable.

The fever that burned during those hours of work gradually did away with Josie's ideas of being an existential threat. She had not, after all, shot Will. Jaylene's death was a terrible accident. But it *was* an accident. These changes in her concept of the world were hidden by a tempest of creativity. Only after she stopped working and put away her brushes and paints in a haze of fatigue did she become aware of what was taking place. She had held on to her conviction of her guilt until it smoldered and burned itself out, exposing the real poison underneath. *How could Jaylene have betrayed her that way?* Not only had she taken away the future, she'd taken away the past as well. Every second, every step, every birthday, every shared experience, every milestone, and mundane event led them closer and closer to the moment when Jaylene and Will turned away from her and toward each other. When that thought rose to the surface of her mind, Josie returned to the mist. She longed for the rain barrel. She wanted to go to bed with her dog beside her.

Dobbs knew the dark places within her. He was always teasing her away from the edges of sorrow. He challenged her to games of dueling pistols, which she invariably won, and he invariably laughed and said, "I let you win." He encouraged her to go to contests, join a gun club. She became semi-famous in the area, even though she would never go to a match where they used silhouettes of animals or humans as targets. No one wanted to see her name on the list of contestants unless she was in their club and going as part of the team. She liked a few of her fellow sharpshooters but not many.

It wasn't companionship or Dobbs' teasing that kept her shooting. It wasn't the victories, and certainly not the trophies that compelled her. It was the seconds just before she pulled the trigger. That moment when the world went away. The target didn't exist, she didn't exist. In all the universe, there was only a sweet, still emptiness.

The summer rolled on. The porch ended up being a simple affair: evenly spaced four by fours, plank flooring, rolled screening, asphalt shingles for the roof. Dobbs made a flimsy door out of slats that didn't plumb, leaving a gap between itself and the frame big enough to let Rambles open it with her nose and admit a few gnats in as she did. Nonetheless, it served its purpose and was well used. The rains came back, and Tristan glowed over his verdant leaves while Dobbs kept a nervous eye on the size of the boy's crop. It was true, if he rounded up all the home growers in his jurisdiction, he wouldn't be re-elected but there were still limits to what even this county would tolerate. Tristan had a sixth sense, however, as to how far he could push and expanded to a size just within ignorable limits.

Shadaisy grew more and more comfortable moving from tree to tree, reaching the top-most places others couldn't and became good friends with her fellow workers who appreciated her taking up their slack. She went to Lucia's for dinner often enough to accept the food though she never grew to like it. Her admiration for her Mexican friend and her family grew deeper and deeper as the summers wore on. She wanted to be like them, putting family above everything.

In mid-August, Josie took the kids to Hollandtown Central School to enroll them for the fall. The principal, Mrs. Bird, was the same old battle axe who taught Josie science in high school. She could have been a double for Maggie Smith. Her nose was a little beakier, her eyes a little less poppy, and her accent a little less English, but her hair, piled on the top of her head, her bosom, large and low, and her erect posture were straight out of Downton Abbey. Now she sat behind the principal's desk.

She'd always had a soft spot for the young woman in front of her. She would have called her, as a teenager, joyful, even shimmering if she used such words. Which she didn't. She was the most fey child she had ever known, and Mrs. Bird saw the value in that though she never showed it. Now she listened as Josie spun a preposterous tale about nomadic parents living in a beat-up RV driving around somewhere out west going from desert camp to desert camp, no forwarding address, no way to find them. Apparently at the beginning of this journey, they had come across Hollandtown and decided it was as good a place as any to drop off the children, telling them they were old enough to take care of themselves. No, there was no paperwork of any kind to reveal who these children were or where they came from. Certainly, there were no school records. The children, of course, had been home schooled. After a fashion.

Mrs. Bird knew of the tragedy that had befallen Josie and had seen for herself the light go out of the young woman. She'd heard rumors that Will had left town after the terrible accident. She'd never liked the boy, though she never showed it. A man with a lot of lashes. He had girls trailing after him like cats after a fish monger. There was a nasty rumor about the twins and him, but she didn't believe it. Now she looked down her beaked nose at Josie and the two children alongside her and pondered what to do. She glanced at the empty folders on her desk; one for each child. They didn't even have names on their tabs yet. Why had Mrs. Matone put them on her desk? Did she expect Mrs. Bird to fill them out? She looked from the girl to the boy. "What did you say your last name was?"

"Jones," said Josie.

"Jones?"

"Yes."

New York State had regulations regarding admittance to school just like every other state did. The key word was regulations. Not laws. These regulations included but were not limited to: a photo ID for the parent or guardian, birth certificate, immunization record, custody documentation.

The parent or guardian had to have proof of residency. An electric bill, for example. But this was Hollandtown where migrant workers came to school for a month or six weeks and then left. Sometimes all the parents could show the school officials was a green card. Sometimes they produced a document from their employer and sometimes, but not often, a birth certificate. Something to show they, in fact, worked in this county, at least for the time being, and the children were not victims of the slave trade or kidnappers. Josie, of course, was not guilty of anything nefarious. Rumor had it that she had moved into the remotest part of the county. What she was doing with these children the principal couldn't imagine. But at least they were company for her. Mrs. Bird hoped they didn't turn out to be thieves and break her heart.

The Family Planning Committee, a multidisciplinary group that controlled the money, was in charge of school admittance and told the registrar what to do. Mrs. Bird knew for a fact that this group considered residency the only real concern and anywhere the child slept was considered their residence. Members had been known to drive around at night knocking on doors to find out if the child was really where they were supposed to be. They would not need to do all that driving for these two urchins. If Josie said they slept at her place, that was good enough for the principal, and she was the one who told the TFPC what to do. Mrs. Bird folded her hands. "They will have to take tests so they can be placed in the proper class." She turned to call Mrs. Matone from the room off the office. "Come get these folders and put labels on them. One for... Shadaisy Jones and one for Tristan Jones."

Shadaisy tested into the senior class, Tristen into tenth grade. Shadaisy was an immediate social success. She was pretty, foreign, exotic, and from the city. Both boys and girls vied for her favor. After high school graduation, she started at the community college and received her AA degree in two years. She had enjoyed Columbia County Community

College even more than high school. The day after graduation, she slept until past noon then stumbled sleepily to the porch where Josie was painting. If the weather permitted, she always painted on the porch now. Her work had changed. It had become more like her ancestor Sanford Gifford's, which was known for its luminosity. Josie was painting the golden field beyond the garden, trying to capture the way the tall grasses shifted in the breeze, casting interesting shadows created by the June sunlight. Most of her previous followers had dropped her. Dark with a touch of nasty was the rage now. After two small shows, she picked up a new group of patrons, enough to keep her relevant.

"You got home late," she said. This was merely an observation. Josie had never taken the role of disciplinarian with the kids.

Shadaisy rested her elbow on the picnic table and her head in the palm of her hand. "Yeah, we wanted to see the sun rise over Lake Taconic."

Finished for the day, Josie cleaned her brushes with turpentine. She was meticulous, dipping them into the pungent liquid and gently rubbing it off with a clean white cloth. "Do you have plans for the summer?"

Shadaisy sat up. "As a matter of fact, I do. I'm joining the police academy."

Josie stopped inspecting her brush and stared into the distance. It made sense really. The girl had always pursued justice in her own way.

"There's another thing."

Josie turned to look at her.

"I've been seeing John Bond."

"What?"

"Uh huh."

"For how long?"

"A couple months."

Josie shook her head. "I remember a young woman who said she'd never fall in love."

"I'm not talking about love. I'm talking about sex. And I've been a virgin. Till now. I'm twenty-one, and a twenty-one-year-old virgin is just creepy. I mean *everyone* does it. Even little kids, thirteen and fourteen. The foster kids were always sneaking around, but I thought it was cause they were in foster care and lonely. But even kids from regular homes do it. It doesn't mean you're in love or anything. Or even going steady."

"What about you and John?"

"Oh, we're serious. We're not seeing anyone else."

"Are you in… um, love?"

"Sure. I think."

"Think? And what is it that makes you think so?"

"You've seen him. He's gorgeous."

Josie laughed. "I hope there's more than that."

"Sure. He's so solid. Like the rock of Gibraltar. I can calm myself down when I'm with him."

Solid. Rock of Gibraltar. These seemed like strange words for a girl to use.

Acutely aware that her small stature put her at a disadvantage, Shadaisy trained harder than any other recruit. She spent more time on the shooting range than anyone else and more time in the gym. The academics came easier. She read the rules, agreed with what they said and therefore found them easy to remember. She graduated third in her class and was given a job in a precinct in Hudson. Hudson was a small city, but it was a port city and had enough hard-core drug related crime to keep her from getting bored. She worked overtime and double shifts. John continued as Deputy Sheriff, taking on more responsibility as Dobbs spent more time at Willow Bark. Bond married Shadaisy, and they bought a run-down row house in Hudson which they talked about fixing up but never did. Their most domestic activity was going to Josie's for dinner every Sunday night.

Tristan didn't fare as well at school as Shadaisy had. He was teased and bullied from the first day. Mrs. Bird kept a watchful eye on him and punished the culprits to the maximum allowed but did nothing else to protect him, knowing it would only make things worse. Toward the middle of December, she called the boy into her office. He sat before her, pale and terrified.

"How old are you now, Tristan?"

"Sixteen. I just had a birthday November twenty-ninth."

"Good. Would you like to take your GED? You would not get a high school diploma, but you'd get a diploma."

Tristan's eyes grew wide. "Yes, ma'am!"

Mrs. Bird sent an email to all the members of the board stating she wanted to give Tristan his GED test before Christmas vacation. The board members gave a collective sigh then emailed back saying they were willing to allow it as long as she took responsibility. When they received a second email from her saying it was arranged, they gave another collective sigh, this time one of relief.

Tristan passed with flying colors and returned to Willow Bark and his business. He devoured everything he could about harvesting, drying, preparing flowers and packaging from the iPad Josie had given him for Christmas. He spent a great deal of time at Erik's, where presumably he received lessons in producing product. The student soon surpassed the teacher. Tristan kept the size of his crop small enough not to draw attention from the law or the big-time dealers. But his product was so pure, so fine, and consistent, and he was so honest and reliable he had a large, loyal following, some of whom wouldn't buy from anyone else even though his prices were a little high. When Tristan turned twenty-one, he married a girl, Maria, who had worked for him over the summer. Josie hired a contractor to build him a cottage just far enough away from her to support privacy. He and Maria filled it with two children, a girl, Polly, and eighteen months later, a boy, Alfred. They were both exquisite, with Maria's dark wavy hair, big brown eyes, and Tristan's delicate build and pale skin.

CHAPTER FORTY

It was the first Sunday in August, and the land had begun to take on the tired, dusty look of summer's end. Josie used a fitted white sheet to cover the picnic table. That way if a breeze came along the cloth wouldn't flutter into the food or knock over glasses. She disliked plastic knives and forks, paper plates and plastic glasses. She set the table with the sterling silver flat wear and porcelain dishes her mother had given her and Jaylene. The wine glasses were Lunesta and came in a box from Target. They had long stems and were large enough to hold half a bottle of wine if filled to the brim. Only the babies used plastic.

Maria had made pesto pasta from the basil growing in her garden and a large bowl of home-grown peas with mint. She kept a large farmer's garden and sold her produce, with considerable success, to local grocers and vegetable stands. She had arranged the turkey platter piled high with slices of tomatoes just picked from the garden and a bowl of mayonnaise to go with it.

Josie opened the oven door and pulled out the bottom rack where a large blue and white enamel roasting pan rested, the kind used for a Thanksgiving turkey. She lifted off the lid and put it on top of the stove. Taking a fork from the counter, she stuck it into a rack of ribs. The Food Network and barbeque judges said the meat should be tender and juicy but firm enough to stick to the bone. Josie didn't agree. She liked the meat to slip from the rack as soon as she touched it. These ribs did just that. She tasted a small piece. Despite its sweet and spicy flavor, it left that strange metallic taste she had been experiencing lately, but it only lasted a moment. Other than that, the meat was succulent with just the right amount of sauce. Satisfied, she pushed her hands into cooking mitts and hoisted the bottom of the roaster out of the oven and onto the kitchen table. After replacing the lid, she put a folded bath towel over it to keep it warm. Looking up, she saw Dobbs standing outside the screen door holding a large white box tied with butcher's twine. A brown bag sat precariously on top of it. Josie opened the door for him. He put the box on the table and a gallon of ice cream in the freezer. The sheriff always brought dessert and corn on the cob when in season. He turned to Josie. "You should have let me do that," he said, nodding toward the heavy roasting pan.

"I can manage."

"Smells great in here. May I?" Dobbs inclined his head toward the ribs and without waiting for an answer, lifted the towel and top off the pan. So much steam rolled out he had to step back. Josie used her fork to pull away a strand of pork and held it in front of Dobbs' lips. He blew on it then opened his mouth. When she put the morsel in his mouth, he closed his eyes a few seconds for dramatic effect. "Delicious. Best ever."

Josie laughed. "You always say that." The phrase that had lately been plaguing her popped into her head again. A line from a song. Sometimes it played over and over like a broken record, and no matter how often she tried to mind control it away, it would only leave of its own accord when it was good and ready. Fortunately, Shadaisy and John arrived at that moment, emptying her head of everything else. They, or more accurately, Shadaisy, always arrived in a flurry of activity and now drove the words in Josie's head right away. Using her foot to open the screen door, she came into the kitchen holding two bottles of wine over her head. "Hello, hello," she called out. "I've brought a chardonnay, my new favorite. It's called

Eco, isn't that cool? These have to go in the fridge right away. John will bring the other two." She kissed Maria on the cheek. "Is that ribs I smell? They smell delicious. Best ribs in the county, in the country, in the world," she caroled as she headed to the fridge. John followed behind with the other bottles and a small, pleased smile on his face. He wasn't in uniform, but his green and white checked shirt was ironed within an inch of its life. Josie always wanted to snatch these crisp clothes off him, wash them, tie them in knots and hang them on the line to dry. She liked him, though. As Rob said, he was a good man.

"My God," Shadaisy said, "it's sweltering in here." She fanned her face with her hands then turned to Dobbs. "You bring the usual?"

"Always."

"What kind of cake?"

"Chocolate."

"Good man. Did the stand have any corn?"

"They sure did, and it looks like it's at its peak."

Shadaisy pushed her hair behind her ears. "So, Sheriff, when is the county going to say something about all the miles you put on that cruiser driving it back and forth from town to here? You can catch bad guys from Willow Bark as well as from Hollandtown."

They had this discussion every Sunday.

"Never," Josie said.

Shadaisy raised her eyebrows then reached out and pulled Josie into a hug. After giving her a squeeze, she backed away. "Jeez, Josie, you're soaking wet from sweat. Don't you feel all icky? Go change into something dry and nice."

Dobbs put his hand on Shadaisy's shoulder. "While she's doing that, help me bring in the corn. Is the water boiling?"

Josie, who had been heading to her bedroom, turned around. "I forgot." Retrieving a soup pot from under the counter, she ran water into it, put it on the stove and turned on the burner.

"My God!" said Shadaisy. "With that thing going, it will be like a sauna in here. I'll be on the porch."

Dobbs followed behind her. "Shucking corn, I hope."

John had already settled himself there, drinking a beer he'd brought with him.

Josie chose a sleeveless sundress she'd made from fine cotton with periwinkle blue splotches on a white background. It fit around her shoulders and chest then dropped fluidly to her knees. She turned sideways to the mirror to see herself. She ran her hand down her torso. The fabric really was top notch: soft and smooth as silk only better because it didn't feel slippery. Josie loved the way it swirled around her when she walked. Not really the sort of dress for a barbeque. She lifted an apron off a hook on the door, put the loop over her head and tied the sashes at the waist. She looked at herself again in the mirror.

Erik and Greta had arrived and were sitting on the porch drinking wine when Josie returned. Erik was dating a local sculptor. She always brought a bean or lentil salad to Sunday dinner, something that could be a main course if you were a vegetarian, which she was. Erik brought himself. Josie couldn't imagine those two living together in sin or any other way. The woman was so different from the city-thin, smart looking women he usually had affairs with. Tall, large-boned, Rubenesque and laconic, she was the personification of mother earth. Her name was Greta, but both Josie and Dobbs thought of her as Demeter and even slipped and called her that a few times. If she minded, she didn't show it. When she first met her, Josie said, "That will never last," but Bob thought she was perfect for Erik. He said, "She will astonish him with her magnificent breasts, cradle him in her wide hips, enclose him with her round thighs, and enthrall him forever." He thought it wonderful Demeter made beautiful and useful things from the earth. "Perfect," he said. "She's iconic."

Josie brought out two tubs of butter and two cylinders of paper towels and put them at each end of the table. Maria stood, hands on her hips, inspecting the food. "Salt," she said and went back into the kitchen. Josie turned to get the ribs and noticed Tristan walking along the path between the two cottages, a child on either side of him holding his hand.

Tristan. Mouse. No one had called him Mouse in years. Not even Shadaisy. His clients called him The Grocer because of Maria's garden. It was not a nickname. It was a title. All the established sellers had some kind of AKA. Obviously, one didn't call one's source by their real name. Josie liked the slow way Tristan walked toward them, not hurrying the babies. He was naturally considerate. Soft spoken, he only complained when the weather had been bad for a very long time.

He wasn't necessarily a handsome man, but his dark round eyes were deeper in his face and when he turned them full on someone, it was hard to look away. His shyness had turned into a reserved self-containment, which some of his clients found intimidating. That and the fact that he grew the best cannabis in the county, possibly the state, gave him a position of importance. It was considered a privilege to be his customer. The young man was unaware of his status. He cared only that he produced good stuff. He smoked occasionally, solely to test the goods. As he told a friend once, marijuana wasn't addicting but growing it was.

Most of the time people came to him to buy, but occasionally, if someone had no transportation, he'd deliver. One night, he received a call from a young couple living in Hollandtown. Their names were Keith and Susan. Their car had broken down and was in the repair shop, and they were having a party that night and unfortunately had let their supply get low. Tristan told them it would be no trouble to bring them some, he had to pick up something in Hollandtown anyway. Maria needed a special kind of flour for a special kind of bread. The local grocer carried the brand for her.

The couple lived in a duplex on a lovely street off Main, occupied mostly by up-and-coming young people and a few old folks who had been there forever. His customers lived in the upstairs apartment. He climbed the outside stairs and used the knocker. The door flew open, and the husband snatched him inside. "Did anybody see you?"

"I don't think so."

"Keith! You're so rude. I can't believe you. Forgive him…sir. He was raised by wolves." A woman, whom Tristan assumed was the wife, tugged the man's shirt sleeve.

Keith clapped Tristan on the back. "Judge Norton lives just up the street." He guided him out of the hall into the kitchen. "You can't know how much we appreciate this. You've really saved our bacon." He shook Tristan's hand.

"No problem. I had to come to pick up something in Hollandtown anyway."

Keith retrieved his wallet off a built-in kitchen desk and pulled out some bills. He gave them to Tristan. "I put something extra in there for the delivery."

"No need. Like I said I was already coming here." Tristan peeled two twenties to give back, but Keith put up his hand. "No, no, keep it."

The transaction over, Tristen turned to go.

"Oh, since you're going downstairs could you take this garbage bag with you and put it in the bin?"

"Keith! You can't ask him to take out the garbage."

"No bother, really." Tristan opened the door, garbage bag in tow. Before he closed it, he heard the woman say in a low voice, "You asshole. You can't ask The Grocer to take out the trash. Have you lost your mind?"

He shut the door, but a window must have been open because he could still hear words and phrases as he went down the stairs: "…show respect… don't you know anything… I do but… sense of decorum."

This last made him smile. He was so bemused by the whole experience he forgot about the flour, drove right past the grocery store, and had to turn around five minutes later when he finally remembered.

Dobbs carried the ribs out and placed them beside him at the head of the table. The pan was too hot to pass, so people handed their plates to him. Shadaisy made sure the wine kept flowing, sometimes getting up, going into the cottage for more and walking around pouring it into people's glasses, ignoring them if they demurred. Dobbs was on call, so he went easy, though Sundays were rarely busy. The bar brawls and domestic violence of Saturday night had burned themselves out, and the perpetrators were either in jail or home trying to recover. Shadaisy always called off on Sundays, and John would only have to leave if there was a crisis and Dobbs needed him, which so far had never happened.

The conversation started when the last person was seated and continued unbroken as people passed dishes back and forth. Shadaisy put two ears of corn on John's plate and when he was out of ribs, she handed his plate down to Dobbs to be refilled. The locusts had arrived and as the sun lowered, their metallic hum filled the background behind the sound of voices, birds getting ready for bed and the breeze moving across the summer plants. "Locusts," Erik said. "The sound of August and summer's end."

Tristan pulled the pork off a rib for Alfred who sat next to him. He then shredded it into strips. The boy picked up a strand between his thumb and forefinger and put it in his mouth, chewed and smiled up at his father. He picked up another with equal care, frowned then tapped his fingers together and looked at his father and began to whimper. Lately Alfred had taken a strong aversion to sticky fingers and would cry and wave his offending hands around until someone cleaned them for him. Tristan reached for the washcloth he kept at his side and wiped his son's hands. Satisfied, the little boy picked up a pea. Polly, who sat across from him, watched her brother as though he were a racoon who had invited itself to dinner. Alfred had recently been freed from his highchair and allowed to sit at the table on a booster seat. His sister did not approve. Polly returned to her ear of corn which had two precise rows of kernels eaten off. With her white baby teeth, she started on a third row, stopping every bit to make sure she did not stray into the next row until the one she was working on was finished.

The sheriff was a good host, merry and helpful in an unobtrusive way.

Josie kept her eyes on him through-out most of the meal. She noticed him watching the scene play out between Tristan and Alfred. He poured more water into each child's plastic cup. When she looked away, she saw Shadaisy staring at her.

The last to leave were John and Shadaisy.

Josie sighed and sat in a rocker. "Do you think John had too much to drink? He's driving."

"He's all right. He can hold it. He's as big as Sasquatch."

"Sasquatch? More like Clark Kent, you mean."

They sat side by side looking at the sun going down. Josie said, "Demeter was quiet, and Erik appeared wistful."

"You always say that. Did you notice the bowl she brought? Made it herself. How do you suppose she got it that color blue? I think it might be the most beautiful blue I've ever seen."

"Nobody ever eats her hippie food. I wonder why she keeps bringing it."

"Maybe she's oblivious. Maybe she doesn't care. Maybe she goes home and eats the whole bowl herself." Dobbs held his cupped hands in front of his chest, indicating enormous breasts and wiggled his eyebrows.

Josie cuffed him on the shoulder. "Cut it out. I'm beginning to think you're in love with her yourself."

"Oh, no. That's Erik's job." He leaned his head back against the chair. "You know who I missed today. Jess. Do you think he'll ever come back?" Shortly after Josie had gone to Rochester, Jess took a vacation to Bali and never returned. He called her on her birthday and at Christmas. He managed to keep his doings vague, sometimes revealing he was living in an ashram, sometimes talking about a job fixing bikes or learning a new instrument, innuendos, nothing solid. What he was clear about was how much he loved the Balinese. "They have a prayer for everything," he told her. "They bless their bicycles before they get on them. They bless the road they travel on. They have no word for art because art is everything, everywhere, life itself."

Josie tapped back and forth in the rocking chair. She realized more days than not, she wondered if she'd ever see him again. She let her breath out slowly. "I don't know. Maybe. But probably not. What I hope is that he's met some sweet Balinese girl who will love him forever."

There was that annoying phrase filling Josie's head again. *The easiest thing I've ever done is loving you.* She pushed the rocker faster.

Love. Loving. What did the song writer mean? Maybe the phrase referred to making love, not the day-to-day business of living together. Making love to Will had turned her into a wild thing. Making love to Rob could not be more different. It began with relaxing into a state of liquidity, a growing luxurious ease, open to the electricity between her hips, building its tension without urgency, the final thrill sweet and inevitable.

When she thought about the other kind of love, the love of family, she thought of Shadaisy and Tristan, Maria, the babies, and Erik.

Josie never allowed the word love and Rob to appear in the same sentence.

And then there was *easiest*. Easy, ease. Josie remembered a day when she was stuffing the sheets, feed bags, and various shapeless dresses she had worn in the beginning into garbage bags. Rob had knocked then walked through the kitchen door. He watched her for a while before asking, "What're you doing?"

"Getting rid of these old rags."

He picked up one of the sheet dresses. "Don't do that. This is pure cotton. Nice. You can always use it for something else." He gathered up the dresses lying on the kitchen table then pulled out the ones already in the garbage bags and put the whole pile in the washing machine. When the load was done, he took the dresses outside and hung them on the clothesline Josie had tied between two trees. It was a brilliant morning, clear and sparkling. The fabric looked beautiful when a slight breeze picked it up and billowed the make-shift dresses against a Carolina blue sky.

Josie used the material to make pinafores with ruffles and embroidery for Polly. The little girl loved these fancy garments made just for her by her auntie Josie. She wore them whenever she was allowed and had one on today for the barbeque.

How easily Dobbs had nudged her forward one more notch.

There Polly was now, walking purposefully down the path toward Josie's house. She must have escaped her parents because she was wearing only spanky pants. Rob and Josie watched in silence as she approached. She stopped just outside the screen in front of them.

"Do you want to come inside?" Josie started to rise to open the door, but Polly shook her head. The little girl watched them solemnly while scratching the place where her thigh met her torso.

Maria came trotting down the path. "Come back here," she called out. Polly turned and walked to her mother as purposefully as she had approached Josie and Dobbs.

"She's an odd little thing," Dobbs said.

"Odd! Everything about this place is odd. Two aliens drop into my life, and I say by all means move in, stay for the rest of your lives. The sheriff of the county spends half his life out here in the middle of a marijuana plantation and one of the waifs I've adopted marries his deputy, the other waif becomes a drug lord. And then there's the bathroom sinking into the ground." Dobbs and Erik had put an addition off the bathroom so they could bring the tub inside and hadn't gotten the concrete slab right. It cracked and now the floor slanted in such a way that she faced up when she bathed and the Plexi-glass wall at the end of the room was coming away from its frame. Sometimes snow blew in through the cracks. "The only things that aren't odd are those two children," Josie leaned back against the rocker, moving it forward and back.

Dobbs looked at her carefully. "Where did that come from?"

"I don't know. Leave me alone. No, don't. I didn't mean that."

"You must be tired."

"I'm not tired. Why would I be tired?"

"Fixing a big dinner like you did."

"We have dinner here every Sunday."

"True." Dobbs looked at the horizon. The sun had almost disappeared, and the hills were black silhouettes. He turned toward Josie. "You planning a trip to the moon tonight?"

"What? Why do you say that?"

"If you rock any faster, you'll achieve lift-off."

Josie put both feet solidly on the floor and stopped the chair from moving. "I have something I need to tell you."

"Uh huh." Dobbs sat perfectly still.

"I'm pregnant."

"How do you—"

"Believe me, I know. It's either yours or Jesus is about to have a half sibling."

"What I was going to say is how do you feel about it."

Josie was silent for so long, Dobbs checked to see if she was crying.

She wasn't. "Actually, I'm glad. I hope you don't mind, but I'm very glad. There's one thing you must know though. Turn your chair to face me." Josie turned hers so it sat squarely facing his.

Dobbs did the same. "Okay. Let me have it."

Josie leaned forward and took hold of both his hands. Dobbs was so surprised he almost pulled away. Josie tightened her grip. "I did not trick you into this. It's very important that you know that. We're not like that, you and me. Will and I wanted children right away, but it didn't happen. Then I find out he got Jaylene pregnant. So, it must be me, right? I'm the one who is infertile. I didn't give pregnancy a thought."

Dobbs rubbed his thumb over her fingers. "I've never known you to lie. You're honest to a fault. I assumed you were taking care of it but that doesn't matter now. Actually, it would be sort of be flattering if you did. Trick me. Meaning you picked me as the father of your child."

"You're a very strange man."

"Am I? I'm not going to start dissembling now. I'm not going to say something just to make you feel better. I don't think you tricked me, but if you did, that's okay too. But I do like it better thinking you didn't." They were both still leaning forward, holding hands. Josie sat upright and withdrew hers. "I feel like an ass sitting like this. Let's turn the chairs back."

"Well," said Dobbs. Once they were facing the outdoors, he exhaled deeply. He hadn't realized he'd been holding his breath.

"Here's the other thing. I don't expect you to change your life because of this. If you don't want to come here anymore, I understand. You know I can handle this myself."

"I want to marry you."

"Oh, Rob."

"I don't want some little… is it a boy or a girl, do you know?"

"It's a girl."

"A girl. Well, here's the thing. I don't want some little girl going around not having a daddy. I want her to shine with the knowledge that Sheriff Dobbs is her father. I want to go to her little league games. I want to go to school conferences. I want to see her go to the prom. Go off to college"

"We don't have to get married to do that."

"Yes, we do. She is not going to be some illegitimate child with half a family. I've never understood why people think you can do it halfway. Here's my 'baby daddy.' Disgusting phrase. Can you see yourself saying that to someone?"

Josie wrapped her arms around her waist and leaned over, her head nearly touching her knees. "You have no idea how terrified I am at the idea of getting married. I like it just the way it is. When I think of you moving all your stuff into my little house and never leaving, being here all the time, I feel like the weight of the world is coming down on me."

"Oh, is that all." Dobb's voice was light. He started rocking again. "Of course, I'm not going to move lock stock and barrel out here. I can't leave my house in town. I have to be close to the office at least part of the time. Most of the time. Requirements of the job."

Still bent over, Josie turned her head to look at Dobbs. "Isn't that a little weird? What happens when she goes to school, and the other kids make fun of her. 'Your daddy lives in town and your mom is way out in the country'."

"Are you serious? Half the parents in the county don't live together. Divorced, separated, never married in the first place. Some kids don't even know who their father is. Half the time neither does their mother for that matter. She won't stand out at all."

Josie sat up straight. The porch light had come on. "What if she misses you while you're gone? Doesn't understand why her daddy goes away overnight?"

Dobbs kept his face averted. "Um… you could… not all the time, just sometimes, when you felt like it, come into town and stay with me."

"I can't do that." She hugged herself and bent over again. Speaking to her knees, she said, "I start to sweat when I think about being around a lot of people. I'm sweating now."

"We're talking about Hollandtown here. You were born there. You're a native. People already know your story, and they'll respect your wishes. They'll give you space if you want it."

"That's just it. I don't want to be around a lot of people who know my story."

Dobbs stared at her. "Are you feeling sick? Am I making you feel sick?"

Josie sat up straight. "No, I'm not sick."

Dobbs looked at her until she returned his gaze. He chose his words carefully. "Okay. One step at a time, right? We've got a few years yet before we need to think about that." He smiled a small smile.

Josie's expression remained grim. "I know if you say things will stay the way they are then they will. And I don't want our daughter to be illegitimate either. I'll marry you. No big affair. We'll go to the registrar's office. Just Shadaisy, Tristan and Maria, John, and Erik. And if I see you haul one piece of furniture out here, I'll burn it."

Dobbs turned away. "Wow. Can you hear that?"

"What?"

"The sound of my heart banging against my chest." He felt tears prick his eyes and wanted to get up and turn off the porch light but didn't dare bring attention to himself. He felt as though he were in the presence of a fox. One wrong move and it would scare off. Instead of getting up, he took a deep breath and said as casually as he could, "What a night huh? I find I'm a father-to-be and then a few seconds later, I get engaged." He shook his head. "What a night. By the way, have you thought of a name yet?"

"I was thinking Daisy might be nice. Tristan could be her middle name."

Dobbs pondered the darkness beyond the screen for a long moment. Eventually, he said, "I like it. Shadaisy sounds a little too, I don't know… ghetto. But Daisy is very nice. Those little aliens saved your life, after all. They deserve to have the baby named after them. Daisy Tristan Dobbs."

"I wasn't planning on changing my name. She would be Daisy Tristan Whitt."

The sheriff rocked his chair. He rocked it forward and back, back and forward. He continued, pondering the night. Finally, he said. "You're right. Daisy Dobbs is a little silly." If he was disappointed, it didn't show.

The locusts and crickets raised their song a decibel or two. Here and there, a few fireflies rose sweetly from the ground. An owl hooted in the distance, and all around, the breeze was moist and warm. Maybe it was the idyllic setting that tempted Dobbs to let his caution slide. At any rate, he knew the unbearable freight the words he was about to speak carried. But he said them anyway. "I love you, Josie Whitt. I have for a long time."

Josie bent her head, put the bottom of her hands against her eyes. The plump flesh around the base of the thumb cut out all light. "I told you right from the beginning, Will was the love of my life. I can't love anyone like that again. I won't. I told you that." Her voice was a thready whisper.

"Yes. You did. I haven't forgotten."

She sat up and took her hands away, let them fall to her lap. "And then there's Jaylene."

Dobbs snapped a glance at her. Josie hadn't spoken her sister's name since she returned from Syracuse. Neither had anyone else within her hearing.

Her voice took on a thoughtful tone as though she were telling a story. "I often wonder if the accident hadn't happened, and Jaylene had lived, and I'd found out later about her and Will and the baby, what would have happened. I loved Will, yes, in a mad carnal way but loving Jaylene went beyond that. I didn't even think about loving her because it was like loving myself. Everything I did, said, thought was fine because we were connected in every way. If I had to make a choice between her life and mine, I would have said kill me because without her, I didn't exist."

Josie pushed back her shoulders. Her tone turned hard. "And she reached right around me and all my devotion and grabbed onto Will because she wanted him. Even though she knew that besides her, he was the most important thing in the world to me. She wanted him, and she took him, and she kept him. And not only that, she felt no remorse. If you had read that text on Jaylene's phone, you would know neither of them felt any remorse at all. They were gleeful, giddy with each other and the thought of their future." Josie stopped talking. Too often, she had thought of the two of them in their hidden world where the only thing that existed was each other: their smooth round flesh, the texture of each other's skin, her luscious breasts, the weight of his penis, the nobs of her backbones making a path to that precious valley. And afterwards they would lie coiled together, her dark head on his shoulder, her arm flung across his chest and her hand under his waist, dreamily planning how they would keep this from her. She could see it all.

"During those months before the accident, Jaylene was especially sweet to me. She'd come to my house two, three times a day bringing me homemade jam, her famous chicken Alfredo, a pie. She'd lean over and kiss me and say, 'Oh, Josie, you are so good.'

"And Will. He wanted to make love every day. Sometimes he'd come home from work in the afternoon and take me right to bed. He was unbelievably tender and stroked my shoulder or my hair and kissed me over and over again. I had no idea what was going on, just that I couldn't believe how lucky I was. And all along it was guilt. Both were acting out of guilty pleasure. Or maybe it was a way to keep me at bay, to keep me from being suspicious. Or maybe they were just so bursting with sexuality they couldn't keep from hugging or kissing or fucking anyone who got it their path."

"Josie, I am so sorry."

"So, I wonder if the accident hadn't happened, and I found out a year ago or even this summer, what I would do. Would I want to kill Jaylene as well as Will? And the answer is hell yes. I'd want to kill her more. And not only would I want to kill her, I'd plot a way to do it. My weapon of choice would be a gun. I don't know if I would try to get away with it or just say the law be damned and go to jail. But I would kill her with a gun, and my goal would be to shoot her right through the heart." Josie managed a small wry smile. "And we both know what a good shot I am." She waited as though giving Rob a chance to say something. When he didn't, she turned and fixed her gaze on his face. "So, you see, Rob, you are in love with a cold-blooded killer who also happens to be the mother of your child. Still want to be the happy family man?"

Dobbs remained silent. He turned back to the darkness all around the porch. It was true, the end of summer was not pretty with its dusty plants and dried grass. The flowers seemed to have given up, to send out the message enough was enough. But at night, when everything was cloaked, the air, heavy and sensual, wrapped people with its living presence. Dobbs said, "Tragedy changes people. Right down to the cellular level. The cells change shape, the strands of your DNA twist into a different form. Your genomes mutate. The synapses in your brain change. I am sure a hundred years from now, this will be common knowledge and big pharma will have pills to hide any manifestation of this change. So properly numbed people can continue to be productive. But the changes, the physiological changes, will still be there underneath the drugs. Whatever that crabby German philosopher said, trauma does not make you stronger. It just makes you different. Remember, the first time I really got to know you was the day after you didn't kill Will."

"It wasn't Will I wanted to kill. It was Jaylene. I just didn't realize it at the time. I'd kill her now if she were alive, with a bullet right through the heart." Josie looked up at the black sky. It was a new moon, lying on its side. South moon under, or south moon rising. She wasn't sure. Another phrase from nowhere or maybe from Marjorie Rawlings. Josie had no idea what it meant. Stars dripped from and around its pointed end, stood out the against the dark, cold, distant, and beautiful.

"I don't think you would when it came right down to it."

"I do."

Dobbs tipped his head upward facing the roof of the porch. "Josie, you're not unique. There's a small black vile of poison within all of us." He ran his fingers through his hair, waited for Josie to reply. When she didn't, he began to sing.

"*Daisy, Daisy give me your answer true, for I'm half crazy, all for the love of you. It will be a happy marriage and we'll push you in a carriage, da dah, da dah, etcetera.*"

Josie put her hand on the arm of his chair. "You are a man of many parts, Sheriff Dobbs."

"And don't I know it!" he said and smiled his magnificent smile.

The End

Acknowledgements

I want to thank Alma Kendall, the woman who makes my authorship possible.

Next, thanks to my fellow writers and critics who keep me honest by sharing their wisdom: Peter Stipe, Susan Williamson, Bob Archibald, Dave Pistorese, Chris Pascale, Mark Green, Tim Holland, Patti Procopi and Sonja McGiboney.

About the Author

E. Compton Lee began her writing career as a freelance writer of nature and human-interest articles for magazines such as *Mother Earth News, Practical Horseman, American Country and Horseman.*

Her first novel, *Native,* takes place in the backwoods of Appalachia, and portrays a woman struggling to overcome misogyny and bigotry to find her place in the cutthroat world of the horse industry.

My Name Is Sloan, a companion to *Native,* tells of a mother fighting to rescue her daughter from foster care. She is helped by good people handcuffed by bureaucracy and the blindness that takes place in agencies meant to help children.

Born and raised in the Hudson River Valley, she left this region at the age of eighteen and embarked upon a journey which immersed her in a multitude of cultures. The knowledge gained from those experiences is what is used when she writes her novels.

E. Compton Lee lived in the Allegheny Mountains of Pennsylvania and western Maryland for fifteen years, where she worked as a therapist and ran a horse business. She currently lives in Williamsburg, Virginia, where she writes full time.

CPSIA information can be obtained
at www.ICGtesting.com
Printed in the USA
BVHW082306210922
647551BV00005B/300

9 781948 979818